BLOOD OF THE LAMB

MICHAEL LISTER

BLEAK HOUSE BOOKS

MADISON | WISCONSIN

Published by Bleak House Books, Inc.
953 E. Johnson St.
Madison, WI 53703
www.bleakhousebooks.com

Copyright © 2004 by Michael Lister

Published 2004.
07 06 05 04 03   1 2 3 4 5

This is a work of fiction. Any similarities to people or places, living or dead, is purely coincidental.

ISBN 1-932557-05-9
Library of Congress Control Number: 2004100858

Jacket and book design: Peter Streicher www.shushudesign.com
Text set in Adobe Garamond

Printed in the United States of America by McNaughton & Gunn

To my grandmothers:

*Gladys McKnight, who as far as I know,
never gave up on anyone,*

&

*Fatima Barry, a fellow mystery lover,
who now knows the greatest mystery of all.*

Acknowledgments

I would like to thank the following people for their sustaining support and endless encouragement: Mark Ryan, Cricket Pechstein, Lynn Wallace, Lou Boxer, Kim Ludlam, Margaret Coel, Mike and Judi Lister, Bobbie Palmer, my friends and family of Calhoun and Gulf Correctional Institutions. Very special thanks goes to Micah and Meleah Lister for all the pennies flung in fountains and prayers flung to heaven, Pam Lister for her faith and true faithfulness, Van Willis for compassionate and wise counsel, Bette Powell, my literary mother, for caring for these pages as if they were her own, and my family at Bleak House Books, Kate Fletcher, Julie Kuczynski, Alison Janssen, and especially Blake Stewart and Ben LeRoy for not being afraid of the dark.

BLOOD OF THE LAMB

MICHAEL LISTER

CHAPTER 1

On the day Nicole Caldwell died, I awoke as if from a night of bad dreams with a nagging sense of dread, which only intensified as I arrived at Potter Correctional Institution and was told to report to the warden's office.

When I opened the door to the admin building, I saw long black cables snaking down the hallway and a bright swath of light, both of which spilled out of Edward Stone's office. I was greeted by Betty Costin, Stone's secretary, and a young, menacing-looking black man with an expensive suit and perfect teeth, both of whom held a finger to their lips signaling me to be quiet.

I had never met him, but I recognized the young man as DeAndré Stone, the warden's nephew. His thuggish posture, expression, and demeanor let everyone know he was hardcore—that no matter where he was or how he dressed, he was never far from the street. Though his designer suit was cut to conceal it, I was sure I detected a holster beneath his arm.

When I took a closer look, he shifted his weight and turned slightly, but it was too late. I was certain now. DeAndré Stone had a firearm on state prison property—a felony punishable by fines and jail time.

Beyond Betty's office, and inside the inner sanctum of Edward Stone's, a local TV news crew was busy recording an interview with Stone and three people who looked only vaguely familiar. As I listened, I learned that the man was Bobby Earl Caldwell, a televangelist from New Orleans, his wife, Bunny, and their adopted daughter Nicole.

Bobby Earl and Bunny Caldwell looked like televangelists—flashy clothes, big, perfectly coifed hair, and liberally applied make-up, though that was the only thing liberal about them. They were also white. Nicole, like Stone, was black. Though not as overly made-up as her adoptive parents, it was obvious Nicole had been dressed to be seen, the bow on her ponytail coordinating with her preppy dress and the matching socks folded just above her patent leather shoes.

I recalled flipping past Bobby Earl on more than one occasion in the solitude of sleepless nights. His message was one of guilt and shame, preached from a pulpit of fear and anger, which was why I was alarmed to hear the reporter announce that he would be conducting a crusade in my chapel later that night.

Bobby Earl's anti-intellectual religiosity and sentimental spirituality were shallow and filled with clichés. They were the first things most of the inmates gravitated toward and the last things they really needed.

I shook my head as I thought these things. I was doing to Bobby Earl what bothered me most about what he did—passing judgement. Maybe we were far more alike than I wanted to believe.

The reporter had to be mistaken. All religious programs performed at the prison had to be approved and scheduled by me. I had neither approved nor scheduled Bobby Earl Caldwell. And I would never even consider letting a child inside the institution—for any reason. Yet, according to him, Nicole was coming in with them.

"Do you sing, Nicole?" Nancy Springfield, the reporter asked.

Nicole was seated on Bunny's lap, but Bunny barely touched her, and certainly not in any way that could be called nurturing. In fact, the whole family's interaction looked staged and stilted, more like amateur actors rehearsing a scene than people who loved each other.

Before Nicole could answer, Bobby Earl said, "Yes, she does. She's got the voice of an angel. In fact, she and her mother will sing in our service tonight. We've found that the men really appreciate the fact that we have an African-American daughter. They appreciate the life we saved her from and can see we're about breaking down racial walls and setting the captives free."

"Mr. Stone," Springfield said, "tell me what a program like this does for your institution."

"Well, first, it gives the offenders something positive to do," he said, leaning forward slightly, the vest of his three-piece suit gathering as he did, his deep voice and careful enunciation giving authority and weight to his words. "Inmate idleness is a serious concern. But it does far more than fill time. Bobby Earl also gives hope. The men will hear a powerful message of redemption and forgiveness and will see living proof of the real thing—a man of God who practices what he preaches."

Nancy thanked them and told her viewers one more time when Bobby Earl's telecast aired in our area, then rushed out of the room, her crew trailing after her, equipment in tow.

"Chaplain Jordan," Stone said, his furrowed brow and squinting eyes parental and chastising. "Where have you been? I wanted you to take part in the interview."

"Traffic," I said, though there wasn't much to speak of in our little part of Florida's forgotten coast.

His brow furrowed even more deeply, his mouth twisting in disbelief, but he decided not to press it. Instead, he introduced me to Bobby Earl, Bunny, and Nicole, who had obviously captured his heart—proof at long last he had one.

"I want to thank you for allowing this humble preacher and his family into your chapel tonight," Bobby Earl said.

I tried not to laugh at his use of the word humble while referring to himself in the third person. He reminded me of a pro athlete who does the same thing—taking all the credit while saying it was a team effort. It seemed my first impression of the man had been accurate.

"Actually," I said. "I didn't know anything about it. In fact, I'd already scheduled a program for tonight—over a month ago."

I now had the full gaze of Bunny Caldwell as well, her blue eyes taking me in between the fluttering of her thickly-coated lashes. She moved into my space, which is probably all she usually had to do to get her way. "It would mean so much to the men," she said, "if they could hear Bobby Earl preach."

"Cancel it," Stone said simply to me, then looked at Bunny. "Excuse me for interrupting, Mrs. Caldwell," then looking back at me, "but it's not every day we can welcome the Reverend Bobby Earl Caldwell into our institution. Do you know how many places are on a waiting list to get him to preach?"

"Speaking of which," I said, "how can I get him in? It takes a minimum of two weeks to complete the FCIC/NCIC checks, obtain authorization, put the clearance paperwork in the control room, and brief security. Not to mention notifying the inmate population of the program. I didn't know anything about this and haven't done—"

Edward Stone lifted his hand, signaling me to be quiet. "I've taken care of everything," he said. "All of this will take place under my authorization. You don't even have to be here during the program."

Nicole Caldwell, the five-year-old little brandy-eyed beauty, had wandered away from our small group and was staring at the crayon drawing hanging on the wall behind Stone's desk. Her head tilted side to side as she closely examined the drawing of an African-American family. No one in the room seemed even vaguely aware of her, least of all her parents. When her examination of the picture was complete, she nodded her head as in approval.

Watching Nicole made me again long to have children of my own. Early in our marriage, I had wanted children, but Susan hadn't. Then when she finally decided she did, more as an attempt to save our marriage than anything else, I was still grieving the death of

Martin Fisher (an unsolved that haunts more than any other) and could not imagine bringing a child into a world where such things happened. It wasn't long before I reconsidered and we began trying to get pregnant. Thankfully, we weren't successful, because within a year we were filing for divorce.

"May I speak with you alone for a moment?" I asked.

Stone shook his head. "Don't have time. We have a meeting with the secretary, the regional director, and the governor in just a few minutes. Then a luncheon at central office."

I shook my head.

"What is it, Chaplain?" Stone asked angrily.

"During the interview it was mentioned that Nicole was coming into the institution as a part of the program tonight," I said. "That can't be—"

"It's all taken care of," he said. "As soon as Mrs. Caldwell and Nicole have sung their songs, they will go into your office for the remainder of the program. They will stay in there with both doors locked until the inmates have been escorted from the building."

"I can't—"

"You have nothing to do with it," Stone said and, turning his back to me, looked at the others. "We've got to get going. Can't keep the governor waiting."

Only when it was time to go did Bunny look for Nicole; Bobby Earl not even then. As she gathered Nicole and her things, I noticed bruises on Bunny's upper arms and wrists. It looked as if she had attempted to cover them with makeup and clothes, but the makeup was wearing off and the clothes shifted as she moved.

I glanced back at Bobby Earl, wondering if he were responsible. Did he beat his wife?

They made their way to the door before Stone turned around and said, "Have everything ready when we return. We'll be on a very tight schedule and they have a plane to catch tonight."

I didn't say anything, only smiled at Nicole. When she smiled back, I knelt down beside her and said, "Hi. I'm John. Do you like that drawing?"

"Uh huh," she said, nodding her head vigorously. Her hair had been straightened and put up in a ponytail that bounced as she nodded. "Who drew it?"

"I don't know," I said. "But Mr. Stone can tell you. Do you draw?"

"Uh huh."

"I'd like to see one of your drawings." I said.

"You would?"

"Uh huh," I said enthusiastically.

Her face brightened into a large smile, her dark eyes sparkling as she said, "I'll color one just for you. Do you want one of Jesus?"

"I'd love one of Jesus," I said.

"Chaplain Jordan, I know we'll be running on a very tight schedule this afternoon," Stone said impatiently, "but if we happen to get back early, I want you to sit down with Bobby Earl and discuss some ideas he's got for your chapel program."

I stood up and looked at them, stunned, bristling at even the suggestion.

"I want to help in any way I can," Bobby Earl said, then winked at me as they all walked out.

CHAPTER 2

After unlocking the chapel and letting Officer Whitfield into the library to listen to some preaching tapes, I met briefly with my inmate orderly, Mr. Smith. Once in my office, I popped in a cassette of Gregorian chants and spent some time in thought and prayer.

I felt frustrated and angry at my reaction to Bobby Earl and what I suspected his brand of religion would do to the inmate population. Many of the men who attended chapel teetered on the precipice between genuine faith and love, and irresponsibility and over-simplicity. I was afraid the apocalyptic excitement of Bobby Earl's hellfire and brimstone preaching would cause them to plunge to their spiritual deaths.

What was a man like Bobby Earl even doing here? There was nothing the inmates could do to expand his television empire.

I picked up my phone and punched in Anna Rodden's extension in Classification. It rang several times, but there was no answer. I hung up, and like the unexpected answer to a prayer, Anna walked into my office.

"Hey, stranger," she said, closing the door behind her.

As I came around my desk, she dropped the envelopes and inmate requests she was carrying into a chair, and we embraced. She was tall and athletic, and our bodies fit together like they were made to. The hug was quick, but the connection immediate and intense, and I had to release her and step back while I still could.

"I've missed you," she said. "Doin' time's not nearly as much fun when you're not around."

"Thanks," I said. "It's good to be back."

"How was training?"

"I can think of more fun ways to waste time," I said.

And then, for a long moment, we stood there, neither of us seeming able to move.

On the right side of Anna's neck, a thin scar ran down at a jagged angle. Slowly, I reached up and gently traced it with my fingertip. I liked to feel the small rise of the scar tissue beneath the skin, the vulnerability of the wound, the power of healing. It was the wound that caused this scar, and the blood it shed, that had saved my life, and had given me the opportunity to save hers.

She breathed in deeply and swallowed hard.

"Sorry," I said.

She shook her head, waving off my apology, and I somehow made it back to my chair and sat down, while she took the empty chair across from my desk.

After being away from the institution for two weeks in chaplaincy training, I had more to do than I could fathom, but all I wanted was to be with Anna.

"I had a lot of people ask me about us while you were away this time," she said.

"*Us?*" I asked, instinctively glancing at her ring finger before I realized what I was doing.

"If we're having an affair," she said. "They can't understand us."

I said, "Neither can I."

She smiled and her dark brown eyes lit up.

The faint chant of prayers rising from the chapel drifted through the air like incense—Muslim prayers, prayed to Allah in Arabic.

Allaahu Akbar, Allaahu Akbar... Ash hadu allaa ilaaha ill Allah.

Tossing back her shoulder-length brown hair, she pulled a small plastic bag from the pile of mail and inmate requests on the chair beside her. "I got you a little something. Two little somethings actually."

She handed me a small plastic bag with blue musical notes on it.

I withdrew two CDs from the bag. The first one was Dan Fogelberg's latest, which I had picked up along with Jann Arden's to enjoy on my drive back from central Florida.

"I wanted you to have them the moment you got back," she said.

"Thank you," I said, as if I didn't already have them.

"The other one is Jann Arden, and you're going to love her. She's so honest and... well, melancholy, yet with an underlying optimism, or at least hope."

I couldn't have described her better. "I can't wait to listen to them," I said. "Thanks again."

Allahu Akbar, Allahu Akbar... Laa ilaaha ill Allah.

An inmate passed slowly by my office door, lingering near the narrow panel of glass, staring at Anna as he did. A moment later, when he walked back by, I could see that it was Harmless Harry, one of the most notorious rapists the state of Florida had ever known. My fists clenched involuntarily.

Hayya' alal Falaah... Qad qaamatis Salaah... Qad qaamatis Salaah.

I heard the conversation of two Latino inmates from somewhere in the hall. Their Spanish, the Latin of the Gregorian chants, the English we spoke, and the Arabic of the Muslim prayers swirled together into a linguistic potpourri that permeated the air.

"I did a lot of thinking while I was away," I said.

It sounded more ominous than I had intended.

"Yeah?" she said, tilting her head and raising her thick brown eyebrows. I had her complete attention.

"I'm not sure I can be an effective chaplain if I'm spending so much time investigating."

Her expression encouraged me to continue.

"Things always get out of control," I said. "I change... and if I have to choose..."

"But—"

"I came very close to taking a drink last summer when I was in the middle of the Ike Johnson case," I said.

Her face registered her surprise. "You should've said something."

I didn't respond.

Harmless appeared at the door again, and I waved him away. She turned, but he was gone.

"How close did you come, really?" she asked when she turned back around.

I shrugged. "The thing is, even though I maintained my sobriety," I said, "I lost my serenity."

When Harmless appeared at the door again, I jumped up and rushed over to it. He pulled back from the door and started walking toward the sanctuary.

"What are you doing, Harry?" I asked.

He spun around and stepped back toward me, his dull eyes blinking rapidly behind his thick glasses. "Waiting to see you," he said impatiently, the severe lisp only adding to his annoying tone. "I've been trying to see you for a long time."

Harry actually looked harmless with his small build, graying crewcut, and thick glasses, his speech impediment only adding to the facade.

"I'm with someone right now," I said. "If you want to see me, have a seat in the library. If I see you hanging outside my office door again, I'm going to have you locked up."

"For what?" he asked belligerently.

"You hear that tick tock sound?" Anna asked, coming up behind me and staring Harry down. "That's the gain time you're losing. Like sands in the hourglass... I'm taking away days of your life outside."

He stalked away, muttering something under his breath, and we both made our way back to our seats, shaking our heads as we did.

"Why do you do this?" she asked.

"I was about to ask you the same thing."

When I moved back home to northwest Florida after being a cop and a cleric in Atlanta, I never would've imagined I'd become a prison chaplain. But God works in mysterious ways, and when I fell from grace in Atlanta, this is the grace I fell into.

"I've thought about that a lot lately, too," I said. "I became a chaplain at a time when I was scrambling to put my life back together, probably would've taken anything, and the combination of forensics and ministry seemed a natural. But now I really think this is exactly where I'm supposed to be—for now at least."

She started to say something, but the phone rang.

When I answered, a friendly voice said, "Chaplain Jordan, this is Chuck in the warehouse. We have a special delivery for you and need to see you right away."

"I'm kind of busy right now. Can I come over after lunch?"

"No, you have to personally sign for it and it's here now."

"Okay, I'm on my way," I said. "Thanks."

"I've got to go to the warehouse," I said to Anna as I stood. "Can I drop by your office after lunch?"

After sending the inmates back down on the compound, Anna and I walked over to the library where Bobby Earl Caldwell's thunderous preaching could be heard.

I wasn't aware of it, but I must have been making my eating-broccoli face.

"Makes you cringe, doesn't it?" Anna asked.

"Doesn't it you?"

"Well, yeah, but I bet it bothers you more."

I tried to get Officer Whitfield's attention, but his back was to us and the tape was so loud he couldn't hear me.

As soon as Bobby Earl Caldwell brought his message to a frenzied finish, Bunny came on and made a tearful appeal for money.

I looked at Anna. She was laughing.

Whitfield jumped when I tapped him on the shoulder, stopped the tape, and spun around to face me.

"Sorry," I said. "I didn't mean to startle you. I've got to go down to the warehouse, so I need to lock up."

"Sure," he said. "No problem. The message is over anyway."

As we walked out of the chapel, and I paused to lock the door, Whitfield said, "I'm ready to face the enemy on his own territory now." He nodded toward the compound. "I've got my shield of faith, helmet of salvation, breastplate of righteousness… "

When he finally finished, I said, "Well, go fight the good fight."

It sounded more sarcastic than I intended, and, as he walked away, Anna laughed. When I was sure he was too far away to hear me, I did too.

"He should be the chaplain here," I said. "Not me."

The great irony for a man in my position is how little use I have for organized religion. I am essentially a member of the unchurched. Yet, since high school I've felt a strong sense of vocation, a paradoxical longing and belonging which somehow resulted in my becoming a nonreligious religious leader. I was on the very fringe of religion, but so far prison chaplaincy had worked for me.

Anna shot me a look. "I'm not saying he's not a good, well-meaning guy, but the last thing the repressed religious simpletons around here need is a repressed religious simpleton as a chaplain."

"Thanks," I said, and let out a small ironic laugh at the madness of it all.

"Don't tell me you didn't miss all this while you were in training," she said.

I looked at her for a long moment. "I missed some things more than others."

Chapter 3

Leaving Anna wasn't easy. It had never been, and every time it got more difficult.

The first time I left her after high school, I had fled to Atlanta, trying to escape the painful and nearly sobering reflection I saw in my mother's glazed and unfocused eyes.

It was almost two years before I came home again to visit, and having heard that Anna was married, I avoided her. But, just like the song, I ran into her in the grocery store on Christmas Eve, and we had our own bittersweet *Same Old Lang Syne*. I started listening to Dan Fogelberg then, and have been ever since.

On my walk over to the warehouse, I was joined by Dexter Freeman, a young black inmate with closely shaven hair, a three-inch part cut into the front of it. He was thin, but muscular, and held himself in such a way that even the biggest predators left him alone. He had recently transferred to this institution and had been attending my Bible class and weekly worship service.

"Chaplain, I've got a question for you," he said, as he walked along beside me. "Can I walk with you?"

"Sure," I said.

A loud burst of laughter erupted to my left, and I turned to see a small group of inmates seated behind the food service building, wearing soiled aprons and white plastic hair covers. The laughter came from a squat, balding black man leaning against the gray cinder block wall. I guessed he was attempting to entertain the others who were seated on over-turned plastic milk crates, but it was obvious that he found himself much more amusing than they did.

"Is the Bible true?" Dexter asked.

"How do you mean?"

"Did all those things really happen?" he asked. "The flood, the tower of Babel, Jonah and the whale?"

Unlike most of the inmates in this facility—or in any state facility—Dexter was well educated, and spoke with no discernable accent or dialect.

I knew what he was asking. It's what most people of faith ask themselves at one time or another—are our stories true?

"The truth of a story isn't contingent on its being a factual account of actual events," I said. "Think about Jesus' parables. Is there anything more true than them?"

He squinted as he thought about it for a long moment. "It doesn't have to have happened to be true?"

"What is truth?" I said. "Is it the shallow assurance that something literally took place, or is it about something far deeper, something that is profoundly true—on all levels? Not just the literal one. It's like poetry."

His face lit up, his eyes brightening. "Religion as poetry," he said. "I like that."

"Why do you think sacred texts are filled with so much figurative language?" I said.

"Yeah," he said, nodding his head and smiling. He got it. Then, suddenly, he began to frown. "But so many people just take it literally. They're missing so much."

"It's how they can believe they have truth and everybody else has superstition."

He looked down and shook his head.

At the end of the food service building, a rust-and-grime-covered green dumpster sat reeking of sour milk and rotting vegetables.

It reminded me of grammar school. That same pungent smell had floated around the rear of the lunchroom like a tormented apparition—presumably one that died of food poisoning. From somewhere beneath the violated metal mass bled a thin milky substance, as if from an open wound.

Dexter and I both carefully stepped over the sludge that seeped across the width of the asphalt street. It puddled like some primordial pool that would soon spawn a horrific new species.

He started to say something, but hesitated, and I could tell he wanted to say more.

"What is it?" I asked.

He smiled. "Is it wrong? I mean does…," he began, then trailed off.

"Just spit it out," I said, "I can guarantee I've heard it before."

"Does the Bible say masturbation's a sin?" he asked quickly without looking at me. "All the brothers on the compound say it does. Now don't get me wrong. I'm not a member of the gun club."

I smiled at Dexter's reference to the PCI Gun Club. Gunners were inmates, usually sex offenders, who masturbated while looking at female officers in the dorms. They'd simply whip it out and get busy regardless of who was around. Each day the gun club received new members. It was getting out of hand (so to speak) and I felt sorry for the female officers who had to endure such violations.

"Actually, the Bible doesn't say anything about masturbation," I said, adding, "unless you count, 'Whatever you find to do with your hand, verily I say, do it with all your might.'"

He looked perplexed.

I smiled. "It's a joke. The Bible doesn't say anything about it."

"What about the dude in Genesis they keep talking about? What's his name?"

I smiled. "Onan?"

"Yeah?"

"Not the same thing," I said.

The sounds of young men playing drifted over from the rec yard, mixing with gunshots from the firing range, creating an auditory paradox that otherwise only existed in war and inner-city housing projects.

"So it's not a sin?"

I shrugged. "I guess it can be."

"They act like it's really against God—sexual impurity and all."

I nodded as he spoke, thinking about the hypocrisy of rapists and child-molesters feeling righteous about themselves for abstaining while they were in prison, but didn't respond when he finished.

"Well, is it?"

"What? Against God? I sure hope not."

His face filled with relief.

"I think you'll find that most of the ones saying how evil and sinful sex is are the very ones with the greatest sexual dysfunctions and addictions."

He was about to respond when we reached the gate. "Well, this is my stop. They won't let me go any further."

I smiled. "Come up to my office when you can and we'll talk about it some more."

"Okay," he said. "Thanks."

When Dexter was gone, I proceeded through the south gate. Emerging on the other side, I noticed a large panel van with Bobby Earl Caldwell Ministries painted on it parked near the warehouse.

I soon discovered that the truck was filled with an unsolicited shipment of Bobby Earl Caldwell preaching tapes and books for our chapel library. The tapes—both audio and video—were unedited recordings of his television program and crusades, the books, self-published transcripts of his sermons. The materials were in cardboard boxes stacked on pallets that had to be unloaded with our forklift.

As the truck was being unloaded and each box being carefully searched for contraband, Chuck, the warehouse manager, read what was printed below Bobby Earl's logo on each of the boxes. "Man incarcerates. God liberates."

"As Bobby Earl's ego *in*flates," I said, and we both laughed.

CHAPTER 4

After working through lunch, I had caught up enough to take a break and finish my conversation with Anna. Walking down toward the classification department, the heat of the afternoon sun bearing down on my back, I spotted Warden Stone, his nephew, and the Caldwells near the center gate. I was shocked to see that Nicole was with them.

The center gate separated the upper compound of service buildings—the library, chow hall, medical, the chapel, and classification—from the lower compound of inmate dorms and the rec yard. The majority of inmates were on the lower compound, but there were enough on the upper to be a serious threat to Nicole.

What was wrong with Stone? Had he been behind a desk outside the institution too long? Was he that out of touch? Or was it just that, unlike me, he had never heard the detailed confessions of the predators we held captive, never looked into the abyss of their dark hearts?

"Chaplain," the warden said by way of greeting as I walked up. "We got back earlier than we expected and I was just giving the Caldwells a tour of the institution. They're very impressed. Would you like to join us? It'd give you and Bobby Earl a chance to talk," meaning a chance for Bobby Earl to talk and me to listen.

"What is Nicole doing on the compound? Shouldn't she be—"

"If anyone even looks at Nicole the wrong way," Stone said, "my nephew will put him in the hospital."

I glanced around the compound at all the inmates who were gawking in our direction and knew that, even as appealing as many of them would find Bunny, they weren't all looking at her.

When Paul Register, a sex offender I had been counseling, saw me, he quickly looked away.

"She's safe, Chaplain Jordan," Bunny said. "Mr. Stone wouldn't let anything happen to her in his institution."

"That's right," Stone said.

"You worry too much, John," Bobby Earl said with the smarmy smile of a door-to-door Bible salesman. "You've got to learn to trust God more."

"It isn't God I don't trust," I said. "Why don't I take Nicole up to the admin conference room and let her color while you finish the tour?"

"Chaplain, you're being silly," Stone said. "I assure you she's—"

"Mama, I'm hot," Nicole said. "I want to go with Chaplain JJ inside to color."

I smiled. Not very many people called me JJ anymore, and I wondered who she had heard refer to me by my initials. Adding chaplain to them was purely her own invention. No one had ever called me Chaplain JJ before, but coming from her it sounded cute, and hinted at what I suspected was a delightful personality.

Bunny looked at me. "You're sure you don't mind?"

"Not at all."

"Okay," she said.

"Have her quote Scripture for you," Bobby Earl said. "I guarantee she knows it better than you. I'll put hard-earned money on it."

Not pointing out that quoting and knowing aren't the same things or the fact that, though he had plenty of money, none of it was hard-earned—not by him anyway—I took Nicole's hand and we walked as quickly as we could off the compound, through the front gate, and into the admin building.

"You're a preacher like my daddy?" she asked.

I smiled. "Not *exactly* like him."

"Are you on TV?" she asked.

"That would be one of the ways I'm not like him."

The cool air and shelter from the sun felt refreshing, but couldn't compare to the relief I felt at having Nicole on this side of the chainlink and razor wire. I still couldn't believe they had taken her down on the compound. Perhaps the Caldwells were just naive. Not everyone was as sensitized as I was to the danger the concrete and steel held, but it was unimaginable they could put her on display like that, parading her around for all the molesters to see, and Edward Stone should have known better.

"Are you saved, sanctified, and filled with the Holy Ghost?" she asked.

"Not so much," I said.

She looked puzzled, but let out a small laugh. "You're silly."

Once we had retrieved her coloring book and crayons from Stone's office, she settled in the head chair at the conference table with them and got right to work.

For a long moment, I just sat and watched her, finding her intensity and concentration fascinating. As she worked, she narrowed her eyes, furrowed her brow, and talked very softly to herself about what she was doing.

"Would you like a Coke or a candy bar?" I asked.

Without looking up, she said, "Mom says caffeine and chocolate make me hyper."

I was struck again by the way she spoke. Like her straightened hair and preppy dress, the only thing about her that was black was her skin—and it was very light. Was it just the inevitable byproduct of being adopted by Caucasian parents, or were Bobby Earl and Bunny consciously raising her to be white?

"CHAPLAIN," one of the ladies from the business office yelled from down the hall. "THERE'S A CALL FOR YOU. ARE YOU UP HERE?"

"TRANSFER IT TO THE CONFERENCE ROOM, PLEASE," I called. "THANKS."

I picked up the phone almost the moment it rang.

"I thought you were gonna come see me this afternoon," Anna said.

"I got a better offer," I said.

Watching Nicole color so intently, I realized again just how stunning she was and how wrong it was for her to be here.

"Rumor has it you're with another woman," she said.

"Why don't you come see for yourself?"

Though she never looked up, Nicole leaned toward me slightly, turning her ear in my direction, and began to color with less enthusiasm, and I could tell she was listening to our conversation.

"I think I will," Anna said, and hung up.

When she arrived a few minutes later, I made the proper introductions.

"It's nice to meet you," Nicole said to Anna, then turning to me, asked, "Is she your girlfriend?"

"Only in my dreams," I said.

"You're silly," she said again.

"May we color with you?" Anna asked.

"Sure," Nicole said. "I have a whole book of pictures."

She let each of us tear a page from her book and told us to help ourselves to her crayons.

"Thanks for being so generous," Anna said.

"It's more blessed to give than receive," she said.

"So I've heard," Anna said, smiling at me.

"Sprite doesn't have caffeine," Nicole said.

Unaware of my previous offer and Nicole's response, Anna smiled at what she thought was the typical non sequitur of a small child. "No, it doesn't," she said.

"A Sprite it is then," I said. "Anna?"

"No, thank you," Anna said, continuing to color, "*I'm* starving for my art."

As I was walking from the room, Nicole said, "Chips don't have chocolate."

When I returned with the Sprite and chips from the vending machine, seeing Anna and Nicole together, I wondered what it would be like to have children with such a woman. Though aware of and attentive to Nicole like I had yet to see Bunny be, she had thrown herself into coloring her masterpiece with the same child-like abandon Nicole had.

"Thank you, Chaplain JJ," Nicole said, as I popped the top and opened the bag for her.

"My pleasure," I said.

After a few chips and sips, she looked up at Anna and said, "You should marry him. I'm gonna marry a preacher."

"If she were my wife," I said, "I might just get my own TV show."

"My mom's pretty," she said.

"She sure is," Anna said.

Before I could say anything, the phone rang again and I picked it up.

"Chaplain Jordan, this is Kate at the switchboard. An inmate in A-dorm just tried to commit suicide and they need you down there right away."

I stood as I placed the receiver back in the cradle.

"I've gotta go to A-dorm," I said. "Can you stay with Nicole until her parents get back?"

"Sure," she said. "What is it?"

"Attempted suicide."

She nodded.

"Call me if you need anything."

Without looking up from her work, Nicole said, "We'll pray for you, Chaplain JJ."

They were the last words she ever said to me, and their simplicity and sincerity would haunt me long after she was dead.

CHAPTER 5

That night when I reached the chapel, Bunny and Nicole were singing "Consider the Lilies." Bobby Earl looked on with pride from his seat on the platform, and it was disconcerting to see him sitting in the chair I had come to think of as mine.

Crisis counseling wasn't something that could be rushed, and I was much later getting to the chapel than I would've liked.

I slipped into the sanctuary past Officer Roger Coel, who gave me a strained nod, and walked to the center aisle to get a better idea of the attendance. The chapel was packed, inmates filling the pews and spilling over into chairs beyond the drawn divider into the overflow room.

"Good turnout," I whispered when I had eased back over to Coel.

He was a tall, lean, ex-military man with thin blond hair that had a tendency to stand up.

"Someone circulated a picture of Bunny Caldwell around the compound this afternoon," he said.

"You sayin' their reasons for being here are more carnal than spiritual?" I asked with mock surprise.

"It's why *I'm* here. I volunteered for this assignment."

The nondescript chapel, meant to accommodate all religions, bore the symbols of none. It was large, with pews on either side of a wide center aisle and had a platform with a wooden pulpit centered at the front. The pews and the pulpit had been built by inmates who lacked the precision their construction required. The tops of the pews were different heights and the pulpit leaned to the left a little.

"Are you the only officer here?" I asked, unable to keep the surprise and anger out of my voice.

He nodded. "Whitfield was here—he loves this shit, but he got pulled to escort the GED class back down to the dorms. Almost made him lose his religion," he added with an appreciative smile. "He should be back soon."

Bunny and Nicole finished their song and received a standing ovation. Bunny took several bows, but looked over at Bobby Earl uneasily. Nicole just smiled. Then, as the men were being seated and Bobby Earl was taking the pulpit, Bunny and Nicole slipped into my office through the door near the platform.

"Do you need any help?" I asked Coel.

"You can check the bathrooms," he said. "I can't be here and there at the same time, and it's probably full of these randy bastards beatin' off to Bunny."

I nodded, and started to walk out when Coel grabbed my arm.

"Why didn't you put out a memo for security about this service?" he whispered, his voice harsh, his face pinched. "Control didn't have anything on it. Were they cleared through the proper channels?"

"I didn't have anything to do with this program," I said. "Stone set it up. He said he took care of everything."

"Yeah, with a phone call at the time they arrived. No advance warning. No chance for us to prepare. Nothing."

"I'll look into it," I said.

My pulse started pounding when I found several inmates, one of whom was a child molester, lurking around the hallway near the water fountain and my office, and I realized again just how vulnerable Nicole really was.

"You need to get back in the sanctuary now," I said.

Paul Register seemed to shrink in on himself, his short, boyish form becoming even smaller. His eyes blinked sheepishly at me like a small puppy expecting another whack with a newspaper.

"Yes, sir," he said softly. "My knee's hurting. I was trying to stretch it out some."

"You can stand in the back if you need to," I said. "But you need to be in the sanctuary."

"Yes, sir," he said. "I'm going." He glanced through the glass pane in my office door, then limped back into the sanctuary under the hard glare of Officer Coel.

Once Register was out of the front hallway, I walked over and made sure the door to my office was locked. It was. Then I headed to the inmate bathroom next to the kitchen and multi-purpose room in the back.

Obviously designed by someone who had never worked in a prison, the chapel's inmate and visitor bathrooms were down a short L-shaped hallway that led to the kitchen and meeting room in the back. It was a blind spot, difficult to supervise, and, if not watched closely, the place where the more criminal of our criminal element congregated. For an event like this, there should be a minimum of three officers on duty.

Inside the bathroom, to my shock, I discovered Abdul Muhammin, one of the clerks assigned to the chapel. I had never seen him or any other Muslim at a Christian worship service.

"What're you doing here?"

"Using the bathroom," he said. He posture and tone were defiant and challenging, his muscular body flexing as he began to bow up.

"No," I said. "In the chapel?"

"Hearin' Bobby Earl," he said. "Dog's doin' good for hisself."

Suddenly, he was different, his demeanor relaxed and playful, as if he and I were friends just hanging out, talking about old times and people we knew.

"You're a fan?" I asked.

"Shit," he said, "I shared a cell with 'im at Lake Butler. I came to make sure he don't forget a nigga'."

"You and Bobby Earl—"

"Yeah," he said. "Bobby Earl's my boy. He like the Jimmy Swaggart of jailhouse religion."

"Well, you need to get back in there," I said. "You wouldn't want to miss him."

He nodded slowly, rubbing his chin as if contemplating something profound. "All right, Chap. I'm on my way."

"Is anybody else in here?" I asked.

"I am," a disembodied voice rose from within the stall.

"Who's that?"

"Inmate Cedric Porter, sir," he said.

"It's time to get back to the chapel," I said.

"Yes, sir," he said.

When I left the bathroom, I checked on Bunny and Nicole through the window of my office door. Nicole appeared bored, Bunny sad and restless, and I wondered how much of their lives were spent waiting on Bobby Earl's seemingly eternal sermons to end.

I stepped out of the air-conditioned chapel into the humidity and heat of the dark night, and walked up to the control room where I asked to see the memo giving Bobby Earl and his family authorization to enter the institution and conduct the special program.

There wasn't one. Never had been. No one knew anything about it until Mr. Stone called and told them to let Bobby Earl and his family through the gate and to escort them to the chapel.

I borrowed the phone and called Anna at home.

"Sorry to disturb you," I said, thinking *but you do me all the time.*

"Are you okay?" she asked, her voice full of concern. I never call her at home.

"Did you run a FCIC/NCIC check on Bobby Earl and Bunny Caldwell?"

"Not yet," she said. "When're they supposed to be coming in?"

"Tonight," I said.

"Not gonna happen," she said. "I haven't—"

"It already has."

"What?" she asked in shock. "I haven't seen anything on it."

"You still the only one who runs the checks?" I asked.

"Yeah," she said. "Which means they shouldn't be there tonight. So how the hell'd they get in?"

"Stone," I said.

"Well, he can do that."

"Even without a background check?"

"Not supposed to," she said. "But he can. He has the authority."

"Why wouldn't he?"

"Check?" she asked. "Maybe because he knows Bobby Earl so well. Knows he's not related to any of our inmates. Knows he's not a convicted felon."

"Or knows he is."

"What?"

I told her. As I did, I stared absently into the control room.

The dark night made the light in the control room seem even brighter, putting the two officers inside on display like fish in an aquarium, the condensation on the glass reinforcing the illusion.

"And an inmate in the chapel says he was Bobby Earl's cell mate at Lake Butler."

"Oh, my God," she said. "John, you better keep a close eye on him."

"I will," I said. "Thanks."

Once in the chapel again, I looked into my office. Bunny Caldwell, who was sitting in my chair, waved to me. She smiled, too, which was something to see, and for just a moment the sadness left her eyes. I waved back. She smiled even bigger and I motioned her over to the door, which was still locked.

"You okay?" I asked after she had unlocked the door and I stepped inside.

She nodded, but looked away. When she looked back, she said, "I'm just a little tired. I don't have Bobby Earl's stamina."

"Where's Nicole?"

"In the bathroom," she said, nodding toward the narrow door in the corner.

"I'm sorry to do this," I said, "but I may never see you again."

As though she knew where I was going with this, tears began to fill her eyes. Blinking them back, she said, "What?"

"I couldn't help but notice the bruises on your wrists."

Instantly, she jerked her arms back, and began to shake and move, as if no longer in full control of her body.

"I'm sorry," I said. "But I had to ask. Are you okay?"

She nodded, her eyes flattening, her face becoming a impenetrable mask. "I'm fine. But it's sweet of you to ask." She glanced down a moment, then back at me. "They look worse than they are. I bruise very easily."

"They look like they were made by someone grabbing you," I said.

"Even men of God can lose their tempers," she said. "Besides, I can be nagging and disrespectful."

"If—" I began, but she put her fingers over my mouth in a gesture that expressed an intimacy we didn't share.

"I'm fine," she said. "Really. Please don't make a big deal out of it. It's very sweet of you to care, but they really look worse than they are."

"Okay," I said. "But if it ever gets—"

"Then I have friends and family I can call," she said.

I nodded, embarrassed.

When I walked into the sanctuary, I found Coel still alone and Bobby Earl giving an impassioned altar call.

"Where's Whitfield?" I asked.

Coel shrugged and shook his head.

"I'm going to check the bathroom again," I said.

"Ten-four," he said.

Two steps into the back hallway, I bumped into Theo Malcolm, the institution's only literacy and GED teacher. Without a word, he shoved past me and rushed out the door.

I turned and considered him, wondering what he was doing here, and why he was in such a hurry to leave. I called after him, but he didn't even pause, so I decided to go ahead and check the bathroom. I could always talk to him later.

In the bathroom, I found Officer Whitfield washing the sweat off his face with water he splashed from his cupped hands.

"I'm glad you're back," I said. "Coel needs some help."

"I'm heading in there now," he said.

Tim Whitfield was tall and lean, but seemed soft. His dark brown hair was thick and wavy and sat high on his head. The front of his hair was damp and small rivulets of water snaked out of it and down his long forehead.

"Anyone else in here?"

"Just two convicts," he said, looking at the dull reflection of the stalls behind him in the sheet-metal mirror bolted above the sink. "You convicts get back in the service."

"Yes, sir," Dexter Freeman said, stepping out of the stall.

"Just a minute," the voice of what sounded like a young black guy called from inside the other stall.

"Just make it fast," Whitfield said.

When I walked back into the sanctuary, Bunny was singing "Just As I Am" while Bobby Earl finished his altar call.

I searched the stage for Nicole, but she wasn't there.

"Where's Nicole?" I asked Coel.

"Who?" he said.

"The little girl," I said.

"The black one?" he asked.

Making no attempt to mask my anger, I said, "There's only one little girl in this entire institution."

"She's still in your office, I guess," he said. "She didn't come out with her mother."

"Who's with her?" I asked.

"No one right now," he said. "The preacher went in while his wife was singing, and since he came back out for the altar call, I've had my eyes on both doors. He hasn't been out of your office long."

Relief washed over me when I saw that the altar call was over and Bunny was slipping back into my office, Bobby Earl remaining behind to say one last prayer.

Bobby Earl's prayer was simple, but passionate and persuasive, and I could see why he did well on television. His prayer, which had started off loudly, had now become a whisper and the sanctuary fell into a reverent hush as well.

"In Jesus' name," he whispered. "Through the shed blood of the lamb—"

He broke off as the scream erupted.

The entire congregation turned to see Bunny Caldwell stumbling backwards out of my office, her staccato shrieks piercing the silence like stabs. Her screams were not those of fear, but of absolute horror, a horror so dark it seemed to echo from some sudden void in her soul.

For a moment, perhaps as she took a breath, there was absolute silence, and in that one quiet moment, no one moved. Like children slapped for the first time, everyone was too stunned to do anything. Then, after the initial shock subsided, everyone began to scramble as hesitation gave way to panic.

As I ran down the side aisle toward her, I somehow knew what I was going to find. Her scream had told me that, and my mind, as if divided into two parts, was simultaneously telling me it was so and absolutely rejecting that it could be.

Bobby Earl reached Bunny before I did, wrapping her up in his arms while looking into my office. His knees buckled and they both fell as the inmates began gathering around them, all straining to see what the small office held that could elicit such strong reactions.

"Get back in your seats," I yelled, but no one moved. They stood there transfixed like the Caldwells had been, and when I reached the doorway, I knew why.

Beyond the open door of my office was the crumpled, lifeless body of Nicole Caldwell.

CHAPTER 6

"Go home, Chaplain," Colonel Patterson said. "The inspector can take your statement in the morning."

My nerves were humming like high-voltage lines, my eyes and fingers twitching like an addict in need of a fix. Head aching, heart pounding, adrenaline-rich blood coursing through my veins, home was the last place I wanted or needed to be.

It had taken a while to quell the overwrought crowd of inmates, most of whom had rushed my office door in an attempt to see Nicole's body. By the time they were cajoled and, in some cases, beaten into submission and securely locked in their dorms, Colonel Patterson and Inspector Fortner had arrived.

With the Caldwells being cared for and interviewed by the trauma response team, I had made the mistake of stepping out of the empty chapel to take in some fresh air and collect my thoughts. Now, the colonel was refusing to let me back inside.

"We've got a lot to do tonight, Chaplain," Patterson said, adding, "We know you're not goin' anywhere," as if I were a suspect. "Pete can take your statement tomorrow."

He knew it wasn't my statement but the investigation I was worried about, and I could tell he was enjoying my frustration almost as much as the tobacco juice that trickled from the corner of his mouth.

I had to laugh at him trying to be so tough. He just didn't have the physique to pull it off. He had the body of a bird, his thin, stick-like legs looking incapable of supporting the weight of his enormous belly. The white shirt of his uniform, holding back his belly above his belt, always appeared about to burst open. Like his legs, the strength of his buttons was a mystery. And he wore boots for height, but they only made him look and walk funny.

All I could think about was Nicole, how I had failed to protect her, how I had let her get killed—in my office. I should've never left her. I had to get back in there, had to find out who had done this profane thing.

I stepped forward and said, "But I—"

"You're not going back inside tonight," he said. "This is a crime scene now. Whatever you've left inside you can get tomorrow." Then, very slowly, he said, "We will see you tomorrow."

The previous summer I had been part of an investigation into the death of an inmate that had not only uncovered the illegal activities of some of his officers, but cast him as either inept or corrupt. In fact, my ex-father-in-law, the inspector general of the department, was still investigating him.

"I didn't leave anything inside," I said. "I thought the inspector might need my help."

I could feel myself falling apart, but I was powerless to stop it.

Suddenly, getting inside the chapel became all that mattered, all I could think about. If I could just see her, just be with her, look at the crime scene, examine the evidence, attempt to redeem my negligence by finding her killer.

"I'll get him all the help he needs," he said, patronizing me and enjoying it. "You don't have to worry about it. Just go home and—"

"But I'm a—"

"A *what?*" he asked, as if he had been waiting for this. "You're a chaplain. A preacher. You're not an inspector. You're not an officer. You're not an investigator. You are a chaplain. If you don't like being a chaplain and want to be something else, then maybe you should quit, but until you *are* one of those other things, you are not going into my crime scene."

A nearby group of officers perked up when they heard Patterson's rebuke and a couple of them—his boys, as they were referred to—began to edge toward us.

"You mean Inspector Fortner's crime scene?" I said.

"My institution," he said. "My crime scene."

"What are you afraid of?" I asked.

Stepping forward and bowing up his short, fat body, he got very close to me, looked up and said, "I ain't afraid of *you*. I tell you that."

"You afraid an officer's involved again? Is that it?" I asked. "What are you trying to cover up?"

"I'm giving you five seconds to leave this institution on your own," he said, "and then I'm gonna have you escorted out. And if you resist, I'll have you locked up."

"Just step inside and ask the inspector if he wants my help," I said.

"The inspector's not in charge here," he said. "I—"

"He's in charge of the crime scene," I said. "He has full—"

"Boys," Patterson said.

The two officers grabbed my arms, and I struggled against them. Breaking free, I pushed Patterson and tried to get in the chapel, but they grabbed me again—this time with both hands and no matter what I did, I could not free myself.

"Show the chaplain the way out," Patterson said. "And if he gives you any more trouble, cuff him and put him in the holding cell."

They tugged at me, but I didn't move.

"Some chaplain we got," one of them said.

"He's as bad as some of the convicts," the other one replied.

They dragged me to the front gate and pushed me through it. As soon as I was on the other side, I tried to turn to keep the gate from closing, but my feet got tangled and I fell hard onto the concrete.

The two officers who had pushed me and the two inside the control room began to laugh.

"Walk much, Grace?" one of them asked.

"Maybe he's had too much communion wine again," the other one said.

With the pain and guilt I felt over Nicole's death, the frustration and powerlessness of not being involved in the investigation, I lay there in my anger and embarrassment after being tossed out like trash. It was just too much. All I could think about was my first drink—the first of many.

CHAPTER 7

When I arrived at Rudy's just before three in the morning, I drained the remainder of my bottle and threw it toward the dumpster. Clanging off the side, the bottle hit the powdered oyster shell parking lot and shot up a small puff of white dust.

I sprayed my mouth with breath freshener and opened the door to the diner quietly, hoping not to wake Carla who was slumped on a barstool, her head resting on her outstretched arm next to open school books on the counter. My coordination wasn't as trustworthy as it usually was and I was unable to prevent the cowbell above the door from clanging.

She bolted upright and spun around toward me.

Her blond hair was mussed and stuck out on the side, her brilliant green eyes soft and vulnerable, their sleepy quality only adding to the sublimity of her beauty. At just seventeen she had the old soul of a motherless daughter trapped in a small town with an alcoholic father.

"I tried to wait up for you," she said. "I heard what happened. Are you okay?"

"Can I have some coffee?" I asked as I made my way to my booth in the back.

"Sure," she said, studying me for a moment before adding, "I'll bring the pot."

I made it to the booth and pitched into it.

The thick smell of old grease and stale cigarette smoke hung in the air.

"Anna's called looking for you," she said from behind the counter where she was preparing a fresh pot of coffee. "She told me what happened."

As usual, Rudy's was cold. According to Rudy, it caused people to eat more and had tripled his coffee sales. The way I figured it, the increased revenue might almost be enough to pay for his increased electric bill. The condensation covering the plate glass widows in front made them look like sheets of ice and blurred everything seen through them.

"What'd you tell her?"

"Just that I hadn't seen you," she said.

"If she calls again, tell her the same thing," I said.

Carla turned toward me, her brow furrowed, eyes questioning.

My eyebrows shot up. Challenging.

She looked back down at the coffee pot. "Sure," she said softly.

Since I'd moved back to Pottersville, I had spent many nights here in this booth in the back, reading, studying, making case notes and sermon outlines, and talking to Carla. Most of the time, it was just the two of us, which is why I came. The café sat on the highway and Rudy, Carla's single father, insisted that it stay open twenty-four hours. And since Rudy was in the back passed out most nights, Carla was the one to keep it open, napping at the bar throughout the night before getting ready and going to school the next morning.

Like the Pinkertons, I didn't sleep, not much anyway, so when I was here, Carla could. She often thanked me for keeping an eye on the place, never seeming to realize it was her I had come to watch over.

She brought over the coffee pot and two cups.

Wearing faded jeans and an Evanescence T-shirt, inexpensive white tennis shoes, no make-up or jewelry, she moved like she was on the runway—a carriage imbued with such elegance and dignity she made Dollar Store clothes look designer.

"You can go back to sleep," I said. "I'll be here."

"But—"

"In fact," I said, "you can go in the back and lie down. I can make a pot of coffee if someone comes in. And if something has to be cooked, I'll come get you."

Her sad sea-green eyes were full of compassion and I could tell she wanted to talk, but I didn't want to be around anyone, not even her. All I wanted to do was drink my coffee and not sleep it off.

"You don't want to talk?" she asked.

"I'll gladly listen to anything you want to tell me," I said. "But I have nothing to say."

She hesitated before speaking and I added, "Do you have anything you need to talk about?"

She shook her head very slowly. "No," she said softly, "not really."

"Then get some sleep," I said.

As she turned and began to walk away, I called after her. She turned quickly, a hopeful, even expectant look on her face. "Yeah?"

"Thanks."

"You're welcome," she said with a small smile. She then continued walking away another step or two before turning around and coming back, taking a seat in the booth across from me.

"I know you're… well… anyway, I *do* need to talk—if you can," she said.

"Sure," I said.

As far as I knew, I was the only adult she really had to talk to.

Looking at her so closely in the harsh light of the diner, I realized she was not nearly as pretty as I thought she was—not physically anyway. Her eyes were just slightly too close together and her nose was a little on the long side. Perhaps if I were seeing her for the first time—or looking at a photograph of her—I would say she was a little above average at best, but I wasn't. I was seeing her after knowing her. I was seeing, if not nearly all of her, far more than a first glance or picture could ever reveal. And I still say she was beautiful in a profoundly subtle way.

She took a deep breath and let it out. "I know we've talked about a lot of stuff, but this is hard."

I waited. I should have encouraged her to continue, reassured her in some way, but I was in no condition to do either.

"I've got a couple of friends whose boyfriends are pressuring them to…" she began, then hesitated a moment, before dropping her voice and adding, "have sex with them."

I nodded. Nothing new there.

"But they want to be virgins when they get married—or at least when they really fall in love and think the guy's the one. So they're considering alternatives—"

"The girls?" I asked.

"Yeah, but only because the boys are begging them to," she said. "Do you know what I mean by alternatives?"

"Well, unless your generation has come up with some new ones, I only know of three," I said.

A small smile twitched on her lips, then she raised her eyebrows and nodded slightly, trying to get me to elaborate.

"You want me to say them?" I asked.

I felt myself getting frustrated, but remembered how much I could have used someone to talk to besides my friends when I was her age.

Wincing slightly, she asked, "Would you?"

"Well," I said, finding it more difficult to say than I thought it would be, "there's manual, oral, and anal."

She nodded, a look of relief filling her face. "The third one," she said. "They already do the first two. They think if they do it—the other thing—their boyfriends will be satisfied and they'll still be virgins."

I shook my head. "They might be virgins—depending on how you define it, I guess—but their boyfriends will never be satisfied. At least not for more than a few minutes at a time. And if the, ah, standard way becomes the thing they can't do, it will become the thing they most want to."

She nodded. "I told them that," she said. "Well, something kind of like that."

"Are we really talking about friends of yours?" I asked.

She nodded slowly. "Yeah," she said. "I mean, I've thought about it some, too, but I don't even have a very serious boyfriend."

"Just be very, very careful," I said. "You're all making decisions that can affect the rest of your lives."

"It really is about two of my friends," she said. "I thought if I told them you said it, they'd listen."

I laughed.

"You're very influential," she said with a wry, self-satisfied smile. She patted my hand and stood up.

"I'll leave you alone now," she said. "Thanks."

When she had climbed back onto the bar chair and laid her head down on the counter next to her school books, I said, "Go get in bed. At least get a couple of good hours."

She glanced toward the back and the small living quarters she refused to call home, then back at me. "I'd rather just stay here."

I nodded and smiled at her.

Before I finished my first cup and just about the time Carla dozed off, the cowbell above the door clanged and Anna walked in.

It was the only time in my life I could recall not being happy to see her.

She spoke to Carla, then walked over and slid into the booth across from me.

We sat in silence for a long moment, staring at each other. Her huge brown eyes took me in, and though there was only acceptance and compassion in them, I didn't like the reflection I saw.

My embarrassment at her seeing my weakness was compounded by how much I needed her, but the self-loathing I felt couldn't compare to the pain her presence inflicted.

"You okay?" she asked.

"No," I said bluntly.

"Can I do anything?"

"No," I said again, shaking my head.

"Have you been drinking?" she asked.

"Yes," I said. "And more than just coffee."

"I'm sorry," she said.

I shot her a quizzical look.

"For what you saw," she explained. "For what you're feeling."

I couldn't tell her that part of what I was feeling was anger and frustration at not being allowed to stay and investigate, at being treated like a chaplain and not a cop. In the light of what had happened to Nicole, my self-centered, sophomoric feelings seemed even more silly and superfluous, my hypocrisy more pathetic. Less than twenty-four hours earlier, I was telling her how I wanted to stop investigating so I could concentrate on chaplaincy.

"I can't know what you've seen or what it's done to you," she said, "or how much pain you must be feeling."

I didn't say anything, just tried to get some of what I needed from the energy of her full attention. Desiring her so strongly and not being able to have her hurt so badly that I couldn't tell which was stronger, the wounds or the wanting, and I wondered if I had the ability to inflict the same unseen injuries on her.

"But it's just an excuse you're using," she said.

"What?" I asked, my anger flaring.

"You're drinking because you want to," she said. "Fine. But don't use that precious little girl to justify it."

I looked at my watch. "It's late," I said. "I'm a single man. You're a married woman."

"*John*—"she started before I cut her off.

"I'm not your concern," I said. "Don't come chasing after me in the middle of the night. Have some self-respect."

"*John,*" she said, her stunned tone filling the single syllable with more pain than I thought possible.

"Go home to your husband," I said.

Which she did, and, as I sat there alone in the comfortless silence, her absence was as palpable as her presence had been.

CHAPTER 8

After waking up late at Rudy's following a fitful few hours sleep in my booth, I raced down the empty stretch of pine tree-lined highway between my trailer and the prison. White clouds filled the sky and the air was fresh and cool, especially for May.

A quick shower had helped revive me, but my head throbbed, aching with every beat of my heart. As I drove, I thought about Nicole and the nightmares her death had resurrected. Like an old black and white film in an empty auditorium, they flickered in the theater of my mind.

I'm running up Stone Mountain, my heart slamming against my breast bone from exertion and the fear of what I'd find when I reached the top. I'm weary and unsteady, a mixed drink of bone-tired fatigue, mental exhaustion, and vodka coursing through my veins. Still I run as fast as I can, but I'm too late. When I reach the top, he releases her, and her body slides down the cold solid granite, following its contours like a tear in the crevices of a wrinkled face.

It was why I didn't sleep much… why it wasn't restful when I did, and why I was speeding to work on the empty highway with a hangover and didn't see the flashing blue lights until they were suddenly reflecting off my rearview mirror.

I pulled my truck to the side of the road and rolled down my window by hand since my old Chevy S10 didn't have power anything, even when it was new nearly two decades before.

Since my dad was the sheriff of Potter County, and everyone in the small county recognized my truck, I had never been pulled over before. I glanced at my watch. When I looked back up, I caught sight of a young deputy in an ill-fitting green uniform swaggering toward me like John Wayne. The walk alone was enough to let me know it was my younger brother, Jake.

When he reached my window, he flipped open his ticket book and withdrew the small piece of toothpick from the corner of his mouth.

"This ain't I-75, hot shot," he said. "You ain't in Atlanta anymore."

I shook my head in disbelief. The only thing more absurd than the obviousness of his observation was the fact that it came from Jake, who more than anyone reminded me of just how true it was.

I found his slow, thick drawl more grating than usual, and though the last thing I needed this morning was getting into it with him, I lacked the restraint to resist.

"Thanks for the reminder, Officer," I said, the sarcasm coming out with an edge that had nothing to do with Jake.

In my mirrors, the official lights on top of his car blinked ominously like silent alarm signals, and the passing drivers slowed to look, shaking their heads or blowing their horns when they recognized us.

Jake and I had never been close, but the enormous gulf between us had grown to infinity because I had moved away and he had not. Before, I had simply not quite fit in. Now, I was an outsider, and in addition to everything else, the gap between us had in many ways become cultural.

"Are you giving me a ticket or what?" I asked in frustration. "I really need to go."

"What's the rush?" he asked. "Inmates can't wait until they've had their breakfast to get their religion?"

Sighing heavily and shaking my head, I cranked the truck and put it into gear.

"It's Dad," he said.

I killed the engine.

"He radioed and told me to stop you. He said he needs to talk to us. He's on the way."

He then swaggered back to his car, where he stayed, his lights still flashing, until Dad arrived a few minutes later.

My first thought was that something had happened to Mom, for it wouldn't be much longer until someone's needing to talk to me would involve the news no child wanted to hear. When Dad pulled up without the lights of his Blazer flashing, I could feel a little of the tension leave my body.

As he pulled in behind Jake, I got out of my truck, and we met beside Jake's car where he leaned against it the way cool cops do, the toothpick back in his mouth.

"Sorry to hold you up, Son," he said.

"That's okay," I said. "What is it?"

Jack Jordan, the longtime sheriff of Potter County, Florida, looked younger than he was, his thick gray hair parted on the side, his dark skin deeply lined, but not wrinkled, and his deer-brown eyes soft and kind. He was fit and trim, especially for a man his age, and strong, but humble, content with a simple life of service, his authority resting gently on him like comfortable clothes.

"Tell me about what happened last night," he said.

I did.

"Why weren't we included in the investigation?"

I shrugged. "I wasn't either," I said. "They sent me home."

"Do you know how I found out?"

I shook my head.

"At the coffee shop," he said. "I'm tired of not being included in the cases that involve the prison."

"It's as bad as havin' a fuckin' military base in our jurisdiction," Jake said.

Waiting with nothing to say, I shifted my weight, noticing the wet grains of sand that stuck to the sides of my shoes and the dew-beaded grass blades clinging to the tassels on top. All around us, in the midst of seemingly endless rows of pine trees, the forest was waking up. Birds darted between the trees, piercing the last of the sun-filtering fog.

"I'm not saying I have to run the investigations," Dad said, "but not to ever even be included makes me wonder if maybe something's being covered up. I don't know, it's just disrespectful and…"

"You're right. It is," I said. "I should've called you, but I was in no condition. I'm sorry."

The peaceful morning sounds of the rousing woods were interrupted by the crude mechanical noises of a diesel engine as a loaded log truck flew past us. We all turned our heads and closed our eyes as its wind-wake swirled sand and bits of trash around us, stinging our faces and tossing our hair.

"I'm not blaming you," he said.

"I know," I said, "but you're right. You should be included."

"Hell, yeah, he should," Jake said. "It's his county."

Ignoring Jake, Dad said, "I've got a meeting scheduled with your warden, the secretary of the department, and a representative from the governor's office."

I nodded, not knowing quite what to say.

"Sorry to hold you up," he said again, hesitating, and I knew there was something else he wanted to say.

I waited.

He looked down the long stretch of empty highway, then back at me. "In the meantime we'll be doing a little investigation of our own."

I nodded.

"And I'd like your help," he said.

I could tell he found it difficult to ask, and I felt an awkward embarrassment for him.

"You helping with their investigation?" he asked.

"Whether they want me to or not."

"Will you keep me informed?" he asked. "Let me do my job and be involved?"

How could I say no to the man who had never said no to me?

Nodding vigorously, I was amazed at how, even as a grown man, I still longed to please him and yearned for his approval.

CHAPTER 9

"Have you seen the news?" Pete Fortner, the institutional inspector asked.

Obviously uncomfortable in dress shirt and tie, Pete was a short man with a round middle, thick wavy black hair going gray, glasses, and a couple of chins. He looked like a little boy playing grownup as he sat in Stone's enormous executive chair at the head of the table.

I shook my head wearily.

We were sitting in the conference room in the admin building where, in a few minutes, he was going to take my witness statement and interview me, recording both on audio and video tape.

Pete was sitting where Nicole had, and my mind intermittently superimposed her image over his. When we weren't talking, I could hear the sounds of crayons rubbing paper and the echo of Nicole's voice in the room.

"Top story on every station," he said. "Front page of several papers. Governor issued the Caldwells an official apology and condolences and thanked them for all they're doing for God and our great country."

I shook my aching head in disbelief. I still couldn't believe it. Perhaps I was in shock. Maybe it was just denial. Whatever it was, I was experiencing a disconnect, a form of spiritual self-preservation, for nothing made me question my faith in goodness—in God—like the death of a child.

The admin conference room was adjacent to the warden's office. In fact, one of Stone's doors opened into it. It was a large, plush room with an oak bookcase with glass doors built into the back wall and a massive matching conference table in the center. The handcrafted table and bookcase, with their detailed carvings and smooth, glossy finish, were far too extravagant for a state agency, especially a prison, but it was precisely because this was a prison that we had them. Like most things around here, including the prison itself, the furniture had been built by inmates—these by the best craftsmen available at the time.

"Amazingly enough, Stone's still got a job," Pete continued. "Somebody's lookin' out for him. Regional director, I guess. Of course, if he hadn't followed proper procedure to the letter, no one could've saved him."

"Proper procedure?" I asked.

"NCICs, clearance memos, approval of the regional director."

"He had all that, did he?" I asked.

"Yeah," he said. "Unless you know something I don't, which has been known to happen from time to time."

"He didn't do the background checks or run a single thing through the proper channels."

Behind his glasses, Pete's eyes slowly grew wide.

"You know Bobby Earl's head of security is Stone's nephew," I said.

He nodded. "What I just learned this morning is that Bobby Earl's related to the regional director."

"So they let their relatives come into a maximum security prison with a minor without following proper procedure and a little girl got killed," I said, more to myself than Pete.

We were silent for a moment, then I said, "I know you don't have to, but I'd appreciate it if you'd call Dad occasionally and let him know what's going on out here—especially when there's a murder."

"Sure, no problem," he said. "I've thought I should do that, but I just forget. I'll start doing it. I promise."

"Thanks."

As usual, the conference room was cold, its window covered with condensation. Through it, the officers standing in front of the control room and the inmates cleaning the visiting park looked distorted, like objects seen through a raindrop-dotted windshield.

"Okay. You ready?" he asked.

I nodded, and he turned on the recorders, introduced himself, noting the date and time.

"Let's start with what you did when Mrs. Caldwell came out of your office screaming," he said.

And, cognizant of the red record lights on the audio and video devices, I told him my story:

"I motioned for Coel to get backup, my mind splitting into two halves, and I heard two distinct voices. One said, preserve the crime scene. The other, preserve her dignity. So, I tried my best to do both.

"I stepped into the office and closed the door. I then knelt beside her and checked her pulse, though it was purely academic. There was no question that the battered body before me was lifeless.

"Reaching into the garbage can next to my desk, I withdrew part of a plastic sandwich bag and used it to pick up the receiver and punch in the security emergency number.

"Within seconds, security officers poured into the chapel and helped Coel quiet the crowd of unruly and upset inmates, a few of whom had gathered around Bobby Earl and Bunny and had begun to pray for them.

"In a matter of minutes, the chapel was empty of inmates, and only Coel, myself, and the Caldwells remained. I helped them up off the floor and onto the front pew where they sat in silence, tears rolling down their cheeks.

"I stepped back into my office to look around when the trauma support team's first responders ushered the Caldwells out of the chapel.

"Then I heard a sound like someone attempting to open the door, which was followed by a quick knock and I looked up to see the institutional inspector, Pete Fortner, through the glass pane in the door that opened in from the hall. I noted that the door was locked. The inspector came in. You know the rest."

Through the moist window behind Pete, I could see that the small group of officers standing in front of the control room were laughing and cutting up like this was any other day. Their insensitivity and the inappropriateness of their actions enraged me, and I had the urge to go out and pick a fight with them so they could beat me up.

"Did you notice anything unusual at the crime scene?" he asked. "Or on or about the victim?"

The victim.

I thought about Nicole again—saw her drawing, pictured her wide smile, heard her small voice.

"The corner of something sticking out from underneath her left side."

"Any idea what it was?" he asked.

"A greeting card, I think. I give them out to the inmates each month. There was a stack on my desk at the time of... the murder. I assume they're still there."

"Anything else?"

"Yeah," I said. "Over on the floor under the window was what looked to be a small pink marble."

"Do you know what it was?" he asked.

"No," I said.

"Could it have been a piece of candy?"

I thought about it. "Yeah," I said. "I guess it could've."

"Okay," he said. "Good. . . Had you worked with the Caldwells before?"

"No," I said. "I didn't know them. Still don't, not really. I mean, I've seen them on TV a time or two, but Mr. Stone set up this program. I wasn't notified about it until the day it was scheduled to take place."

"So you had nothing to do with the program?"

"Nothing."

"Why were you there?"

"Just checking in on them," I said. "When a program's being conducted by someone I don't know, I try to stop by. And since this service had the unprecedented dimension of having a child involved…"

"Did you disturb anything at the crime scene?"

I shook my head. "Just what I told you. I closed the door, felt for a pulse, and used the phone."

"Thank you," he said. He then switched off both recording devices and sat back down. "So what the hell really happened?"

"The warden approved an ex-offender and a minor to enter the institution without going through the proper procedure or providing adequate security," I said, "and the minor got killed."

"While in a locked room by herself," he added.

"Exactly," I said.

"Oh, shit," he said.

"Exactly," I said.

"Was there anybody in the room when you went in?"

I shook my head. "The only places to hide are the bathroom and under the desk," I said. "I checked both."

"And?"

"And there was a killer, but I failed to mention it until now," I said, the sarcasm in my voice harsh and angry.

"Jeez," he said.

"Sorry," I said. "I just… I'm sorry."

He nodded. "I know I ask stupid questions," he said. "But I'm lost. I don't even know where to begin."

I nodded my understanding without saying anything.

"So," he said, "tell me where to begin."

"With the parents," I said. "Their statements. And any physical evidence gathered off them or from the scene."

He looked as though I were speaking a language he didn't understand. "You suspect them?" he said at last.

"Of course, " I said. "You know the drill, it could be anyone, but statistically they're far more likely to have done it than anyone else. Plus, they were the only ones—that we know of anyway—who were in there alone with her."

He fell quiet for a long time.

When I let my weary eyes fall shut, I pictured Nicole sitting at the end of the table coloring with the passion of an artist, her small fingers curled around the crayon. Is she your girlfriend? Chips don't have chocolate. You're silly. We'll pray for you, Chaplain JJ.

"They were treated as victims—grieving parents, not suspects," he said. "They weren't checked for evidence. Hell, we didn't even make them give statements."

Suddenly, I no longer had the strength to hold my head up, and it fell into my hands.

"Maybe I need a new job," he said.

"Have you considered the Boulder Police Department?" I said.

A former football coach at Pottersville high school, Pete had no previous investigative experience. Like many locals, he saw the building of the prison in our area as the best job opportunity he was likely to ever have. His only qualifications for the job were a losing season and a county commissioner cousin.

"But she was like a zombie," he said. He then shook his head and sat in silence for a long time before saying, "My case is over before it began. Is there anything I can do?"

"You can still get a statement from them," I said.

"The governor issued them a personal apology for not protecting their daughter while they were our guests," he said.

"Still has to be done," I said. "But you could start with the inmates."

"What inmates?"

"The ones who went out in the hall that night during the time Nicole was in my office," I said. "We know only Bobby Earl and Bunny went in the door from the sanctuary, but what about the hallway door?"

"It was locked," he said.

We were quiet a moment, then he lowered his voice and said, "We found a stack of hundred dollar bills near the body."

"What?" I asked, the surprise obvious in my voice. Money wasn't something you saw much of in prison.

"Yeah," he said. "They were under your desk. It looks like they may've been knocked off along with a greeting card and some papers during the struggle."

"I don't see how," I said. "I don't keep hundreds on my desk."

"You think someone was paid to kill her?" he asked.

"Then decided to do it for free and left the money?" I asked.

"Maybe they just didn't see it. It appeared to have been in an envelope. Some of the bills still were. It was a lot of money."

I was silent a moment, thinking about what he had said and its implications.

"We're pretty much finished here," he said. "If you want to go, you can."

"Have you taken Coel's statement?" I asked.

"It's next," he said. "You wanna sit in on it?"

"Yes, I do," I said.

"Why?" he asked.

"Because," I said, "he was the only one in the whole building who could see both of my office doors at the same time."

CHAPTER 10

Before Fortner could begin his interview, Edward Stone barged in and began firing questions at Coel. In stark contrast to his normal immaculate appearance, he looked ragged and unkempt, on edge. His eyes were bloodshot beneath drooping lids, and his countenance was that of an old and weary man.

"How the hell could you let this happen?" he asked.

Coel spun around, eyes widening, mouth dropping open, face reddening, and started to say something, but stopped himself, shook his head and sighed heavily.

Fortner had just turned on the recording equipment and he let it continue to run.

"You were responsible for her safety," Stone continued.

Having gathered himself, Coel sat perfectly still, his rigid composure the result of many years of military discipline. With great restraint, he seemed to be showing Stone the respect a senior officer was entitled. Swallowing hard, he didn't say anything, just simmered in silence, but I could tell Stone's words were fanning his smoldering anger into flames.

The wall behind Coel was filled with various plaques, all of which were engraved with the FDC logo and small employee nameplates. I saw my name on the Employee of the Year plaque and wondered how long it would be before it was on the Deceased plaque. I thought about death often. Probably because for most of my adult life I've been surrounded by it. You can't conduct murder investigations and funeral services without being reminded of just how short life is, how quickly death comes.

For me, the contemplation of my mortality is not morbid, not an obsession with death, but a call to life. Living with a sense of the brevity of my existence and a heightened awareness of the fragility of life reminds me to live each day to its fullest, to learn, become, and experience all I can, to truly live before I die. As far as we know, in the carnival of life we only get to ride once. The problem is, I've yet to figure out how to live that way on any kind of consistent basis. As with most things, my intentions far exceed my actions.

Nicole's ride had been far too short, and I grieved inside for the child who would never grow up, never be a boy-crazy adolescent, or a passionate young woman, a wife or a mother, never know the unspeakable joy and exquisite pain the seasons of life bring.

I became aware of Stone continuing to pour his wrath and rage all over Coel.

"Our number one priority is public safety," Stone yelled.

Finally, Coel had had enough. Casting off restraint, he slammed his hands on the table and jumped up. "So why the hell did you let a child into the institution?" Coel shot back. "What were you thinking? I've got to live with this the rest of my life. But I wasn't the one who put her at risk."

None of us could believe what had happened, and we were all looking for someone to blame—anyone, though deep down we all knew we were each responsible in our own way.

"By not doing your job you most certainly did," Stone said. "It wasn't going in that got her killed. It was not being adequately protected." Stone jerked his head around at Fortner and saw me for the first time. To Fortner, he said, "Get this over with and get him out of here." To me, "I want to see you in my office when y'all are done."

I nodded.

When he had stormed out of the room, Fortner looked at Coel. "You need a minute before we do this?"

He shook his head. "He should've never let her in," he said. "That's my statement. And that's all I'm saying without my lawyer."

"What?" Fortner said. "Come on. I'm just trying to find out what happened."

"It sounds like y'all're lookin' for someone to hang this on," Coel said.

Fortner continued to plead and reason with him, but he refused to reconsider. Finally, I stood up and switched off both recording devices. "Okay," I said. "No statements. Nothing official, just some information off the record. How about just answering a few simple questions?"

"Like what?" he said.

"Like who were the inmates who went to the bathroom or the water fountain or into the hallway for any reason while Nicole was in my office?"

He nodded slowly. "I want y'all to find who killed her. Hell, I'd like to find the bastard myself, but I'm not gonna take the fall for somethin' that was Stone's fault."

I nodded.

He studied me for a long moment, then nodded to himself as if agreeing with himself about some internal decision we were not privy to.

"Abdul Muhammin," he said. "I remember him because I couldn't believe he was attending a Christian service, and it was the first time I'd ever seen him without his koofi."

"Yeah," I said. "I thought that was strange, too."

"He's a chapel clerk, isn't he?"

I nodded.

"You need to ask him about it," he said.

"Plan to," I said. "Who else?"

"Paul Register," he said.

"The one they call Chester the molester?" Fortner shouted.
"Good God. How could you let him out there with her?"

"She wasn't out there," he yelled. "She was inside a locked room
with her mother. And I was standing at the sanctuary door watching. But the point is, she should have never been inside here in the
first place."

"We all agree on that," I said. "Who else?"

"Cedric Porter," he said.

"Inmate from public works?" Fortner asked. "I thought he was
an atheist. Does he come to church?"

"I've never seen him there before," I said.

"Probably just came to see Bunny like the rest of 'em," Coel
said. "Hell, a lot of them stayed in the bathroom during most of
the sermon."

"Why'd you let 'em?" Fortner asked.

"Because I was by myself," he said. "They pulled Whitfield
to help get education back to the dorms. At the sanctuary door, I
could see the hallway, the sanctuary, and both office doors."

"Sorry," Fortner said. "You did good. You were in a no-win
situation."

Obviously grateful for what Pete had said, Coel looked at him
for a long moment, then slowly nodded his head, a grave expression
on his face.

"Any other inmates come or go?" I asked.

"Dexter Freeman," he said. "Y'all know him?"

"I do," I said. "I've worked with both him and Register."

"They're both in on sex charges," Fortner said.

I nodded, then looked back at Coel. "Did you ever leave your
position at the door?"

He shook his head.

"Not even for a moment?" I asked.

"One time," he said. "Bunny opened your office door and
motioned for me to come over."

"Which door?" I asked.

"The one in the sanctuary," he said. "I walked over and she asked me how to place an outside call. I told her, then went back to where I was. But I saw her and the little girl at that point and they were fine."

"And no one else came or went?" I asked.

He shook his head.

"What about staff?"

"Well, let's see," he said. "There was you."

"I know I was there," I said, and I heard a harsh sarcasm in my voice that reminded me that Stone wasn't the only one on edge. "I meant anyone else."

"And Theo Malcolm."

"The school teacher?" Pete asked in surprise, his eyebrows and glasses shooting up again.

He looked over at me.

"Yeah," Coel said. "He must've stopped by after his class, on his way out or somethin'. He didn't stay too long."

"What the hell was he doin' there?" Pete asked.

Coel shrugged.

"I wondered the same thing," I said. "As far as I know, he's never been in the chapel before. And he was in a big hurry to get out. He nearly knocked me down on his way to the door."

"He didn't stay long," Coel repeated. "At least, I don't think he did. I didn't actually see him leave."

"Could he have killed her?" Fortner asked.

I shrugged. "We've got to talk to him. He was coming from the back when I saw him."

"I never saw him close to your office door," Coel said.

"And Officer Whitfield came in at the end," I said.

"Oh, that's right," he said. "I forgot. He got back just in time for the... well, you know."

"So," Pete said, "you got any idea who did it?"

"No," he said, "but Stone might as well have. He's the one who tied her to a stake like bait down there with all the predators."

CHAPTER 11

When Edward Stone welcomed me into his office, something he had never done, he closed the door, something he had often done. He then invited me to take a seat and offered me coffee, something he never did, and when I declined, he frowned deeply, something he often did.

"I assume your father and Inspector Fortner have both asked for your help," he said.

I didn't respond. He had warned me not to investigate after the last case I had worked.

"It's okay," he said. "I'm about to do the same thing. We need your help on this one. You're a good investigator, you have a unique position that allows you to move about between both the inmates and the staff comfortably, and you are respected by both groups."

"What was she doing in here?" I asked, my voice raw and accusatory. "How could you have let her? Why would the people who're supposed to be her parents even want to—"

"They weren't supposed to be her parents," he said. "They were her parents. She was loved and cared for by—"

"People who used her race to further their cause? People who subjected her to the fatal dangers of prison to gain greater acceptance from the large black population?"

He shook his head. "You of all people should understand ministry," he said. "You do anything for God."

"For God?" I asked in shock. "Bobby Earl's ego is his God."

He winced, the furrow between his eyes deepening into dark crevices, and I could tell that my words had seemed blasphemous to him.

"Bobby Earl serves the same God I do," he said. "And there's nothing we wouldn't do for him."

"Including offering up your child?" I asked.

I knew it was a low blow before I said it, but I didn't realize how low I was for saying it until I saw the anguish in his eyes. Though I was unaware of any of the details, I knew he had lost a son as a child and I wanted to wound him for what he—what I—had allowed to happen to Nicole. The outrage I felt at his culpability in Nicole's death filled me with a self-righteous indignation that made me thoughtless and cruel, and, gripped by a familiar guilt, I cringed to come face to face with the man I had so often told myself I no longer was.

He took a deep breath and sat more upright in his chair. As he straightened the vest of his dark suit, the bony fingers of his hands shook. He always wore a three-piece suit, and I had never seen him take off his coat. His suits weren't expensive or particularly nice, but they didn't have to be. The way he held himself, the way they fit him, made them look as though they were—at least until today. Today his suit looked cheap and ill-fitted for his narrow frame, as if in the course of one night he had shrunk somehow.

"Why not?" he asked. "Abraham did."

"God wasn't asking for Isaac's blood, but for Abraham's love. In the story God provides a lamb."

"That reminds me," he said, opening the center drawer of his desk and withdrawing a page from a coloring book. "This is for you. It was found in your office near… ah, her body. They gathered it with the rest of the evidence."

Tears stung the edges of my eyes as I took the wrinkled picture from him. The color-crayon image, made blurry by my tears, was of Jesus just as Nicole had promised. It was her rendition of the portrait that hung in the Sunday School rooms of my youth: Jesus, his dark eyes intense, his long dark hair flowing, with a lamb draped across his shoulders. In the bottom corner in red that glistened like blood as one of my tears fell on it, it read: To: Chaplin JJ. From: Nicole.

Images of Jesus praying alone in the Garden of Gethsemane flashed in my mind. I heard his trembling voice begging for his life, and the cold, cruel silence that followed. Where was God then? Where was God now?

Where are you?

"I realize you have a job to protect," I said. "One that would be in jeopardy if central office finds out what really happened, but why did you let an ex-offender and a minor into the institution without proper background checks and safety procedures?"

"So you know," he said, shrinking in his chair without any outward movement.

I nodded, waiting, watching, measuring his response.

"You're right, I did all that, but there's a good reason. I've known Bobby Earl for many years. He's conducted services in all my institutions."

"And he's related to—"

"The regional director," he said.

"Your boss?"

His nonverbal admission was a few small nods of his head.

I waited for a moment, but instead of saying anything, he took off his glasses, withdrew a silk handkerchief from his inside coat pocket, and slowly wiped them with it. Without his large glasses to cover much of it, I could see more of his face. His skin was dark—not quite the blued-black of a Nigerian, but very black, and shiny, and far more lined than I remembered.

"But your enthusiastic endorsement of him led me to believe that you two—"

"He was incarcerated at Lake Butler when I was the assistant warden there," he said. "I've never seen such a dramatic change in anyone. He made a believer out of me. He's the real deal."

"Still," I said, "it seems more personal than that."

Stone glanced down at the picture I held in my hands and then turned and looked at the one behind him on the wall. "Bobby Earl helped me and my wife through a very difficult time in our lives."

I nodded, even though he couldn't see me.

Still staring at the picture as though it gave him the strength to be vulnerable, he said, "He's given my nephew, DeAndré, who became like a son to me when mine died, a place to belong, a purpose. Got him off the streets. Kept him out of prison. I owe Bobby Earl Caldwell more than…"

"I understand," I said.

"I made a mistake," he said, as he turned back to face me. "And I don't want to lose my job, my career, over it. But more than that I want to find and punish the man who did it."

He paused for a moment, took a deep breath, and let out a long sigh. "Will you—"

"I will," I said. "No matter who it is or how it makes you, me, or this institution look."

He swallowed hard without saying anything, his nod seeming not one of approval, but of recognition, as if reconciling himself to the statement's inevitability.

CHAPTER 12

When I got to the chapel, I tried to say my morning prayers, but found I was unable to concentrate on anything except what had happened to Nicole. Leaving the silence of the sanctuary, I walked to the storage closet next to the unoccupied office I was using since mine became a crime scene and grabbed a handful of sharpened pencils and a new legal pad. Back in the small office, I sat down at the desk and began to make some notes on the case.

Making a list of the suspects, I considered each of them carefully.

Paul Register, Dexter Freeman, Cedric Porter, Bobby Earl and/or Bunny Caldwell, Abdul Muhammin, Roger Coel, Theo Malcolm, Tim Whitfield, and DeAndré Stone.

The Caldwells were the most likely of the lot.

Even if they didn't actually kill their daughter, they could be behind it. Why didn't DeAndré come back in with them? Why have security if you're not going to guard your daughter when she's surrounded by several hundred convicted felons?

And then it hit me like the hardest punch in boxing—the one you don't see coming.

What if Bobby Earl gave DeAndré the night off precisely because he didn't want his daughter to be guarded? Could he be that wicked? Was this crime that calculated and premeditated?

I'd have to figure out a way to ask Bobby Earl, but for now I could start with the suspects at my door.

I found Abdul Muhammin at his post in the chapel library, preparing to open it to the inmate population. Like most inmate orderlies in the prison, he had a proprietary interest in what he believed to be his library, but that was okay, because it motivated him to do a good job. Only on occasion did I have to remind him that the people using the library were more important than the library itself.

"Bet we'll be busy today. Everybody wantin' to see the scene of the crime," he said, shaking his head to himself. "Sick bastards. I still can't believe it happened."

"Me neither," I said.

"It's all they're talkin' about on the pound."

"I bet."

I sat on the edge of a folding table across from the small desk where he continued to stamp cards and insert them into books.

"How did it happen?" he asked.

Muhammin was a thick, light-skinned black man in his late twenties. He had bulk, but no muscle, and he was fleshy, almost puffy, without being fat.

"I'm still not sure," I said. "You have any ideas?"

"Has to be Bobby's bitch, doesn't it?" he asked, and I could tell he wasn't even conscious of how demeaning he was being to Bunny. In fact, I was sure to him he wasn't being. In his world the sky is blue, water is wet, and women are mamas, bitches, or whores. "Who else could've done it?"

Like most libraries, this quiet room smelled of dust, glue, and ink, but unlike most libraries, there was a monotonous uniformity to the materials it held. Try as I did to compensate with the small budget I was given each year, the majority of books and tapes that lined the shelves were donated by puritanical people with a particular point of view—for the evangelistic compulsion to convert and proselytize was felt most strongly by those most conservative. Ironically, those with the least to say usually say the most and the most outwardly religious were often the most theologically unsophisticated.

"What about Bobby Earl?" I asked.

His face wrinkled into a slack-jawed mask of incredulity, as if what I had suggested defied a natural law that everyone knew to be as certain as gravity.

"Bobby's no child killer," he said. "His conversion was real—I saw it—but even before he was born-again or whatever y'all call it, he was no killer. People either are or they ain't, and he ain't."

"Did you get to talk to him?" I asked.

He shook his head and frowned. "After what happened, I didn't even try."

An unopened box from Bobby Earl Caldwell Ministries sat next to a rack of pamphlets and tracts, and I wondered again about the complex motivations of a man like him—why he did what he did the way he did it, but soon found myself contemplating the more pertinent subject of what a man like him was capable of doing.

"I was surprised to see you without your koofi," I said, attempting to make it sound like curiosity and not accusation.

"Just showin' a little respect," he said. "Keepin' everything on the down low."

I nodded as if I not only understood but appreciated what he had done.

As if just making a casual observation, I said, "I saw a lot of people last night I don't normally see—especially in those type services."

"Lotsa men here to see Bunny," he said. "But a few of the sick pricks were here to see that little girl. Did you see the way that little Chester was hanging around outside your door? Hell, he's pressing his nose against the glass like it's the fuckin' candy store."

"Paul Register?"

"You shoulda seen the bulge in his pants when she was singing on stage," he said. "He looked like he was goin' to whip it out any minute and lay hands on it. Hell, if the door wasn't locked, I'd say he did it. You know how those nasty bastards can't resist little chicken tenders. Break in there, Chuck and Buck her, then ice her ass so she can't tell."

I could tell he was disappointed that I didn't react to his callous comments or ask what Chuck and Buck meant, but long before I heard the term on the compound, I'd seen the low-budget independent film it had come from. Even if I hadn't been familiar with it, I wouldn't have asked. I wasn't about to give him the perverse pleasure of saying anything else so crude about Nicole.

"I ain't tellin' you how to do your job—or whatever it is you're doin', Chap," he said, "but you see a little Chester motherfucker dry humpin' the door a little girl's on the other side of, and a few minutes later she dead, you start with him."

CHAPTER 13

Paul Register was the kind of inmate for whom prison was most difficult. He was small, resembling a teenage boy more than a twenty-three year old man, and, like his hands, his voice was soft. His pale skin, curly light blond hair, and weak gray eyes made him look colorless, which is what he might as well have been, for he remained nearly invisible among the colorful inmates at PCI, as nondescript as the pale gray walls of the institution.

But he preferred it that way. When unable to blend into the nothing gray of uniformity, he stuck out like a small buck in an open field during hunting season, which at PCI was year-round.

He was easy prey.

Paul Register was a sex offender, not a vicious rapist of women who demanded jailhouse respect, but a molester of the little boys he so closely resembled.

"Hey, Chaplain," he said, the tone of his voice matching his welcoming smile. "What are you doin' here?"

"I need to talk to you," I said.

I had talked to Paul on several occasions, though never in his cell, but more than talking, I had listened to him; listened for hours as he recounted his abuse and how he became an abuser. Tearfully, with what seemed to be a genuinely contrite heart, he had made his confession—telling the truth and finding what I had hoped was at least a spiritual freedom, but now I wasn't so sure.

Suddenly his face clouded over, distress replacing happiness. "Oh, no," he exclaimed. "Is it my mother? It's my mother, isn't it? Oh, God. I thought I'd be ready, but I'm not."

"No," I said. "It's not your mom. Nothing to do with any of your family. I just wanted to ask you some questions about what happened last night."

The relief rose over his face like the sun reappearing after a storm. "Oh, thank God. I'm sorry. It's just I'm so worried about her, and I know it won't be long until I get that call to your office."

That call, I thought. *What would my job be like without that call?* And then I realized again as if for the first time: *I spend my days dealing with other people's crises.* And I wondered if it was just an elaborate way of avoiding my own.

"I'm sorry," I said. "I get that reaction a lot."

"It's okay," he said. "I know one day you'll be calling me up there. I'm obviously not ready. But ready or not, I'm glad you'll be the one."

"Thank you," I said. "How have you been?"

"Okay," he said. "But I'm glad you're back. I've missed our sessions."

I nodded.

The cell seemed smaller than its six by nine foot dimensions— perhaps it was the bunks, sink, and toilet closing in on us—and we stood closer than we normally would have because of it.

Unlike closed custody cells, Paul was in a cell only because the open bay dorms were full, so his door stayed open, permitting him the freedom afforded to the entire open population.

"I wrote some more letters," he said. "And I got three more back. The one from my sister was great. She said she forgave me and that she really believed I was well."

I eyed him suspiciously.

"I already wrote her back and told her I'd never be well, and that she should never think that. I shared with her my commitment to recovery and how it's a lifestyle and not a fix."

"Good," I said.

The cell had the sour sweet smell of sweat and cheap cologne. Occasionally a foul odor from the lidless toilet wafted between us, cutting violently through the other odors like a hostile intruder.

"The other letters weren't so good," he said. "One said I was a bottom feeder and a robber of innocence, and the other one said I should have my, ah, private parts cut off and crammed down my throat."

"And?" I asked.

"And I was expecting it," he said. "It still knocked me for a loop. I mean, I understand their feelings, but… I don't know."

"Why don't you come to my office this afternoon," I said. "Bring the letters and we'll talk about them."

"Thanks," he said. "Now, whatta you want to know about last night? Let me help you for a change."

"When did you go to the bathroom?"

"I didn't," he said. "I just went to get some water. To get out of the service mainly. Bobby Earl was hard for me to take. I just needed a break. I mean, he was so mean-spirited and his solution to everything was an oversimplified formula. You know?"

I nodded.

The huge dorm had an open, airy quality about it outside the cells, the cement floors and high, unfinished ceiling amplifying every sound. It was noisy, but none of the sounds were distinguishable.

"How long were you out there?" I asked.

He shrugged. "About ten minutes," he said. "Long water break, huh? Like I said, I was stalling. Am I a suspect?"

I nodded.

"I guess I got to expect that," he said. "But it doesn't feel any better. Especially having you think it."

He took a deep breath, dug a fire ball out of his pocket, pinched the clear plastic wrapper between his thumb and forefinger, and popped it in his mouth.

"Want one?" he asked.

"No, thanks," I said.

The hard red candy sold in the canteen was all the rage on the compound, but was way too hot for me. I was convinced something that brought tears to my eyes could not be all that good for my taste buds.

"How much—"

And then it hit me. That was what was on my office floor. It looked like a pink marble, but it was a partially dissolved fire ball.

"What?" he asked.

"How much of the sermon did you hear before you got up?" I asked.

"Fifteen minutes, maybe," he said. "Couldn't've been much longer than that. He didn't preach very long, which surprised me."

"That surprised me, too," I said. Was it because he was too busy killing his adopted daughter, I wondered. "Did you see anyone else in the hall?"

"Dexter Freeman was hanging around," he said. "Sort of close to your office door. He was probably trying to get another look at Bunny. A lot of them were."

"Anyone else?" I asked.

"Mr. Malcolm came in," he said. "And Cedric Porter."

"Have you heard anything on the compound since it happened?" I asked.

He nodded. "Everything," he said. "You know how it is. Rumors're flying. I've heard everything from Bunny to Officer Coel to you did it."

"Me?"

"That surprise you?"

I shook my head. "Unfortunately," I said, "nothing much surprises me anymore."

"A lot of inmates say they've been with Bunny before," he said. "Say she's got a thing for black men. Used to be pretty wild when she and Bobby Earl first hooked up. Probably not true, but you never know."

"Anything else?"

"They say Bobby Earl has serious mob money from New Orleans," he said. "That he had to pay some debts, so he brought Nicole in just to murder her. Say he had a lot of life insurance on her. They say that's why he preached such a short message. He really came in just long enough to do it. And then left."

I nodded. "Will you listen out for anything else and let me know what you hear?"

He nodded.

Drifting into the cell with the snippets of inmate conversations that ricocheted off the cinder block walls was the acrid smell of cigarette smoke from the cheap tobacco sold in the canteen. Someone was smoking in his cell, hoping to get a little nicotine in his bloodstream before the dorm officer could determine where it was coming from. Within just a few moments, the inmate conversations bouncing around the dorm halted abruptly as the officer began to yell threats at whoever was stupid enough to smoke in his dorm.

"Who do you think did it?" I asked.

"I don't know," he said. "But a safe bet would be Abdul Muhammin."

I smiled.

"What is it?" he asked. "I know he's one of your chapel clerks, but—"

"No, it's just he said the same thing about you."

"Really?" he asked, his voice full of surprise and a touch of outrage, but he looked away, nervously averting his eyes from mine. "I wonder why."

"Had you heard Bobby Earl preach before?" I asked.

He nodded. "Sure," he said, pausing a moment and forcing himself to look at me. "Lots of times—on TV, on tapes, and here about a year and a half, two years ago. Why?"

"I was just wondering if you were familiar with his message and style."

"Sure," he said. "He's so self-righteous, so rigid, so—"

"So you knew what to expect?"

"Yeah," he said, growing impatient. "Why?"

"Because," I said, "if you knew what to expect and you didn't care for it, I'm wondering what your real reason for going was."

CHAPTER 14

Walking out of G-dorm, I ran into Cedric Porter as he and the other inmates were coming in for the noon count. Porter was about three inches taller than my six feet, and he weighed about one-ninety. He had the height of a basketball player, but the build of a football player, his tall lean body cut with defining lines and rippled with muscles.

"I've been wanting to talk to you," he said, his voice soft and respectful. "You looking into who killed Nicole?"

I nodded.

"Good," he said. "More than anything in this world, I want her killer caught."

Although his voice was respectful, his eyes were distrusting, even scared.

"Really," I said. "Why's that?"

"Because she was…" he started, then looked away.

"She was what?" I asked softly.

"She was my daughter," he said, his eyes softening momentarily to match his voice, tears moistening their corners.

"What?" I asked in shock and disbelief, my mind unable to accept what he was saying. I'd have to follow it up like any lead, but I didn't believe him.

"Yeah," he said.

"Your daughter," I said. "Are you sure?"

He looked at me as if he couldn't believe what I had just asked. "Yeah, I'm sure," he said, and his voice took on an edge that contradicted his eyes.

He then pulled out a folded sheet of paper from his shirt pocket and showed it to me. It was a crayon-colored picture of Jesus like the one Nicole had made for me.

"She sent me one every month," he said.

Maybe she was his daughter. The picture had obviously been done by her. I felt bad for how I had responded when he told me.

"I'm sorry," I said.

He waved off my apology with the sweep of his large hand.

A glazed, faraway glare filled his eyes. "I never really got to know her," he said to himself.

"Do the Caldwells know?" I asked.

"Yeah, they know," he said. "And they know I know a lot about them, too."

"You know them well?" I asked. "When did they adopt her?"

He smiled weakly. "Did time with Bobby Earl when I was down the first time," he said.

Behind Porter, inmates poured into the dorm for count, many of them sweating and panting from playing on the rec field. Like kids letting the screen door slam shut behind them, none of them made any attempt to prevent the massive metal door from ramming the steel frame that held it. A few of them spoke to me. Most did not.

"Were you up there to see Nicole?"

He nodded. "I was gonna try," he said, "but they killed her before I could."

"Who?"

"Just promise me no matter what happens to me, you'll find and punish whoever killed my daughter." Tears formed in his eyes again and he tried unsuccessfully to blink them away. "She was so beautiful. So sweet."

"Yes, she was," I said. "Who do you think killed her?"

"Who else?"

"What might happen to you?"

"Just promise me," he said, his voice filled with desperation and fear. "I'd hate to think he got away with killing us both."

Many of the inmates filing into the dorm had their shirts off, their hard bodies glistening as the sun hit the sheen of sweat covering them, and they looked like oil-covered body builders in the focused beam of a spotlight on center stage.

"Who?" I asked again.

His eyes widened momentarily at something behind me, and he quickly looked away. I turned to see Roger Coel walking toward us.

"Bobby Earl," Porter whispered, then nodding toward Coel, "and he'll probably use one of them to do it, too."

"Coel?" I asked.

"A correctional officer," he said.

Roger Coel walked past us and said, "You need to get in the dorm, Porter. It's almost count time."

"Yes, sir," he said.

The compound had gone from playground to ghost town. The rowdy sounds of mean children in men's bodies were replaced by the eerie sound of the nearly silent wind as it slithered through the structures.

"I was just tellin' Dexter a coupla days ago to watch out for Bunny," he whispered.

"Mrs. Caldwell?" I asked. "Why?"

"She bad news. Nothing but trouble. I's a damn fool. I fell in love with her like no other woman in my life, but she didn't love me. She don't know how to. She's just playin' me."

"You had a relationship with her?" I asked.

He nodded.

"When?"

"Before Bobby Earl," he said. "She was a secretary in the chapel at Lake Butler. That's where she met Bobby Earl. They hooked up while me and him was down the first time. Then when he started coming back in to preach, we'd get together. Usually in the back of the chapel. Sometimes in the bathroom or the kitchen."

"After she was married to Bobby Earl?" I asked, thankful for something verifiable.

He nodded. "For a while. It was good while it lasted," he said. "But when she's finished with you…"

"So Nicole wasn't adopted?" I asked in shock. "She's your and Bunny, ah, Mrs. Caldwell's child?"

"Bobby Earl adopted her, but she's Bunny's and mine's daughter," he said. "They told all they supporters they's adopting some underprivileged little black girl who didn't stand a chance in the world."

"Bunny was with Bobby Earl when she had Nicole?" I asked.

"Yeah," he said. "Fool thought he was havin' a son, an heir to his empire, then a little black girl pops out. They say he beat Bunny black and blue, but she wouldn't tell him who the father was."

The compound was full of inmates who could spin a yarn, but as fantastic as his story sounded, I didn't think that's what this was. It was unbelievable, sure, but I was beginning to believe him, and not just because he was giving me information I could check, but because of his conviction and certainty. He was either telling the truth or genuinely believed he was.

"And you haven't seen her since then?" I asked.

"I see her when they come in, but I ain't messin' with her if that's what you mean."

"And now you think she's seeing Dexter Freeman?"

He shrugged. "She may've moved on from him by now," he said. "Somebody say she with Walter Williams."

"Who?"

"Oh," he said with a contemptuous laugh. "His new Muslim name is Abdul Muhammin. Nigga' say he all spiritual now, but I sure as hell can't tell. Please just find out who killed her. And don't let them get away with it. And if somethin' happen to me, I guarantee Bobby Earl'll be the one what done it."

"Why would he want to kill you?" I asked.

He didn't answer me, just looked around nervously.

"Tell me," I said. "Why do you think he killed Nicole?"

"Because," he said, putting his hand on the door of the dorm and looking away, as Coel walked back by again.

"I said get in that dorm, inmate," Coel said. "Now."

"Because?" I asked as Cedric opened the door and walked into the dorm.

"Because he finally found out I was Nicole's father. He killed her and now he's gonna kill me," he added just before the solid metal door slammed shut, its loud clank reverberating through my body, the way the jolt he had just delivered echoed through my mind.

CHAPTER 15

After searching unsuccessfully for Anna, which it seemed I had been doing my whole life, I finally found her in the records vault in Classification.

Shoes off, long, elegant legs beneath the black sheer of her hose, perfectly painted nails, she had thrown herself into replacing the inmate files she had used over the last few days.

She went about her task with far more aggression than she normally did, violently cramming folders where there wasn't sufficient space. When she noticed me, she stood upright, her body growing rigid. But that was the extent to which she acknowledged my presence.

"There are people paid to do this," I said.

"It doesn't matter," she said without looking at me.

"I told you I'd do it," Lisa, the file clerk, called from her desk just outside of the vault. "I don't have anything else to do."

I glanced out at Lisa, but it was the wall behind her desk that caught my attention. Beneath a wood-framed cork board filled with magazine cutouts of NASCAR drivers rather than the DC Memos it was designed to hold, a small black radio with a broken antenna emitted the grating sounds of slightly distorted country music. In front of her, Lisa's desk was disorganized and cluttered, piled high with inmate files and requests, though I had never once seen her actually working.

I walked over and stood just behind Anna.

Lowering my voice, I said, "I'm sorry I was in no condition to receive you when you called on me last night."

"It doesn't matter," she said.

"Last night?" Lisa asked. "What were the two of you doin' together last night?"

"I just got confused when I saw you," I said. "Or maybe it was the bourbon."

"Bourbon?" Lisa asked in shock.

Anna didn't say anything, just continued to file. Beneath her dark eyes were even darker circles, her hair needed brushing, her clothes were wrinkled, and she wore none of her usual jewelry, save the huge albatross of a wedding ring hung round her finger.

"I'm sorry," I said. "Why won't you talk to me? I'm reasonably sober."

"I don't think I will, John," she said. "And that's nothing to tease about."

"You're right," I said. "I'm sorry."

"Last night, when I saw you like that," she began, but then broke off.

"What?" I asked.

"You sure you don't want me to file for you, Anna?" Lisa asked.

"I've got the damn files," she said. "Go take another break."

"But, I'll—"

"NOW," Anna yelled.

Lisa huffed out of the office, her cheap heels clicking hollowly on the over-waxed tile floor.

The small vault, dusty and smelling of mildew, seemed to shrink in on us, the naked flourescent bulbs above us making everything look flat and dull.

"Last night what?" I asked.

"That's not the John I know," she said, still without looking at me. "It's not anyone I want to know."

I nodded.

"I'm doing my best to forget last night," she said. "I'm gonna try and just remember the John I knew, the John that could never talk to me like that."

"Just a little too flawed for you?" I asked.

"You can believe that if you want," she said, looking up at me for the first time, her eyes swimming in the mixed drink of anger and pain.

"So if it happens again," I said, "you won't come looking for me?"

"No, John," she said. "I won't. I've got a sober husband at home, and though he doesn't need taking care of, I think I'll do it anyway."

CHAPTER 16

At three, when his shift had ended, Merrill Monroe stopped by the chapel.

He found me in the hallway outside my office, looking in.

"Lock yourself out?" he asked with a smile.

I laughed.

We had been friends since junior high school, and though on the surface we had little in common, with the exception of Anna there was no one whose company I enjoyed more.

"Actually," I said, "I was trying to remember where everybody was last night. Walk through it and try to follow everyone's movements. Pete just walked into the library to get Whitfield."

"Library?"

"Listening to Bobby Earl tapes," I said. "Feedin' his soul before he takes his post."

Merrill smiled to himself appreciatively as if at an inside joke.

Standing in front of the main doors, he eclipsed the light coming through their glass panels. His upper body was a perfect V, broad shoulders tapering down into narrow hips. His light brown CO shirt stretched tightly over the dark brown skin that covered the muscles in his shoulders, chest, and arms—especially the large round biceps which appeared perpetually flexed.

A moment later, Pete and Tim joined us in the hallway.

"It'd help me to have a visual as I'm thinking through this whole thing," I said. "I've called for Coel, but until he gets here, why don't you be him, Merrill?"

Merrill snapped to attention, saluted, and did his best white-man's walk into the sanctuary.

"Was the door closed?" he asked.

I nodded, and he closed the door. Through the glass of the door, he could still see the entire main hallway and we could see him, which meant the murderer could, too.

"He can see everything from there," Pete said.

"Yeah, that's the point of the glass," Tim said.

"So how could anyone get into that locked office without him seeing them?" Pete asked.

"That is the question," I said, then, turning to Whitfield, asked, "How long were you here?"

"I got called out almost immediately," he said. "The service hadn't even started yet."

"To escort the education inmates back down to the dorms?"

He nodded.

"And when'd you make it back?" I asked.

"I had just gotten back when you saw me in the bathroom," he said.

"Okay," I said. "For now, you just be one of the inmates."

"Which one?"

"Register," I said. "And, Pete, you be Freeman. Go in the sanctuary, sit down, and then in a moment, slip out here again."

The door behind me opened, and I turned to see Roger Coel walking in. In another moment, Coel was in his place inside the sanctuary and Merrill was playing Muhammin.

One by one, Tim, Pete, and Merrill slipped out of the sanctuary and into the hallway. They got water, stretched their legs, and went down the smaller hallway to the bathroom.

"Now, Bobby Earl was preaching," I said to Coel, who was still in the sanctuary, "and he's pretty loud and dramatic. Could you have gotten wrapped up in his performance and not seen what was going on out here?"

"Hell, no," he said. "I didn't get caught up in Bobby Earl. Not even for a second. Now, Bunny's a different story."

"Okay," I said. "So just watch like you did that night."

He did.

And as he did, Tim Whitfield darted out of the small hallway, crossed the main one, and into my office.

Coel wasn't even looking into the hallway at the time, but still saw him in his peripheral vision.

"He wasn't even looking and he saw him," Pete said. "And that was with the door unlocked, which we know it wasn't."

I nodded.

"I take it you were a little more distracted when Bunny and Nicole were singing." I said.

"Well, yeah," he said. "Bunny's a beautiful woman, but not enough not to see the hallway at all times. Besides, if I ever did get distracted by Bunny, it was when Nicole was on stage with her, and she wasn't killed on stage."

"The only time you left your post was when Bunny called you to the other office door?" I asked.

"Which was less than twenty seconds," he said. "And I was looking in the office at her."

"So no one got in that office from this hallway," Pete said. "Which means we know who killed Nicole."

"Who?" I asked.

"Bobby Earl or Bunny."

"Which one?" I asked.

"Both, maybe," he said with a shrug. "I don't know. But it's got to be one of them. No one else could have."

"That's not necessarily true," I said.

"Of course it is," he said. "No one could've gotten into your office without Coel seeing him."

"Even if that's true, it doesn't mean they did it."

"Who else?" he asked in frustration.

"There're a lot of possibilities," I said. "But the most obvious is that the killer could have already been in there."

Pete looked like he had been hit. He started to say something, but stopped.

"Where?" Tim asked.

"Hiding in the bathroom," I said. "Or under the desk. It's not likely, but it is a possibility. And there are others. We've got to figure out what really happen, not just assume it was Bobby Earl or Bunny by process of elimination."

CHAPTER 17

Since I couldn't work where Nicole's blood still stained the floor, Merrill and I went into the staff chaplain's office, which was vacant now and would be until we actually got funds appropriated to hire a staff chaplain.

Merrill was sweating heavily, and the dark skin of his face and arms glistened under the harsh flourescent light. When he sat down, his large frame dwarfed the chair across from the desk, and he looked like a parent sitting down to a child's tea party.

I opened the bottom right drawer of the desk, withdrew a couple of paper cups, and poured orange juice from a can into them.

"So," he said. "You know whodunit yet?"

I shook my head.

"I can't even get my mind around a motive," I said. "I mean the most obvious would be sexual—"

"She been messed with?" he asked.

I shrugged. "I haven't seen the prelim autopsy report yet, but—"

"I ain't talkin' 'bout her murder," he said.

I had been so focused on her murder, I hadn't even considered that she might be the victim of molestation, which would be a powerful motive.

"Bobby Earl?" I asked.

He nodded.

My mind began to race.

"Whacha thinkin'?" he asked.

"That if a public figure wanted to kill his adopted daughter because she was about to tell the world his dirty little secret, bringing her inside prison to do it would be... brilliant."

"Nobody said Bobby Earl was stupid," he said. "If he was messin' with her—"

"Which is a very big if, but certainly something we need to file away for consideration if the autopsy shows—"

"What's this *we* shit, white boy?" he asked.

I smiled. "I've got to interview them," I said.

"When you talkin' about Bunny, you can say we."

I laughed.

"You notice the way Bobby Earl's handling the death of his daughter?" he asked.

"You mean in as public a way as possible?"

"Yeah," he said. "Now, I hate to be cynical, but I bet he receive one hell of an outpouring of well-wishes and financial support because of it."

"Word on the compound is he had a very large life insurance policy on her, too," I said. "And that he's mobbed up and in need of a quick stimulus package for his struggling economy."

"If he brought that little girl in our house to kill her for money... for any reason..." he began, but was unable to finish.

"I know," I said.

"Just do me a favor and don't be askin' me to give the motherfucker mercy."

I didn't say anything.

My religion, what little I practice of it, is compassion. Merrill's if he has one, is justice. More often than not, they compliment each other, but occasionally they throw us into conflict. I couldn't imagine this would be one of those times, but when they came they almost always surprised me.

"*Could* it have been anybody else?" he asked. "I mean really."

I nodded. "I can think of a couple of ways it could be one of the inmates or staff members that were here."

He nodded. "I almost hope it *is* somebody else."

We both grew silent a moment, retreating into the disturbing thoughts inside our heads, comfortable with each other's quiet company. I thought about what he had said about mercy, and realized I wasn't feeling any at the moment either. I wondered if I would before we caught whoever committed this unimaginably dark deed.

"Cedric Porter says he was Nicole's real father," I said.

"You believe him?"

"Looking into it," I said. "Says Bunny was a chapel secretary at Lake Butler and they had an affair. That's where she met Bobby Earl."

"He saying Bunny was her mother?"

I nodded. "Says Bobby Earl just found out and that's why he killed her and now he's trying to have him killed."

Looking off in the distance as he thought about it, Merrill took another big swallow of his orange juice. It was the way he did everything. Without meaning it to be, most everything Merrill did was big. It wasn't bravado or for show, it wasn't even conscious. Noticing the way the paper cup was nearly completely hidden in his huge hand, I realized again that it could not be otherwise.

"I realize I ain't no ecclesiastical sleuth," he said with a smile, "but I don't see how anybody but Bobby Earl benefits from her death."

"We've got to figure out a way to interview him," I said.

"Big Easy ain't far from here," he said. "Just ride over and pay him a little visit."

"Got no jurisdiction over there," I said.

"If he killed that little girl, fuck jurisdiction," he said.

"Good point," I said.

"And it ain't like we got any jurisdiction here."

"An even better good point," I said.

The phone on my desk rang. I picked up after two rings and no one was there. I hung up and it started ringing again. This time someone was there. But no one I would've ever expected.

"Hey, it's me," she said, and within the split second of recognition came a flood of old familiar feelings. It was as if a secret door somewhere in my heart had been unlocked and all the vanquished spirits it held had rushed out at once.

The 'me' of, "Hey, it's me," was my ex-wife, Susan.

"Hey," I said. "How are you?"

"I'm good," she said, pausing awkwardly before adding, "Really."

"Good," I said. "That's good. Really."

We both laughed small, slightly nervous laughs.

I looked over at Merrill. I was sure he could read the awkwardness in my expression and voice, but he gave no indication, just sat there staring at nothing.

Susan and I had shared a life together once, but that had been a lifetime ago.

"How long's it been?" she asked.

"I'm not sure," I said. "At least a year. I've been down here that long."

"It doesn't seem like that long," she said. "Does it?"

"I don't know," I said. "I guess it doesn't. . . but in some ways it seems a whole lot longer."

"Yeah," she said. "You're right, I guess. I've been going to an ACOA support group for about nine months now."

I was shocked. It hadn't been my drinking as much as my sobriety that had ended our marriage. The child of an alcoholic, Susan knew how to cope with addiction. It was recovery, the absence of problems, that had given her the biggest problem. To hear now, a year after our marriage had ended, that she was in a recovery group of her own left me stunned, my mind reeling.

"Really?"

"Really," she said, adding with a laugh. "I'm not lying."

"I didn't mean it like that," I said, though of course I did. "It's just… I'm so… surprised."

"No one's more surprised than me. I've been in an ALA-NON group, too."

"That's really great," I said.

We were silent for a moment.

"I'm sorry," she said.

"For what?" I asked. "I'm glad you called."

"For everything," she said. "I was wrong."

I was speechless. After a moment, I managed, "I was, too."

"Yeah," she said. "But you've already admitted that. I haven't. You attempted to make amends. I wouldn't let you."

Where's my wife? What have you done with her?

"I'd like for us to get together and talk," she said. "I think we really need to."

"Sure," I said. "But now's not such a good time."

"I can come there," she said. "I've got a couple of days off. I was thinking about going to the beach anyway."

"Okay," I said. "We could have dinner."

She laughed.

"What is it?" I asked.

"Have you noticed anything funny about our divorce papers?"

"No," I said. "I haven't noticed them at all."

"That's what's funny."

"What?"

"We don't have any," she said. "I never signed them. Legally, we're still married."

She was right, that was funny, but not in any way that made me want to laugh.

When I hung up and sat there in stunned silence, Merrill said, "Who was that?"

I told him.

His eyes lit up as a broad smile spread across his face.

I started to say something, but was stopped by a thought about Bobby Earl and Bunny. Snatching up the receiver, I punched in Pete Fortner's extension and waited.

"You callin' an attorney or a marriage counselor?" Merrill asked, a look of self-satisfaction joining the genuine pleasure already on his face.

When Pete answered, I said, "What time did the Caldwells leave the institution last night?"

"You mean this morning," he said.

"So it was late?" I asked.

"Very," he said. "Why?"

I clicked off without answering, called the airport, and asked if they had any flights to New Orleans scheduled.

"Should I pack a bag?" Merrill said.

Before I could answer, the ticket agent came back on the line and said the only flight to New Orleans included a brief stop in Memphis and left at eight.

"You gonna fly over and ask Bobby Earl and Bunny how to make love last so you and Susan get it right this time?"

I laughed.

"They left here too late last night to catch their flight," I said. "The only other flight to New Orleans leaves at eight tonight. Whatta you say we're there to see them off?"

CHAPTER 18

When we reached the Bay County/Panama City International Airport, I jumped out and ran inside while Merrill hunted for a place to park.

The ticket counters to my right were quiet and mostly empty, only two agents helping a handful of passengers check their luggage and confirm their seating, but the left side was crowded and noisy. Recent arrivals and those who had come to meet them enthusiastically greeted, embraced, and conversed as they waited for the buzzer to sound and the conveyer belt to come to life.

There was no sign of the Caldwells in the long center corridor that led past the security checkpoint to the departure gates, nor at the small restaurant on the left, but as I turned to the right and peered into the gift shop, I saw Bunny Caldwell standing alone in front of the magazine rack in the back.

As I walked toward her, I realized she wasn't really looking at the magazines—they just happened to be what were in front of her. She seemed lost and alone, unsure where to go or what to do, so she just stood and stared and saw nothing.

"Mrs. Caldwell," I said.

When she turned around, she squinted at me for a long moment as if finding it difficult to focus. She only vaguely resembled the overly made-up, seductive young woman I had met the day before.

"Chaplain…" she said, and I could tell she was searching for my name.

"Jordan," I said. "John."

She nodded. "Right. What're you doing here?"

"I came to talk to you," I said.

Her long, pale face clouded over in incomprehension, then her eyes widened and it contorted into an expression of alarm. "About what?"

"Nicole."

She tightened her mouth in an unsuccessful attempt to fight off tears. "I can't believe she's gone."

I nodded.

"It doesn't seem real," she said. "I keep looking for her, keep starting to call her. I even started to buy her that." I followed her gaze over to an aqua bear draped in a small American flag. "She loves all those Beanie things."

Beyond the bear, out in the terminal near the rental car counters, I saw a small circle of old ladies huddled around Bobby Earl. Like Bunny, he looked dressed for church—or TV, and he was putting his hands on their heads and praying for them.

"I'm so sorry," I said, turning back to her.

"Why?" she asked.

"Why did it happen?" I asked.

"Yeah."

"Who do you think did it?" I asked.

"Who?" she said softly, and I wondered if the way she was acting was the result of grief, guilt, or medication.

"Are you okay?" I asked.

She shook her head.

Maybe it wasn't grief, guilt or medication, but shock.

She stared at me for a long moment without saying anything, without seeming to even see me. She looked so helpless, so vulnerable, and I felt bad for what I was about to do.

"What could she have done to make somebody do that to her?"
I asked, trying not to let my disgust at the question bleed into my
voice.

Forgive me, Nicole, I prayed.

If she or her husband had done it, she had to believe I was on
their side, that I would understand. She'd need to justify it.

As usual in these situations, I felt indecent and iniquitous. I was
attempting to manipulate someone to whom I should have been
ministering.

She glanced over at the bald black man reading a magazine
behind the counter. He was the only other person in the shop. If
he overheard our conversation, he gave no indication. He looked
bored, the magazine a barely adequate distraction.

"She didn't make anybody do anything," she said. "She didn't
do anything. She didn't deserve this."

"No, I didn't mean…" I said, but of course I did. "I just meant
I know how some children can be."

"Nicole was an angel," she said. "An angel." She then turned
her head to the side and looked up as if thinking of something for
the first time. "Maybe that's why God took her—to join the other
angels."

"There's no doubt she's with God now," I said. "And the angels,
but God didn't kill her. Who do you think killed her?"

"She was too good," she continued, in her own world now, no
longer talking to me. "She was just too good for this fallen, sinful
world."

Over the intercom, a pleasant-sounding woman with only a
slight southern drawl announced the boarding call for their flight,
but Bunny didn't seem to hear her.

"Bunny," I said sternly. "Who killed Nicole?"

She looked at me, our eyes locking, as if she were really seeing
me for the first time. "We did."

"You and Bobby Earl?"

She nodded. "We—" She broke off, her eyes growing wide, her face filling with alarm, as she spotted something over my shoulder.

I turned to see Bobby Earl quickly approaching us, DeAndré Stone following behind him at a distance.

"Honey, it's time for our flight," Bobby Earl said. "Why, Chaplain Jordan, what're you doing here?"

"I came to see you two," I said.

"To minister to us or ask us if we killed our daughter?"

"Both," I said.

He looked at me for a long moment, shaking his head. "DeAndré, take Bunny to the plane. I'll join you there in a minute."

Zombie-like, Bunny stepped forward and DeAndré took her by the arm. When he turned to walk out with her, Merrill was in front of him, blocking the aisle.

"We gonna do this here?" DeAndré asked.

Merrill looked over at me.

I shook my head.

"Guess not," Merrill said to DeAndré, "but I'd like a rain check on that."

"Bet on it," DeAndré said.

Without moving, Merrill relaxed his posture, and DeAndré led Bunny over to another aisle and out of the store.

"I'm sorry again for your loss, Mrs. Caldwell," I called after her.

"Do you really lack spiritual discernment to such an extent that you suspect me or Bunny of killing our daughter?" Bobby Earl asked.

"When I asked Bunny who killed Nicole, she said, 'We did.'"

"She meant by taking her into the prison," he said. "She's very upset right now, as you can imagine. She feels enormous guilt. It's unthinkable that you would come and—"

"Whose daughter is she?" I asked. "Is Mrs. Caldwell her biological mother?"

Before he could prevent it, his eyes widened briefly and flick-ered in confirmation, and he shook his head. "How can you do these things?" he asked. "Talking to another man's devastated wife when he's not around, accusing a man of God of murdering the underprivileged little black girl he's taken in and loved as his own? Sir, I ask you, are you a minister or a... or something else? I have to go now, but I will keep you in my prayers—and the men whose souls you're meant to shepherd."

He turned and began walking toward the terminal.

I followed.

"Weren't you and Bunny the only ones in that locked office with Nicole last night?" I asked.

Without stopping, he said, "Obviously not. She was brutally murdered—and we didn't have anything to do with it."

"Why did you have her in the prison in the first place?" I asked.

He shook his head, but didn't answer.

He walked quickly, weaving in and out of slower moving pas-sengers. A few of the stragglers from recently landed planes headed in our direction, recognized Bobby Earl, reacting to him the way most people respond to celebrities—with wide-eyed excitement, pointing him out to others or with attempted nonchalant coolness, undermined by surreptitious glances.

"Why have security if you're not going to use him to pro-tect your daughter in the most dangerous place she's ever been?" I asked.

We had reached the security checkpoint, beyond which Merrill and I couldn't go, and I realized that was my last question for the night.

"I gave DeAndré the night off so he could visit with his uncle," he said, dropping his bag onto the small conveyer belt and step-ping through the metal detector. "I was assured y'all would provide security for Nicole. Maybe rather than harassing us, you should be asking yourself why your chapel—your own office wasn't safe for my little girl and how culpable you and the Florida Department of Corrections are."

"He actually said 'culpable'?" Merrill asked.

I nodded.

After continued attempts to engage Bobby Earl across the security checkpoint, and making sure they did, in fact, get on the plane and that it did, in fact, leave the ground, Merrill and I were walking back through the mostly empty airport.

"Sound just like an inmate," he said. "You can take the convict out of prison, but..."

I laughed.

The recently deplaned had picked up their luggage and departed, and the airport was much quieter now, though it still had that high-ceiling, tile floor, open-air hum large enclosed spaces like malls get.

"Bobby Earl's put the fear of God in his old lady," Merrill said as we walked back toward his truck. "And that ain't all he's put in her either."

"I didn't smell alcohol on her," I said. "And if she'd been drinking, I'd've known. I can smell booze the way a vampire can smell blood."

"Man like him can get as much script as he want."

I nodded.

"'Course she could be medicating herself," he said.

"Yeah," I said, "but for guilt or grief?"

"Maybe both," he said. "I hear moms make real sensitive murderers. They kill they kid just like anybody else, but then they all 'oh-shit-what-did-I-do?' and tore up about it."

Merrill stopped and looked around the nearly empty building. "Damn, I's hoping we could pick up some stewardesses to party with—do a little layover."

"This is a work trip," I said. "Besides, *I'm* a married man."

"It's not like anybody was gettin' frequent flyer points from you when you thought you wasn't."

I laughed and we started walking again.

"We need to do a real interview with them," I said. "Even if we have to go to New Orleans to do it."

"Just let me know when," he said. "'Cause I wanna conduct a little interview of my own with that nigga' that works for them. And it's gonna be real-real painful for his black ass."

I smiled.

"So which one of them you think did it?"

I shrugged. "Maybe both. Maybe neither."

"You think it could be one of those other fools hangin' out in the hallway?"

I nodded. "I think while we're setting up a real interview with Bobby Earl and Bunny we should try to find out."

CHAPTER 19

When I reached the control room for work the following morning, I was directed by security, along with the other staff, into the visiting park for a contraband search. A long row of tables was set up on which we deposited the contents of our pockets and anything we were carrying—purses, briefcases, and lunch boxes. We were then escorted into the restrooms—men's and women's respectively—and required to remove our shoes and be patted down. These occasional checks for contraband were a good idea in theory—inmate visitors weren't the only ones bringing it in—but most employees were tipped off about them in the parking lot when they still had time to slip something back into their vehicles, and the thoroughness of the search was often dependent on how well the officer doing the searching knew you. They were our coworkers, after all.

Leaving the VP, I ran into Theo Malcolm, the new GED and literacy teacher at PCI. Malcolm was a thin, wiry black man in his early thirties with small dark eyes, the whites of which looked like unstirred chocolate milk. His eyes had an angry, defiant glare, and his posture was one of rigidity and defensiveness.

"You got a minute?" I asked.

He hesitated, then gave one curt nod of his head. Obviously, he didn't want to talk to me, but would, as long as I understood that he was doing me a favor. "In my office," he said and began walking down the compound.

I followed. When I caught up with him, I asked, "Are you enjoying your work here?"

"I'm not here for enjoyment," he said curtly. "I'm here to do my part to free my brothers from their oppressors."

"And to enjoy it would lessen its importance somehow, wouldn't it?" I asked.

He didn't respond, and we walked the rest of the way in silence.

To my surprise, his office, which was filled with kente cloth and African art, was not only unlocked, but there was an inmate inside it.

The inmate, Luther Albright, one of Malcolm's orderlies, was in Malcolm's chair with his feet on the desk.

"Luther, will you please excuse us a moment?" Malcolm asked as if it were Albright's office.

Taking his time getting to his feet, Albright walked very slowly out of the office, glaring at me and bumping my shoulder with his as he passed by.

When he was gone, I said, "Does he work for you?"

"He's one of my—"

"Or do you work for him?"

Malcolm said, "I will allot you ten minutes out of professional courtesy."

"Does that mean you're going to be courteous?" I asked.

On his desk, open file folders revealed photos of several inmates, including Abdul Muhummin, my chapel library clerk. He quickly closed the files when he reached his desk, and I thought his attempt at nonchalance was jerky and awkward.

He shook his head. "I don't have time for this," he said. "I've got work to do. My concentrating on doing my job may be the only hope some of them have."

"I feel the same way," I said. "We're here doing the same thing—trying to achieve the same goals."

The small office and state-issued furniture was all hard, cold surfaces, with no warmth or personality, and was filled with stacks of papers and books and the sloppy clutter that resulted from laziness and disorganization rather than busyness. If it weren't for the kente cloth and African art, it'd look like every other office in the institution.

"Do you have a Band Aid?" he asked.

"What?"

"I may need it if I get cut—oh, but it's the color of white peoples' skin, isn't it? So, because I live in a white world, I have to bandage the wounds white people inflict with something that resembles your pale weakass skin."

"Are you for real?" I asked.

"We don't have the same goals," he continued. "I'm part of the solution. You're part of the problem."

"But some of my best friends are black," I said with a big smile.

"That's not funny," he said.

I shrugged. "I thought it was," I said. "But the fact is, it's true."

"Monroe," he said. "He'd see he didn't need your friendship if he wasn't such a white man's nigga'. You think you're doing us a favor by helping us. It only adds to our dependency."

"Perhaps," I admitted, "but does that mean I should just forget about Nicole?"

"The white preacher's colored show piece," he said. "Well, he finally showed her to the wrong son of a bitch, didn't he? Ironic thing is, whoever killed her did her a favor. Freed her from slavery."

I didn't say anything.

"Wake-up," he said. "Bobby Earl's one of the most racist bastards ever to do time in Florida. I've told my students, he's the one they should've killed. "

"Who's 'they'?" I asked.

He shrugged. "Whoever did it," he said. "I don't know."

"You were there, though, weren't you?" I asked.

He nodded. "You saw me."

His right eye started twitching, and he looked down and began rearranging the objects on his desk as if it were something that had to be done immediately.

"But I've never seen you there before," I said. "Why choose the night before last to go for the first time? It seems a little—"

"Just checkin' things out," he said. "I get a lot of complaints about how racist you and your chapel programs are."

His comment had its desired effect. Suddenly I felt guilty and defensive, my pulse quickening, my hairline sweating, and I wondered who had accused me of such a thing. I had fought the good fight against the rampant racism of the area nearly my whole life, but with one comment I felt the need to defend myself, spouting my record the way a politician does. The race card was a powerful thing, especially when used on someone afflicted with so much white guilt.

"Really?" I asked, my voice flat, calm. "From whom?"

"I can't reveal my sources," he said.

"No, see, that's only reporters," I said very slowly. "You're a teacher in a prison."

"If you don't stop patronizing me, you'll regret it," he said.

"Luckily," I said, "I have experience living with regret, so it shouldn't be a problem."

"Why are you harassing me?" he asked, his voice taking on a whining, wounded-child quality that matched his squinty expression.

"I would think that's obvious to you," I said.

"Because I'm black," he said.

I smiled and shook my head. The persistence of his perception was maddening, and I realized that for all his racist outrage there was very little that was black or Afro-centric about him.

"Could be," I said. "Or maybe it's not harassment at all, but just a few friendly questions."

"But why're you asking me?"

"Because you were there," I said.

"So were a lot of other people," he said.

"That's true, and I'm talking to them, too," I said.

"Oh," he said, and nodded, seeming to relax a little.

"But, unlike you," I added, "the murder didn't happen during their first and only visit to the chapel."

Leaving Theo Malcolm's office, I walked down the long hallway of the empty education building toward the door, my dress shoes echoing loudly on the polished tile. Windows starting half way up the walls revealed dark, empty classrooms, many of which were seldom used. We had the inmate labor to build them, but lacked the budget to staff them.

Theo Malcolm has something to hide, I thought. Something so big, in fact, that he aggressively went on the offensive under the banner of racism in an attempt to distract me from it the moment I spoke to him.

The reverberation of my heels striking the tile was so loud in the long, open corridor that I didn't hear anyone come up behind me—but I felt them. In the split moment before they struck, I knew they were there, but it wasn't soon enough for me to spin around and defend myself.

In an instant, the lights in the hallway were off and someone grabbed my head and slung me into the plate glass window of the classroom to my left.

While one of them pressed my head to the glass, another pinned me to the block wall with his large, muscular body. Two others coming up behind me on either side grabbed my arms and held them in place against the glass.

At first, nothing happened. I was trapped, unable to move, and we all just stood there, only the sound of our breathing to break the silence. Then I heard footsteps coming down the hallway toward us, not clicking the way my street shoes had, but padding the way the rubber soles of the inmate boots did.

When the unseen figure reached us, he leaned in so close that his lips were touching my ear.

"If you're not happy being a chaplain and want to be a cop," he whispered, "join the fuckin' police force."

The voice was vaguely familiar, but shrouded in whisper as it was, I couldn't be certain who it was.

In the back corner of the room I was facing, the red glow of the EXIT sign seemed to float in the darkness as if disembodied from time and place.

"If you go near Mr. Malcolm again, we'll fuck you up so bad you won't be fit to be a cop or a chaplain. Understand?"

I didn't say anything, didn't move or give any indication I had heard him.

"He doesn't understand," he whispered to the group.

The big guy with the muscular body who was pinning the bulk of my body to the wall drove a punch into my kidney so hard that my knees buckled and if they hadn't been holding me I would have gone down.

As the pain surged through me, I saw tiny dots of light like a dark, starry night, and I felt dizzy and nauseated.

"Understand?" he asked again.

"Now I understand," I said, trying to swallow back the acid rising up my throat.

"Good," he said. "'Cause you're only going to get one warning."

The voice receded, the others following one by one, until only the body and head guys remained. Then, as the big guy pressing my mid-section to the block wall held me in place, the guy holding my head grabbed a handful of my hair, jerked my head back, and slammed it into the glass.

This time as my knees buckled there was no one to keep me from falling, so I did.

"I said I understood," I called after them, but they neither spoke nor slowed down, and before I could say anything else, they were gone and I was lying on the cool tile floor of the hallway alone in the dark.

CHAPTER 20

"You okay?" Merrill asked.

"I'll live," I said.

I was back in the chapel, lying on the floor of the staff chaplain's office, holding an ice pack to my eye with one hand and the receiver to my ear with the other.

"How many were there?" he asked.

"Coupla hundred at least," I said.

He laughed.

It was Merrill's day off and he had been washing his truck when I called.

From my unique vantage point on the floor, I could see things that usually went unnoticed for long periods of time—like the small chips and scratches in the ceiling tiles, the marks and proprietary scribblings of "Property of PCI Chapel" beneath the chairs and desk, and the cobwebs in the corners that fluttered like fine hair in a breeze when the central unit kicked on.

"Six, I think," I amended.

"You let six little inmates do that to you?" he asked.

"Embarrassing, isn't it?" I said.

"I wouldn't let it get out."

"Though, in my defense, there was nothing little about them," I said.

"'Cept they brains," he said. "Messin' with a man of God—what were they thinkin'? 'Touch not my anointed and do my prophets no harm' or I a have his handsome sidekick find you and fuck you up."

"That last part was a paraphrase, wasn't it?" I asked. "It's not in any of my translations."

"Gospel according to Merrill," he said. "Thou shalt not fuck with me nor any of my friends, lest thou havest thy ass kick-ithed."

"Amen," I said.

The melting ice shifted in the bag and clinked against the plastic of the receiver.

"What was that?" he asked.

I told him.

"And you have no idea who they were?" he asked.

"I couldn't see anyone," I said, "but the voice sounded a little like Abdul Muhammin."

"Your library clerk?" he asked.

"Yeah," I said, "but when I got back over here, he was sitting at his desk in the library quietly doing his job, so I can't be sure."

"And you think the teacher sent them?"

"Well, they only made a move on me after I talked to him," I said. "And he's the only one they warned me off of."

"They coulda been tryin' to point the finger at him," he said. "Knowing you be lookin' at him a lot harder now."

"That's true," I said. "And I'd be inclined to believe it if it didn't give them too much credit."

"Oh," Anna said as she opened the door and saw me. "I didn't think anyone was in here."

I turned from the copier to see the woman I most enjoyed seeing in all the world, and my breath caught the way it did every time I saw her.

"Hey," I said, heart racing, mouth dry.

"I can come back," she said stiffly. "How long will you be?"

My stomach dropped, and in that moment I felt the pain I must have caused her. "I'm almost finished," I said, my tone begging her not to leave.

It was later in the day, and we were inside the small copy room, which had originally been designed to be a storage closet in the inmate library. A dozen or so inmates sat around reading newspapers and magazines while others worked with the inmate law clerks on appeals, grievances, and law suits in the court-mandated law library.

"I wanted to tell you again how sorry I am," I started.

She held up a hand. "Don't, John," she said. "Let's not."

"Not what?" I asked, my voice hoarse, even desperate. "I just want to tell you how sorry I am."

"I already know," she said.

"Ouch," I said.

"No, I didn't mean it like that," she said. "I know you are genuinely sorry for what happened, and that you want forgiveness, and you'll promise never to do it again, but all that's just part of the sick cycle."

I nodded. "You're right," I said. "I'm sorry."

Her eyes grew wide. It was obvious she didn't want to hear me apologize again.

"Sorry," I said.

"John," she said angrily, but couldn't suppress the small smile dancing at the corners of her lips.

I not only ached to be near her, but I longed to talk to her, to tell her about all that had happened, to think aloud about the case with her like I usually did and get her reactions to the words and deeds of the suspects.

Before I could apologize for apologizing again, Pete Fortner walked in the room.

"I got the prelim results back," he said.

"And?" I said.

He looked at Anna.

"If she's willing," I said, looking over at her, "I want her to stay. We could use her perspective."

She nodded.

He shrugged. "Fine by me," he said.

As he opened the file and began flipping through it, I closed the door. After studying the pages inside a few minutes, he closed the folder and said, "She was beaten to death. Her right arm was broken, the wrist fractured. Her left shoulder was dislocated. She had blunt force trauma to her abdomen that resulted in massive internal hemorrhaging. She was hit so hard that her liver ruptured." His voice caught in his throat, and he glanced down at the folder again, blinking back tears as he did. "Her jaw was broken, and she died from an acute subdural hematoma—the result of a severe blow to the head."

We were all quiet when he finished, shaking our heads and trying to avoid each other's eyes. Suddenly, the small room had become claustrophobic, and I was having trouble breathing.

I saw Martin Fisher's crumpled, seemingly sleeping body again.

"Was there any sign of sexual assault?" I asked after we had each regained our composure.

"ME says he can't tell for sure," Fortner said.

"What does that mean?" I asked. "There was nothing about the way she was killed that would keep him from—"

"He says there was some inflamation and very slight bruising that could either be from normal childhood activity—riding a bike, climbing a jungle gym—or very careful molestation. He's just not sure yet."

"What about old injuries?" I asked. "Any indication of prior abuse or assault?"

"He said she had more old bruises than she should have, but no breaks or fractures," he said. "Nothing like this."

"You suspect the parents?" Anna asked.

I nodded. "Have to," I said. "They were the only ones we know for sure were alone with her inside my locked office."

"John and Patsy," she said to herself.

I nodded.

"Any other suspects?" she asked.

"Dexter Freeman, Paul Register, Cedric Porter, and Abdul Muhammin—"

"Two sex offenders and a murderer," she said. "I can't believe this. What makes them suspects?"

"They were all out in the hallway during the time Nicole was in my office," I said.

She nodded. "But getting from a hallway where they can be seen by an officer into a locked office is..."

"A problem," I said. "We're working on it. But it's not impossible."

"You know how it could've been done?" she asked.

I nodded.

"Because it seems impossible to me," she said.

"The door was locked when I tried to open it," Pete said. "And there was nobody in the office except you."

I nodded.

The copier finished its run and the sorter began clicking as the stacks of paper were shifted to the top to be stapled. We were all quiet for a moment waiting for the noisy cha-chinks of the stapler to stop.

"Suspect anybody else?" she asked.

"Yeah," I said. "Roger Coel, Theo Malcolm, and Tim Whitfield were also near my office at various times throughout the service."

"No shortage of suspects, is there?" she said.

"This is prison," Fortner said.

"Which," I said, "is why Nicole should've never been allowed anywhere near here."

CHAPTER 21

Later that afternoon, I taught a class called "Grace: Still Amazing," and as I did, I noticed several strong reactions from Dexter Freemen, especially when I shared my belief in the absolute, unconditional love of God. It was a strong enough reaction that I felt a follow-up was in order, which also gave me an opportunity to talk to him about the night of the murder, the night when he was one of only a handful of inmates out in the hallway near my office.

I had gotten a haircut recently—as usual from whoever happened to be available at the time—and my too-short hair refused to lie down, a fact that was emphasized by the steady breeze that stood it on end as I was buzzed through the electronic gate and onto the rec yard.

I slowly scanned the penitentiary playground, my eyes searching the blue masses for a black man, who, contrary to his name, was not free.

The fresh air and the warm sunshine were healing, and I knew somehow that the beautiful day was not merely benign, but the evidence of the love, care, and concern of the creator. I closed my eyes and breathed deeply, and as I did the volume of the vibrating world all around me increased, and I realized again how much I missed as I rushed through my days.

The crack of a wooden bat, the tink of an aluminum one, connecting with the softball, followed by shouts and running, and the clank of the bat falling on home plate. The bounce of the rubber basketball slapping the asphalt court to the beat inside the point guard's head. The metal clank of a horseshoe striking and then spinning around the small stake in the sand boxes. The shouts of frustration, the obnoxious trash talk involved in the intimidation of an opponent, and the glorious laughter of men having fun, playing like children, oblivious to the world passing them by.

When I opened my eyes, the vivid colors leapt out at me, the incredibly sharp sounds receding, muffled now by my inability to process all the stimuli life offered. I spotted Dexter on the opposite side of the field, walking around the dirt track encircling it. I waited for him to reach me, and then joined him as he went by, matching the pace he had already set.

"How are you?" I asked.

"Not too good," he said, shaking his head slowly. His face clouded over, his mouth forming a deep, angry, tight-lipped frown. He looked more frustrated than angry.

"What is it?"

"I was disturbed by the class today."

"Really?" I asked, my voice full of sarcasm. "And you hid it so well."

His frown relaxed a little, but his mouth refused to make the leap into a smile.

"I've been thinking about what you said the other day about the Bible not being true," he said.

"I never said that."

"Well, about the events not really happening," he said.

I smiled. I knew what was happening. He had been exposed to the new wine of unfamiliar concepts and the old wineskin of tradition and rigid religion was unable to hold it. I had been there many times myself. Soon he would have to make a choice—pour out the new wine or find new wineskins.

"All I said was that it's irrelevant whether they actually happened or not," I said.

"And what you were saying today," he said. "I mean, I'm supposed to be a Christian, but not if what you said about grace is true."

Two effeminate black inmates in shorts and T-shirts that were several sizes too small jogged past us. They wore pink Keds tennis shoes with matching sweat bands around their heads and white athletic socks that were rolled down around their ankles. They were both extremely thin and ran like awkward prepubescent girls. One of them pulled slightly ahead of the other and began to wiggle his behind as he ran. "Work it, girl," the other one said. "You're looking too fine to dine. I'm gonna have to toss that salad, child."

"Do you remember the story Jesus told about the father and his two sons?"

"The parable of the prodigal son?"

"Yeah," I said. "Which is true, by the way, though it never happened. Remember when the younger son came home after wasting his father's money on prostitutes and parties?"

He nodded.

"The older son was so furious with his dad he wouldn't even go into the house. Not only did his dad not reject or punish his younger brother, but he even threw a party for him. The older son said that it was unjust... and he was right. His brother didn't deserve the warm welcome and the extravagant party. But that's what grace is—what we need... not what we deserve."

"So, God's unjust?"

"Thankfully," I said. "None of us want justice—except for others."

"God's not unjust," he said. "I can't accept that."

"Neither could the older brother," I said. "He thought he had earned his father's love... and he knew his younger brother definitely hadn't... but so did the younger brother. He didn't even *try* to earn his father's love. And because he realized he couldn't, he quit trying… and discovered, perhaps for the first time, what love really was. You have children, don't you?"

He nodded.

The rec yard we were walking around was so enormous that the hundreds of inmates moving about the softball field, the weight pile, the basketball and volleyball courts, playing ping-pong and checkers under the pavilion looked more like ants than people—especially from Tower III, where an officer with one of the few loaded weapons on the compound stood watch, alert for inmates who wander over too close to the fence or low-flying planes or helicopters. Escape attempts by air most often occur on the rec yard because it has plenty of room for a helicopter to land and it's more isolated than anywhere else on the compound.

"Do you love them only when they're perfect?"

He shook his head, and a small smile crept across his face. "I've got a two-year-old son who's a rascal," he said, his whole countenance softening. "That boy stays in time-out. Sometimes his mama has to spank him ten times a day."

"And?"

"And I love him all the time," he said. "But… there's a difference in a two-year-old who's still learning right from wrong and these bastards."

He looked out at the other inmates on the rec field. "You don't know… I live with these people…" he shook his head. "… Most of the time they don't even act human."

I nodded.

A group of about ten inmates, running the opposite way from everyone else, presumably so they could be seen, approached us. They seemed to glide along, as if not quite touching the ground as they moved in unison, in beauty and grace. They spent most of their time on the rec yard, lifting weights and running around the track, and their lean muscular bodies were rippled with hard knots that barely moved as they ran. Their shirts were off, and the slick layer of sweat covering their hard, black bodies made their smooth, hairless skin look like fine silk.

"You're telling me there's not a difference between them and my son?"

"Sure there is," I said, "but not in the way God loves them."

He shook his head.

"If God's love is based on behavior... if it's based on anything, it's conditional," I said. "Perfect love is not based upon whether the one being loved is lovable, but on the lover's ability to love, and in the case of God, the love is perfect and complete."

"So why do we do all the things we do?"

"Like what?" I asked.

"Like praying, studying our Bibles, going to church or a class... doing what's right."

"Not to earn something we've already got," I said. "That's what the father said to the older son when he said he had earned a party, but had never been given one. He told him that he could have had a party anytime... every day at the father's house is a party...but not because he had earned the right. Because that's just the way the father is."

"I'm trying so hard," he said. "And it's not like I wasn't before I ever came here, but now I'm really bustin' my behind to..."

"To what? Earn God's love?"

"And they're still playing the same tired old games," he said, gesturing toward the other inmates. "And..."

"And," I said. "God loves them just as much as he does you."

When we reached the gate, we stopped. I turned back and looked at the activities on the rec yard once more before we continued walking through the first gate and waited for the second one to buzz open.

"I'm going to be honest with you, Chaplain," he said. "I understand what you're saying... and you've made some convincing arguments. But I'm not there yet."

"Me either," I said. "Me either."

We passed through the second gate and onto the compound framed by the enormous dorms on all sides.

"It's hard to believe," I said, looking at him intently, "that God loves Nicole and her killer equally."

He stopped walking abruptly, rage flaring in his eyes.

"You don't think so?" I asked.

"I think there's a special place in hell for him," he said.

"That may be," I said. "But if he or she chooses that, it doesn't change God's love or the fact that it will break God's heart any less than it'd break your heart if one of your children rejected you and did something so self-destructive."

"He should be tortured and killed as painfully and slowly as possible."

"Who?"

"Her killer," he said.

"Who do you think it is?" I asked.

He shrugged, then shook his head. "If I knew," he said. "I'd…"

As we talked, a steady stream of inmates passed by on their way to or from the rec yard. I thought about how few came to the chapel by comparison, and wondered if I was doing any good here at all.

"You were out in the hallway that night for a while, weren't you? Did you see anything?"

"I just went to the bathroom," he said. "I rushed in and out because I didn't want to miss any more of the message than I had to."

"When was this?"

"Near the end," he said.

"Someone said they thought maybe you and Bunny Caldwell had something going on."

Unable to respond, he stood there slack-jawed, stunned into wide-eyed speechlessness.

"What?" he finally said. "No. No way. I would never. I'm married."

I could tell he was lying, but when it came to sex I expected most people to, so I filed it away as a fact that might become important when joined with other the facts I had yet to gather.

"Did you see anyone else out there?" I asked. "In the hallway or the bathroom?"

He looked up and closed his eyes as if trying to remember. "Register," he said.

"Paul?" I asked.

"Yeah," he said. "And Porter."

"Cedric?"

"Yeah."

"Had you ever seen the Caldwells before?" I asked. "I've heard they've been here for the last couple of years."

"I haven't been in long," he said, then hesitated before adding, "Sounds like you're trying to find the killer."

I nodded.

"Why bother if God loves him as much as Nicole?"

"First of all, love doesn't make allowance for lawlessness, doesn't negate the need for justice—in fact, it demands it," I said. "And…"

"And what?" he asked.

"And," I said, "I didn't say I loved him as much as Nicole—or as much as God loves either of them."

That evening I drove down to Mexico Beach for an AA meeting. As the small county road rose slightly to come to an abrupt stop at what seemed to be the end of the world, my breath caught at the beauty, and I felt, as I always did, that this ending was also the beginning, and I had come home somehow.

Beyond the unpolished sunstone-colored sand of the pristine beaches, the Gulf rolled away toward the northwest coast of Cuba, its calm waters the color of uncut Columbian emerald. The setting sun was low in the sky, hanging just above the horizon, and cast a coral-colored shaft of light across the Gulf, as if illuminating a path to another dimension.

I had driven down here to ensure my meeting would be truly anonymous, but already feeling the Gulf's effect on me knew I had been drawn here in ways I could never fully understand.

Pausing at the stop sign as long as I could, I breathed deeply, gazed carefully, felt fully, and once again let the mending begin.

CHAPTER 22

The moment I walked through the chapel doors the next morning, Mr. Smith, my elderly inmate orderly, motioned me past the inmates waiting to see me and down the back hallway to the kitchen.

Mr. Smith was not only the oldest clerk I had, but was the one who had been with me the longest, and the only one I trusted. Unlike most of the inmates in the institution, Mr. Smith was quiet and respectful, his thoughts and actions deliberate, and I wasn't sure if it was his personality or a product of his age. Probably the latter—and the fact that he had been incarcerated for so long.

When we were in the kitchen and the door was closed behind us, he slid the large gray garbage can out from the wall.

The chapel kitchen was small and plain, functional, but not much else. The pine cabinets had been built by inmates and were thin and uneven, their earth-tone counter tops peeling up on the ends.

"I's goin' through the trash, you know, for security purposes—"

I knew he didn't have to go through the garbage, but that he took pride in the chapel and the work he did in it, and that he was constantly looking out for me.

"—and I come across these," he said.

He lifted the clear plastic bag from the can and emptied its contents onto the floor. Withdrawing from his back pocket two of the plastic gloves we kept around for food preparation, he handed me one, and we each slipped a hand in one and knelt down to examine the trash.

"They wrapped 'em in paper towels and shoved 'em down in the middle," he continued, "but they didn't fool nobody."

Beneath his closely cropped gray hair, Mr. Smith's skin seemed dry and paper-thin like parchment, his half-closed eyes wise but weary, as if the one was the price for the other.

"Well, I don't know about that," I said, "but they didn't fool you."

I watched his long bony black fingers beneath the clear plastic glove sifting through the trash, raking it aside until he found what he was looking for.

"When I saw 'em," he said, "I left 'em where they was 'til you seen 'em."

"See what?" I asked.

"There," he said.

Spreading apart the rough brown paper towel, he revealed the two used condoms it was meant to conceal. As he held the paper towel up in the palm of his gloved hand, the condoms unfurled like worms, their elongated forms revealing the moist residue still on them.

"You have a lot better idea of what's on the compound than me," I said. "How available are condoms?"

"They's a lotsa sex, but no condoms," he said. "I been down a long time and these the first I seen." A small, self-amused smile danced across his lips and he added, "No one 'round here practice safe sex."

I nodded.

"I've heard a few hardcore punks talk 'bout a officer usin' a condom before, but they bring one in, use it, and take it out—or flush it."

"These the only ones?" I asked.

He shook his head. "Seein' these got me lookin' closer ever'where, and I found one other in the visitor bathroom."

The visitor's bathroom was in the same small side hallway, just closer to the main hallway door. Unlike the inmate bathroom, which couldn't lock, the visitor's bathroom stayed locked and was only used by staff or visitors during a special program.

Turning around slowly, he opened the cabinet beneath the kitchen sink and pulled out a smaller clear plastic bag.

"This was in the little trash can inside the visitor's bathroom at the bottom of a bunch of tissues, paper towels, and a tampon."

"A tampon?" I asked.

"Uh huh."

Unlike the other two condoms, this one was wrapped in toilet tissue instead of a paper towel.

"It's different from the others," he said.

And he was right. Whereas the others were amazingly clean, blood and fecal matter, judging by the smell of it, streaked this one.

"That shit's rank," he said, jerking his head back when he had fully unwrapped the tissue. "Sorry," he added, and I knew he was apologizing for his language, "but..." He shook his head, wrinkling up his face, beginning to breathe through his mouth.

I reexamined all the condoms, studying them in relationship to each other, trying to account for their differences.

"Why they so different?" he asked. "These used in a woman and this one in a man?"

Vaginal versus anal use would certainly explain the differences, though the one seemingly used for anal intercourse in the visitor's bathroom wouldn't necessarily have had to have been used by two men.

"I'm not sure," I said. "We can't really know until a lab processes them."

Just then the door behind us swung open quickly, and Abdul Muhummin said, "What the hell're y'all doin'?"

I turned to see him straining to see what we were looking at.

"Go back in the library," I said. "I'll be in there in a minute."

"You need any help?" he asked, still not looking at me, but trying to see what was behind me.

"No," I said. "Go back in there now, and keep everybody else away from here until I get there."

"What did you find—a clue or somethin'?"

"Muhummin, if you don't go now I'm gonna have you locked up for disobeying a verbal order."

"I'm goin', I'm goin'," he said, holding his hands up in a placating gesture. "Just relax."

When he was gone, I turned back to Mr. Smith and asked, "When was the last time the trash was picked up?"

"Not since we was cleanin' for the program," he said. "After what happened, we wasn't able to get in here and clean."

My anger at Pete's ineptness and Patterson's obstruction flared as I thought about them not including the two bathrooms back here as part of the crime scene.

"So you're saying all of this is from the night of Nicole's murder?" I asked.

He frowned, the wrinkles snaking across his face like rivers deepening, and he suddenly looked even older. "I'm sayin' that the only night they could be from."

"If the killer wore a condom to rape that little girl before he killed her," Dad said, "how'd it get in the trash in the back of the chapel?"

Though I genuinely believed in the afterlife, and believed Nicole to be in a safe, loving environment now, far from the carnal concerns we were left to deal with, I still shuddered inside when I considered what her last moments in this life had been like.

I shrugged. "The two things may not be related," I said. "Especially since there are three. He could've worn it or carried it into the back in order to dispose of it away from the crime scene. But

Pete says the prelim's inconclusive about whether or not she was sexually assaulted."

"But if she was—" he began.

"I think if she were raped or sodomized there wouldn't be any doubt," I said, cringing to have to think, let alone say, such things.

Dad and I were standing on an old twin-trail logging road beneath rows of slash pines not far from the institution. Pete had agreed to let Dad's department coordinate with the lab to have the evidence processed, and Dad had driven out to collect the evidence. Not wanting to be seen making the exchange, we had opted to meet on the small trail used in years past to harvest the trees growing here previously.

"If not the little girl," he said, "what about the woman? The mother?"

"Could be," I said. "There's talk about her having a thing for black men and she obviously has a history with inmates, but…"

"But what?"

"They were found in the visitor's bathroom and if someone saw her leave my office, they're not saying," I said.

Squinting as he gazed into the distance, I could tell that what he was straining to see was behind, not before, his eyes.

As usual, being caught in the mire of human depravity that accompanies a murder investigation made me feel tainted, my soul soiled, and I longed to be, if not innocent, for surely I would never be that again, at least cleansed.

"What if she weren't meeting an inmate, but an officer?" he said. "Of course Coel would say she never left the office if he was the one she left it for."

The interest on his face and light in his eyes made Dad look younger, and seeing him so fully engaged made me glad we had involved him.

"That's a good point," I said. "Have you ever considered a career in law-enforcement?"

He smiled. "Sometimes I think I should," he said. "Most of the time I feel like a damn politician."

The rows of trees all around us were tall and fat, ready to be harvested again, which probably explained why the logging road was so overgrown. It had been many years since it was last used.

"You thinking these two were used for vaginal intercourse and this one for anal?" he asked, nodding toward the two bags of condoms I had just given him.

"Maybe," I said. "But as far as we know, there were only two females in the chapel that night and they were inside a locked office."

"Inmates?" he asked.

"Possibly," I said, "but a visitor or a staff member had to bring them in."

"What about Bobby Earl?" he asked. "Could he have slipped in the back and had sex with one of the inmates while he was supposed to be in your office?"

"I'm not sure. I don't think there was enough time," I said, "but I guess it's possible."

We both grew quiet a moment.

The midmorning sun was bright and hot, and the tall slash pines offered little shade, and as we both began to sweat, I noticed that we did so in the same places—our hairlines and the bridges of our noses.

"Of course, the condom used for anal intercourse wasn't necessarily used to have sex with a man," I said, and felt awkward talking about such things with my dad.

His eyebrows shot up. "The woman?"

"The presence of a tampon might suggest that Bunny or whoever the hypothetical woman was, was on her period and she and her partner opted for anal intercourse instead."

"That makes sense," he said, a hint of excitement in his voice. "That might just be it."

"It's just one of many possibilities," I said. "I'm hoping the lab can tell us which one it really was."

"Doesn't look like there's much of anything in these two," he said. "Looks like more residue's on the outside than the inside. Maybe our guy can't close the deal."

"It wouldn't be the first time," I said, "but if that's the case, why two?"

"Maybe he wore three—left the outer two and took the one with the evidence," he said. "Bobby Earl's smart enough to do that. We've just got to find out if he, Bunny, or Nicole left your office or if anyone got in."

"There's only one person who can tell us for sure," I said, beginning to ease back toward my truck.

"Where're you goin'?"

"To ask him."

CHAPTER 23

The chow hall of Potter Correctional Institution was a cross between
a cafeteria and an enlisted men's mess hall, combining the very worst
elements of both. Inmates were lined up against the wall and spilling
out the back door where they entered to be served. At the opposite
side, inmates poured out of the exit door after dumping the remainder of their food in a trash can and dropping off their trays.

In between the line of inmates entering and the line of inmates
exiting, the tables were filled with inmates eating. Each stainless
steel table was bolted to the floor and had four stools attached to
it so that neither table nor chairs could be snatched up and used as
weapons.

A few of the inmates scattered throughout the crowd had their
heads down, elbows working, shoveling in their food. However,
most of them ate lazily in between conversation, bursts of laughter,
and making deals under the table. Prison economy is one of beg,
bully, and barter, and every inmate at PCI was well versed in the
art of the deal.

Near the entrance, leaning against the back wall, Roger Coel
stood stiffly, keeping an eye on the inmates as they ate.

"Did you know Stone's blaming me for what happened?" he
asked without preamble.

I shook my head.

"He's written a report that recommends my immediate dismissal," he said. "I'm under investigation. My attorney says if they put this on me, I could face criminal and civil charges in outside court."

Roger Coel had been a soldier before becoming a correctional officer and it still showed in his erect posture, his precision, rigidity, and affinity for uniformity.

"Tell me again exactly what happened that night," I said.

He sighed heavily and shook his head.

From the corner of my eye, I saw an inmate sneak in on the other side of the line and take a place close to the front. I wondered if I should say something to Coel, who seemed to be concentrating on me.

"Excuse me a second," he said, and strode over to the line.

"Gibbs, I told you if I caught you skipping in line again I'd write you up," he said. "Come on."

"But Officer Coel, I—" Suddenly, the inmate saw something in Coel's face that said resistance was futile. He followed Coel, slinging his arms and shaking his head in silent protest. Coel led him over to the corner of the chow hall and stood him in it as if he were the class clown.

"Every inmate gets to eat every time," Coel said when he reached me again. "Every inmate gets the same amount regardless of when he eats. There's no logical reason to break the line. None."

I could tell that the inmates' insistence on breaking the rules offended Coel's military sensibility and bothered him more than it would most.

"Unless there's just something in you that has to break the rules," I said.

"Criminal mentality," he said. "We're surrounded by it. All we do is keep them a while until they get out and rather than skip line, they rob banks. Rather than disrespecting a female officer, they're gang-raping a woman in their neighborhood."

"Some change," I said.

"They're the exception," Coel said.

I didn't say anything. He was right, of course, but if I dwelt on it I wouldn't be able to do my job.

In the silence that followed the grim reality we had just discussed, I could hear numerous inmates complaining about their food, the force of their negativity palpable.

"I don't have anything to add to what I've already said about what happened," he said.

"Well, can I just ask a few questions?"

He shrugged, his eyes leaving mine briefly to scan the noisy chow hall. When he got the attention of a group at a table in the corner, he pointed to his watch signaling their fifteen minutes were up.

"Did Bobby Earl, Bunny, or Nicole go anywhere in the chapel beside my office and the sanctuary?"

He shook his head.

"You're sure?"

He nodded. "Positive."

"They never left my office by the hallway door during the service?"

"How many different ways can I say the same thing?" he said. "No, they didn't leave your office. No one went in and none of them came out—except to go the platform."

"What if I said we found evidence that suggests they might have gone into the back during the service?"

"What if you did?" he asked.

"Listen," I said. "If you're gonna change your story, now's the time to do it. Get in front of this thing and it'll go a lot easier on you."

He turned his attention away from the inmates and fully onto me, his pale, lightly freckled face a mixture of anger and incomprehension.

"You tryin' to help Stone set me up?" he asked. Then patting my chest, asked, "You wearin' a wire?"

"I'm only trying to find out what happened," I said.

"Well, then why won't you hear what I'm sayin'?" he asked.

"I just want you to be sure," I said.

He laughed coldly. "I think I'm the only one who is," he said. "And I am. I'm certain that no one went in and no one came out of that office. Strap me to a polygraph right now and take my statement. I tell the truth all the time. I swear to God what I'm saying is true. And I'm willing to back it up by beating the box."

"Okay," I said, "I believe you."

"Oh, that's such a relief," he said.

Ignoring his sarcasm, I asked, "Did the Caldwells go into the chapel before you got there?"

He shook his head. "I unlocked the chapel for them, let them in, searched the place—including your office and bathroom. No one was in there. No one. I did my job. I did my best to protect that little girl and I'll swear under oath, I'll take a polygraph on national television that everything I've said is the truth, so help me."

"So what do you think happened?" I asked.

"There's only one or two things that could have happened," he said. "Either Bobby Earl or Bunny Caldwell killed their daughter or they did it together. No one else could have."

CHAPTER 24

Tell me about Bobby Earl and Bunny Caldwell," I said into the receiver.

I was seated at the desk in the staff chaplain's office in the chapel, collar and shoes off, enjoying the cool air and solitude.

"I heard what happened," Chaplain Rouse said. "What was that little girl doing in your chapel?"

Jeremiah Rouse, one of the oldest and most respected chaplains in the state of Florida, was a thick-bodied, balding black man of indeterminate age—one of those people who looked middle-aged their whole lives.

We had become fast friends when I met him at a statewide chaplaincy meeting in Orlando, which was why I didn't mind calling him now.

After answering his question, I said, "You were the chaplain when Bobby Earl was there, weren't you?"

As I recalled, he had been the chaplain at Lake Butler for as long as they had a chapel at Lake Butler.

"Uh huh," he said, "and Bunny was my secretary."

"So they met in the chapel?" I asked.

"I'd've never had them working together if I'd known what was happening, but I didn't even suspect anything until he was about to EOS," he said, referring to Bobby Earl's release date or End Of Sentence.

"How long did she stay after he was released?"

"She didn't leave right away," he said. "She had to pay the bills until Bobby Earl could get his ministry established."

"What kind of inmate was Bobby Earl?"

"Perfect in every way but one," he said.

"Which was?"

"He tried to run my chapel."

"And he had an affair with a staff member," I said.

"Okay," he said. "Every way but two."

"So you think his conversion was genuine?"

"Who am I to judge?" he asked. "But look at the fruit. All he's done. I'd say it was genuine. You don't think he killed his..." He trailed off as if unable to say it.

"Do you think he's capable?" I asked.

"I've worked inside too long not to know anybody's capable of anything," he said. "But I'd have to see evidence to be convinced."

"What about Bunny?" I asked. "Could she—"

"Same answer," he said. "I'd have a very hard time believing it of either of them."

"There's a rumor going around that Bunny had or has a thing for black men," I said, "that Nicole was actually her biological daughter."

He hesitated before speaking again. As I waited, I could hear the little bits of static and white noise that were undetectable when we were talking.

"I did see in Bunny an especially strong interest in black men," he said, "but primarily as forbidden fruit. The interest was in illicitness more than anything else, I think. The way she was raised, black men were off limits."

"Did she ever..."

142 | Michael Lister

"Come on to me?" he said. "She did. Which, with our age differences, my position of authority, and me being a married man, confirms what I said about it being stolen bread."

"Do you remember another inmate there around that time named Cedric Porter?" I asked.

"I always suspected they were involved," he said. "He was a chapel clerk for a while, too. He was one smooth dude. Full of himself like nobody's business."

"Cedric Porter?" I asked, my voice conveying my disbelief.

I thought about the broken and beaten-down man I knew and wondered if his transformation was the result of lengthy incarceration or a relationship with Bunny Caldwell.

"Yeah," he said. "He was very charismatic—and I don't mean in the spiritual sense. All the cats who knew him from the street said he was a real player."

"He's nothing like that now," I said. "I know growing up, and especially doing time, can take the starch out of a man, but—"

"He fell apart when I had him reassigned," he said, "and until this moment I never could figure out why it changed him so much, but now..."

"You think it had to do with Bunny?"

"She's the one who asked me to reassign him," he said. "They had been close up until then—a lot closer than I knew at the time, I guess—but then Bobby Earl came to work for me and they began to get close. One day she came to me and said Cedric was making her uncomfortable. Being too familiar and forward with her. I hated to hear it because he was one of my best clerks, but she was staff and I had to let him go."

"So she gets involved with Bobby Earl and, to break it off with Cedric, she has him reassigned, which leaves him devastated because he really loved her?" I asked.

"I'd never thought about it that way until now, but it fits," he said.

We both grew quiet a moment, and as I thought about what he had told me, my other line buzzed.

"Can I put you on hold a moment," I said. "I don't have a secretary—and now I'm not sure I want one."

He laughed and I took the other call. It was the infirmary. They had an inmate who needed to see me.

When I punched in Chaplain Rouse's line again, I said, "If Cedric is Nicole's biological father and Bobby Earl or Bunny killed her, do you think they'd go after him?"

"I don't know," he said. "Why?"

"He's in the infirmary," I said. "He's just been attacked."

CHAPTER 25

I watched from the nurses' station through the steel reinforced glass as Cedric Porter was wheeled into the infirmary and helped onto one of the beds. His head was wrapped in a large white bandage quickly turning red from the blood seeping into it.

The infirmary was a rectangular room with two rows of beds on each side and an open bathroom area at the end. Windows on all sides prevented any privacy, and bright white tile floors made it seem cold, sterile, and uncomfortable. It was not a pleasant place. Inmates were not encouraged to come here. Cedric was the only inmate in the infirmary. Through the windows on the far side I could see that the suicide cells running along the hallway were empty, and in the hushed quiet of the enclosed space there seemed to be no sound.

When the nurse had returned to the station, I asked, "What happened to him?"

"Assault," she said. "Somebody tried to kill him."

Like an unusually high percentage of the nurses at PCI, she was obese, perpetually breathing heavily and moving slowly.

"How?"

"An old standard," she said. "Lock in a sock. Happened in the bathroom of his dorm."

"Do they know who attacked him?" I asked.

She shook her head. "The officer heard something from inside his station—that's how hard the lick was—everyone else was at chow. Anyway, he ran out of the wicker, interrupting the attack, and the killer ran away. The officer saved Porter's life." As I turned to walk back into the infirmary, she added, "He wasn't too happy about it either."

"The officer?"

"Porter."

I understood the feeling well. I often encountered it in the bereaved. But, as much as Cedric may not want it to, the feeling would pass. He would want to live again. We just had to keep him alive until then.

"How are you?" I asked as I walked up to him.

He opened his eyes slightly, closed them again, and said, "Not quite bad enough."

"Did you see who did it?"

He started to shake his head, winced in pain, and said, "No, sir. I didn't."

"Well, I'm gonna find out," I said. "Anything I can do for you in the meantime?"

"Get him to come back and finish the job," he said. "I'd rather be with Nicole."

"You will be," I said. "But let's not rush it. You just lie here and rest. We'll find out who killed her, and though that can't bring her back, it'll help you feel better. I guarantee it."

He frowned his disbelief.

"I just spoke to Chaplain Rouse," I said.

He didn't say anything.

From the open bathroom at the far end, a slow, steady drip echoed out across the tile floor of the mostly empty room, the source, no doubt, of the damp air and the smell of mildew.

"Why haven't you applied for a chapel clerk position since you've been here?" I asked.

"Don't want one."

I nodded. "He said you were never the same again after you lost your position there."

"I didn't lose it," he said. "It was taken away from me so that Bobby Earl and Bunny could have some privacy."

"You loved her, didn't you?"

"Carrying on with him up there when my baby's in her belly," he said. "Yeah, I loved her, but all she love is money. Why they perfect for each other."

CHAPTER 26

Like most small southern towns, there was no shortage of churches or bars in Pottersville. And both institutions were divided along lines of doctrine, class, and race. Some believed in sprinkling; others in baptism by immersion. Some preferred contemporary music while others would accept nothing but traditional. Some were extremely exclusive, while others were inclusive to the point of completely blurring any discernable distinctions. And leading each, whether behind the pine pulpit or the oak bar, were spirit-men who ranged from evangelist to counselor to one of the crowd.

The Sports Oasis was more of a mainline main street establishment, its congregation boasting the upper crust of the faithful. Unlike an east side or south side congregation, there was social status to being a member of the chosen who attended its gatherings. It was located downtown in the second story of a converted turn of the century inn with an assortment of store fronts beneath it attempting to be quaint.

Atop a florist, beauty shop, and antiques boutique, the Sports Oasis had the open feel of a converted warehouse. A curving bar ran the width of one wall and a stage dominated the other, tables and a large dance floor in between. All this, and there was still room for three pool tables and four dart machines along the wall on the left side of the bar.

I arrived at the Oasis at a little after five, hoping to talk to Alice Taylor before she got busy, but the place was already hopping with the after-work crowd. Even before I ascended the stairs, I could hear the distorted blare of Allan Jackson from a jukebox being asked to perform above its volume capacity. When I opened the door, I was enveloped in a whirlwind of country music, spirits, and smoke; and it carried me to the far end of the bar. This was definitely a full immersion congregation.

Scattered along the bar, men and women in their early thirties lounged casually, their loosened neck ties, coat-draped chairs, wrinkled shirts and skirts evidenced their tough day at the office. They all spoke or nodded to me, though I knew most of them only in passing. When I left Pottersville over a decade ago, I knew everyone; now, I seemed to only recognize vague resemblances to founding families in certain faces. Two young guys in jeans and T-shirts earnestly shot pool while a single couple in cowboy boots shuffled across much of the huge dance floor.

Seated around some of the tables were older Pottersvillians whose concerned looks let me know they were old enough to remember my past. The bartender, an early middle-aged man with coarse salt and pepper hair combed back, gave me the same look as he approached though I didn't recognize him. When he reached me, he didn't speak, but merely raised his eyebrows in a wary expression that asked me what I wanted.

"Cherry Coke," I said. I had to say it loudly to compete with Allan, but he seemed to be able to read lips. It was probably a job requirement.

He looked instantly relieved and smiled as he hustled off to fix it. When he brought it back, he said, "On the house," and gave me a wink.

"Thanks," I said and gave him a couple of dollars for his trouble. "Is Alice working tonight?"

"Yeah," he said. He got very close to me, so that he wouldn't have to shout and I smelled Polo Sport on his skin and peppermint on his breath. "She gets here about seven. Serves finger foods and does Karaoke."

"Karaoke?" I said, and feigned embarrassment.

He snickered. "Yeah, I know.… Why?"

"I need to talk to her," I said. "Just for a few minutes. She told me to meet her here."

"She usually gets here early," he said. "You can see her first thing. That way you won't have to be here later when it gets rough."

I nodded and failed to suppress a smile. "It doesn't get much rougher than Karaoke," I said.

"You have no idea," he said, shaking his head wearily. "Are you helping your dad? Alice ain't in no kind of trouble, is she?"

"No kind," I said.

"She's a good girl," he said, adding, "she's single, too," as he walked away to wait on other customers.

Hanging from the ceiling in various conspicuous places around the room, twenty-five inch TVs showed a wide range of sports events, and I got so wrapped up in a Lakers/Celtics game that I didn't notice someone had plopped down on the stool beside me until the bartender approached him. When I turned, I was looking into the familiar blue eyes of a high school acquaintance whose name I couldn't remember.

"Hey, man," he said warmly. "How ya doin'?"

"Good," I said. "How are you?"

He nodded slowly, pursing his lips as he did. "Can't complain. Can't complain. What're you doin' back in this neck of the woods? Just home for a visit?"

"No," I said. "I live here now."

"No shit?"

"None," I said.

"Whatta you do?"

"I'm a chaplain out at PCI," I said.

"I'll be damned," he said.

"Not if he has anything to do with it," the bartender said, nodding toward me as he placed the bottle of Corona in front of my nameless high school friend and another Cherry Coke in front of me.

"Right. Right," he said and started laughing. He took a long drag on his bottle and shook his head. "When we were in school, you were one of the craziest sons a bitches I ever seen. Seems like somebody said you had a religious side, but hell, I never saw it."

"Not many did," I said. "You had to look pretty hard. Some would say you still do."

He laughed. "Nah," he said shaking his head. "I can tell. You're different, man. I mean you still look like good ol' JJ, but... I don't know... just..."

"Sober," I offered.

"Yeah," he said as he started laughing again.

"Whatta you up to these days?" I asked.

"Ah, not enough," he said. "Do a little construction.... I thought about trying to get on out at the prison. Either that or build condos on the beach."

We were quiet a while, each enjoying our drinks. Eventually the music stopped briefly and the voices of people having a good time echoed in the open hall, joined occasionally by the loud clack of the cue ball driving another ball hard into a pocket. The Lakers, a different team than their former run-and-gun Pat Riley selves no longer had a fast-break, but they had Shaq and could beat Boston at their own half-court game.

The music started again—this time it was a pop-sounding song by Shania Twain. "Country music ain't what it used to be," he said.

"Thank God," I said.

"You like her music?" he asked.

"Like her videos better," I said.

He smiled. "I heard that," he said. "You haven't changed that much."

"I still like girls if that's what you mean," I said.

"Then God bless you," he said. He took another big gulp of his beer and seemed surprised to see that it was the last. He placed the bottle back on the bar and signaled the bartender.

"What's his name?" I asked, nodding toward the bartender.

"Same as mine," he said.

"Oh," I said, nodding as if that answered my question.

When the bartender brought him another Corona, he took a big swig from it, sat it down a little too hard on the bar and asked, "How'd you do it?"

"What?"

"Higher Power and all that shit?" he said.

I nodded. "Yeah. That's a big part of it.... Big part of everything."

He seemed to really consider this, after which he turned his head up, tilted the bottle back and finished it off. He carefully stood up, using my shoulder for support and said, "Maybe I'll go to a meeting with you some time."

"Anytime," I said.

"Thanks," he said. "I'll see you around."

He walked over and joined the two guys who were shooting pool, leaning against the table as he did. The bartender walked back over, shaking his head.

"Want another?" he asked.

"Man's got to know his limit."

"I respect that," he said.

"Hey, what's that guy's name?" I asked.

"Same as mine," he said and walked off with the empty glass and bottle.

Not far from me, two guys in their early twenties with FSU T-shirts and caps on began having a drinking contest. They were drinking shots of straight Tequila: salt, shot, lime. Salt, shot, lime. The people nearby cheered them on and as I remembered that taste on my tongue and its burn in my throat and stomach, I missed the quick camaraderie and the easy abandonment of tying one on with friends—and strangers.

I signaled for the bartender.

"I'll have another," I said. "Make it a double.... And whatever she's having," I added when I saw Alice walk into the bar.

He met her on the other end of the bar, pointed at me, and they both reached me at the same time.

"Sorry to have to meet here, Chaplain," she said, "but—"

"Hey," the bartender said, "this is a classy joint." He then placed our drinks in front of us, and moved down the bar.

"Don't be," I said. "I feel right at home."

"I'm not supposed to do this," she said. "This is confidential information."

"If you'd rather not," I said, "I can get it some other way."

"No, it's not that," she said. "I just wanted you to know why I couldn't do it at work."

Alice Taylor worked in the business office of PCI where she was in charge of inmate accounts. When she learned that I was trying to find out who killed Nicole, she got word to me that she had information that might be helpful.

"But I'm serious," I said. "If you're not comfortable, I really can—"

"You kiddin'? I'd love to be a part of catching that bastard," she said.

"You mean whoever killed Nicole?" I asked. "Or did you have a particular bastard in mind?"

She smiled, but there was tension in her eyes, and as she pushed her silky black hair away from her face, her hand trembled. "Bobby Earl."

One by one, the yuppie after-work crowd was being replaced by the less yuppie, more rowdy crowd, as if by an unspoken agreement each knew their allotted time. Mixed drinks were being replaced by bottles of beer as conversations about today's headlines were replaced by small talk about fishing and football.

"Ever wonder why a televangelist with a weekly national broadcast would come into a humble little prison like PCI?"

"I just assumed he was trying not to forget the pit from which he was dug," I said.

"Huh?"

"That he's got a soft spot for inmates or feels a loyalty to Warden Stone."

"That's because you're a good man," she said. "But you're giving Bobby Earl way too much credit."

"Uh oh," I said.

"What is it?"

"I'm thinking maybe Bobby Earl's innocent," I said.

"Why?"

"By admitting you think I'm a good man, you've just lost all credibility as a judge of character."

She smiled and punched me playfully—maybe even flirtatiously. "You are," she said. "Good-looking, good dresser, good chaplain—"

"Good God," I said. "I had no idea you felt this way."

She blushed, her creamy white skin turning a pale pink.

Simultaneously, we both reached for our drinks.

As she smiled up at me, I could see the gold flecks sprinkled throughout the green of her eyes even in the dim light of the bar.

"Do you want to know or not?"

"Yes," I said. "Why does a national televangelist treasure like Bobby Earl come into PCI?"

"To pass the plate," she said.

I shook my head. "We don't have plates in the chapel," I said. "And inmates don't have money."

"Oh, hell, yes, they do," she said, her drink seeming to kick in.

"Well, you ought to know, managing their accounts and all, but there's no money on the compound so—"

"They mail it to him," she said.

"Even so," I said, "they can have—what?—sixty-five bucks a week? How much could they send?"

As she slid a little closer to me, I became conscious of having Coke breath, and slid a piece of Wrigley's Spearmint gum out of my pocket and into my mouth.

"Sixty-five dollars is what they can spend each week with their cashless card in the canteen," she said. "There's no limit to how much they can have in their accounts. Some of them have a quarter of a million dollars or more."

It took me a minute to process that one, and as I thought about it, she went on to explain some things I already knew, which was fine because I wasn't really listening anyway.

"There's no cash on the compound," she said. "They buy food and certain personal items from the canteen by swiping the magnetic strip on their ID badge. By limiting it to sixty-five dollars, we curtail the amount of bribing and bartering that goes on down there, but it doesn't stop it. That has nothing to do with how much they can and do have in their accounts, just how much they can spend in the canteen each week."

"So if one of them wanted to—ah, sow a seed into Bobby Earl's ministry, how would he do it?"

"Simple," she said. "Fill out a withdrawal form and submit it to me with a stamped envelope addressed to where he wants it sent."

"And this happens often?" I asked.

She nodded. "This past year, PCI inmates donated nearly a hundred grand to something called Setting the Captives Free, a Bobby Earl Caldwell Ministry."

"A hundred thousand American dollars?"

"Yes, American," she said and punched me again.

"Does that amount come from just a few large contributions or several small ones?"

"Large ones primarily, but there're more than just a few," she said. "It's funny though—" She paused long enough to take a sip of her drink, a Fuzzy Navel from the look and smell of it, and then continued. "—there are small ones, but they go to a different address than the big ones. The Captives ones go to a P.O. Box in New Orleans, the small ones to a street address that I know is his ministry headquarters address because I've seen it on his literature."

"Is there any way you can get me a list of the inmates who've made contributions?" I asked.

"I don't think I could do that," she said with a smile as she withdrew a sheet of paper folded lengthways from her purse and slid it along the bar to me. "That would be wrong."

"And being the good man I am," I said, "I don't want to encourage you to do anything wrong."

She smiled, obviously enjoying herself.

"Who's his single largest contributor?" I asked.

"Was a drug dealer from Miami named Brawer, but he's no longer with us," she said.

"Transferred?" I asked.

"Yeah," she said. "To hell. He OD'd last weekend."

My eyebrows shot up. "That was him?"

She nodded.

"Sounds like a clue," I said.

"The strange thing is, you'd think there would be a big increase in donations after one of his visits."

"There's not?"

"There's a small increase," she said, "but the majority of contributions are made before he comes."

"Just before?"

"Yeah, why?"

"The clues just keep on coming," I said.

She smiled. "So that helps?"

"More than you'll ever know."

"Good," she said, and when I saw how pleased what I said made her, I was glad I had said it.

She had the same look on her face when she asked, "Are you going to stay for Karaoke?" Which is why an hour later I was wishing I were drunk as I listened to people who were singing songs that they wouldn't have if they weren't.

CHAPTER 27

When I got home, Anna was waiting for me (I never lock my doors—I don't know anyone in Pottersville who does), and I couldn't help but wonder what it would be like to come home to her every night.

Home for me is an old, dilapidated single-wide mobile home—the only thing I could find when I moved back to Pottersville about a year ago, the only thing I could afford after the divorce. After living a very different life for over thirty years, I had become trailer trash, hurricane bait, downwardly mobile. It was as embarrassing as it was liberating.

"Honey, I'm home," I said as I walked through the door, and I realized that finding her here was the first time this little tin box ever felt like home.

She tried to smile, but couldn't quite pull it off.

The new Jann Arden CD she had given me was playing softly in the background, and as I sat down on the couch beside her, I prayed for this moment to last as long as heaven would allow.

Within moments, I had lost myself in the heaven Jann was singing about finding in every breath, under every star, in everything. In the woman sitting next to me.

Anna's softly sweet scent filled the small room, and I breathed through my nose so I could take it in with every inhalation.

"Good CD, isn't it?" she said, nodding toward the CD player.
I nodded.

"You must really think so," she said with a smile. "You have two."

I smiled.

"How many copies of Dan's new one do you have?"

"Two, too," I said. "But I like yours the best."

She laughed, and we listened to the rest of the song in silence.

The couch we sat on had been left in the trailer by the previous tenants. It was uneven and uncomfortable and had one of those covers that bunched and gathered and slid around every time you moved. There was very little furniture besides it in the room—a small folding table that held a TV and other components, an old leather recliner, its back permanently caught between upright and recline, its leather splitting and tearing, a couple of overcrowded bookshelves that leaned into each other for support. Scattered throughout the room, along the walls mainly, were stacks of books in every shape, size, subject, and genre.

When the song was over, she said, "What's new in the investigation?"

I told her.

"I would think Bunny could get all the sex she wanted on the street," she said. "Why run all the risks of having it with inmates inside?"

"Perhaps the risks are what it's about," I said. "But you're right, it's probably not her. As far as I know the only time she left my office was to sing in the sanctuary."

"But then how do you explain the condoms and the tampon?"

"I'm not sure," I said. "The tampon could've belonged to a female volunteer from an earlier night. The condoms could've been brought in by a staff member or an officer."

She didn't say anything and I could tell she was thinking about it, the light of intelligence bright in her dark eyes.

Sitting so close to Anna, I found it hard to breathe. I so wanted to be a good man, to be God's man, belonging fully and completely to her, but how could I when I felt the way I did about this woman? If my love for Anna wasn't idolatry, it certainly bordered on obsession. And yet, paradoxically, I often experienced the passion I felt for her as a metaphor for how God loved me, and through Anna's love, I couldn't help but feel the desire of the God who is the all-consuming fire.

"It's unbelievable Bobby Earl gets that kind of money from our institution," she said. "It might explain the condoms."

I nodded. "The clean ones especially," I said. "If someone's using them to mule drugs inside, the lab should be able to tell us."

"Even so," she said, "it's hard to see what it would have to do with Nicole's death."

I nodded.

"And frontrunners for that?" she asked.

"Bobby Earl and Bunny are certainly still in the lead," I said, "but Coel was in the best position to do something without being seen—and he's the only witness we have who was able to see both doors."

"He could've gone in or be covering for whoever did," she said.

"Uh huh," I said. "But I certainly can't rule out Theo Malcolm. He's working hard to cover up something, and then there's Paul Register—his background alone's enough to keep him near the front of the pack."

Talked out, we sat in silence and listened to the music and each other breathe some more.

"I've had a lot of night classes lately," she said. "And Chris's had a lot of really big cases. Things haven't been the same. It's why what you said the other night did more than hurt me. It devastated me."

"I'm sorry."

"I've heard," she said.

"Really."

"I'm still mad at you."

"You should be."

"Sometimes I hate you," she said, her words four staccato stabs of a serrated blade.

I couldn't respond to that. All I could do was sit there and bleed.

She didn't say anything else, and when I could, I said, "Sometimes I hate myself."

We were quiet for a long moment, Jann's melancholy music holding us hostage, her sultry voice piercing the emptiness around and in us like arrows, the sad lyrics bittersweet poison on their tips.

"Chris thinks we need counseling," she said finally.

"You and me?" I asked.

She smiled. "Me and him."

I nodded.

"What do you think we should do?"

I shook my head. "I'm the last person you should ask," I said, and I wanted to tell her about Susan, but knew it wasn't the time.

"Why?" she said. Her eyes looked big and sad, her face revealing her vulnerability.

"Because," I said, reaching out and sweeping a strand of her thick brown hair from her face, "when it comes to you, I could never be objective."

She smiled warmly. "Thanks," she said. "That's the nicest thing anyone's said to me in a long time."

We sat there in the silence for a long while after Jann had finished her set, our breathing the only sound in the little trailer until the phone rang.

When after a few rings I had made no move to answer it, Anna said, "You gonna get that?"

I shook my head.

Her face lit up again. "That's the second nicest thing anyone's done for me lately."

"I can't tell you how much I've missed you," I said.

"You could try."

"Every time I've wanted to talk about the investigation or share something about my day, I'd pick up the phone and start to punch in your number, or start walking down toward Classification before remembering and…"

"I've done the same things," she said, adding with a wry smile, "except I punched in your number and started up to the chapel. I've wanted so badly to help you like I usually do—especially with this one."

"I've needed your help," I said.

"Well, I'm here now," she said. "How can I help?"

"Just so we're clear," I said, "you are talking about the case—how can you help with the case?"

CHAPTER 28

When I arrived at the chapel the next morning, Dexter Freeman was waiting for me.

"My mom's dead," he said.

"I'm so sorry to hear that, Dexter," I said.

I unlocked the chapel, and eyes red and tired, tears still streaming down his cheeks, he followed me into the spare office and fell heavily into one of the chairs where he sat staring blankly, his body trembling, his head down.

As I watched him, I felt a forceful reminder that before long I'd be experiencing the same thing, and I felt guilty for not spending more of my mom's last days with her.

"They should've called me back in last night," I said. "I'm sorry."

He shook off my apology. "They didn't know."

"How'd you find out?" I asked.

"Called home," he said, looking up. "I asked them why they didn't call you… I guess they just forgot about me. She's been dead three days. My wife would've told me, but they don't talk to her, so she didn't know either. The funeral's this afternoon. I need your help getting a furlough."

"Sure," I said. "How're you holding up?"

He shook his head. "I didn't want her to die while I was inside. You know?"

I nodded.

"She raised me by herself," he said. "She always sacrificed for me. Worked two jobs where I could play sports and have a car and go to college. She was so proud of me. Broke her heart when I was arrested. Knowing I was set up didn't make it any easier for her."

I smiled in response to his smile as the warm thoughts of her flooded his memory. He was quiet for a moment, crying silently, wiping his nose with the back of his hand and the sleeve of his blue uniform.

I handed him some of the cheap, thin, prison-issue tissues I kept in all the offices of the chapel.

"Thanks," he said, then rolled up one of the tissues and dabbed at his eyes with the corner. "I'm okay. I appreciate your time."

"You want to call your family?" I asked.

"Yeah," he said. "But the phones in the dorms—"

"You can call from here," I said. "That'll give you more privacy anyway. Then we can talk some more afterwards if you need to."

"Thanks," he said.

I plugged in a phone for him to use in the room designed for that purpose and closed the door to give him privacy. While he talked, I looked through his file and pulled some more of the information I needed. When he was finished, he came back into the office looking like a different person.

"That really helped," he said. "Thanks a lot. I really appreciate it. Just making contact. Not being so isolated… it helps."

"You're welcome," I said. "I'm glad you were able to talk to them."

He hesitated for a moment, then said, "Can I talk to you about something else while I'm here?"

"Of course."

"I've been wanting to talk to you anyway," he said, and took a deep breath. "I believe I'm here for a reason."

"I do, too," I said.

"Good," he said. "Because I think you're part of it."

"What do you mean?"

"I think I've been put here to learn from you," he said. "And I wanted to see if we could set up a weekly counseling session."

"Sure," I said.

Though he sounded sincere enough, I distrusted the compliments of inmates. Too often, by which I mean nearly a hundred percent of the time, they are the manipulative part of an angle being worked. I wish it were otherwise, but it's the reality of prison, and to forget it, to be vain or blinded by flattery is to invite danger, even disaster. The challenge is to maintain professionalism without developing paranoia, to have compassion without becoming a caretaker who's constantly taken advantage of. It's a precarious position and few of us ever succeed. You get used to the negativity, the hostility, the anger and aggression. It's in the open. You see it coming. What you have to look out for is kindness, is gratitude, is civility.

"Would you pull my file?" he asked. "I want you to see something."

"I already have," I said, tapping one of the folders on the desk. "To arrange the furlough."

"So you know what I'm in here for?"

I nodded. "L and L," I said.

"Yes," he said. "Lewd and lascivious. But I didn't rape or molest or do anything that was lewd or lascivious. You know what I did? I took a leak in a park at night. That's it. I was jogging at night and had to go. So, I found a tree and went."

I picked up his record and glanced over it as he spoke.

"I got sentenced to one year and one day," he continued. "Just one day shorter and I'd've served my time in county jail. Judge probably saved my life. I was supposed to have an accident in their jail. I'm telling you this because I'm not a criminal. But since I've been in, I've had some serious time to evaluate my life, and I want to use this time—all this time I have on my hands—to make some changes. Some core kinds of changes."

"I think that's exactly what you should do," I said. "And I'd be happy to help you in any way I can."

"Exactly," he said. "I want to leave this place in top physical, emotional, and spiritual condition."

"You can start by honestly answering a few questions," I said.

"Sure," he said.

"Are you having an affair with Bunny Caldwell?"

His eyes grew wide. "No," he said emphatically. "Where did you hear that?"

"Have you ever?"

"Never," he said.

"What were you doing in the hall that night?"

"Going to the bathroom," he said. "Honest. I mean, it'd've been all right with me if I got a closer look at her, but I really did have to use the bathroom."

"Like in the park?" I asked. "Seems like your bladder's getting you in some sticky situations."

He let out a small ironic laugh and shook his head to himself.

The banging of the heavy metal door of the chapel and loud conversations announced the arrival of the rest of the inmates, most of whom paused at the office door, straining to see who was in with me, attempting to ascertain the reason for his presence by his posture and body language. I knew the next stop for many of them was my office door. Chapel traffic had increased dramatically since Nicole had been killed, most of the new visitors, voyeurs driven by a morbid curiosity to see the crime scene.

"Is there anything else about that night you can tell me?" I asked. "Anything? No matter how small it seems."

"Well, there is one thing that struck me as funny," he said. "It's probably nothing, but…"

"But what?"

"Remember when we were in the bathroom and Officer Whitfield said there were two convicts in the stalls?"

"Yeah."

"And then he said 'you convicts come out' or something like that."

"And you came out," I said. "And the other man said he wasn't finished or something."

"Exactly," he said.

"What's funny about that?" I asked.

"Just that the man in the other stall wasn't an inmate," he said. "But Officer Whitfield called him one and he didn't correct him."

"You sure he wasn't an inmate?" I asked.

"Positive," he said. "I saw him."

"Who was it?"

"That guy that's supposed to help Bobby Earl with security," he said. "The warden's nephew."

"DeAndré Stone?"

"Yeah," he said. "DeAndré Stone."

CHAPTER 29

"So DeAndré Stone was in the chapel the night Nicole was murdered?" Anna asked.

"According to an inmate," Merrill said.

"Actually, according to the control room logs," I said.

His eyes grew wide. "Oh, my damn."

It was lunchtime. Anna, Merrill, and I were at Rudy's in a booth next to the front window.

"And why exactly did Coel and Whitfield fail to mention this?" Anna asked.

I followed her gaze across the diner to a table in the far corner where Coel and Whitfield sat together.

"They say they never saw him," I said. "Even after I showed them the logs."

"Is that possible?" Anna asked.

"Just ask him," Merrill said, jerking his head toward me. "Anything's possible."

During the day, Rudy's was the quintessential small town diner. Its lunch buffet was a Pottersville standard, evidenced by the trucks parked out front like horses tied to hitching posts. All the meals at Rudy's, like the people who prepared them, were country-fried, and the smell of old grease hung in the air like heavy humidity. The smoking section in Rudy's was flexible—it shifted with the pass of an ashtray—and most of his patrons smoked while they ate, probably because it killed the taste of the food. The waitresses were young girls with nice backsides poured into Levi's jeans, both of which seemed to be job requirements.

"Did he come in with the Caldwells?" Anna asked.

"A good bit later."

"And you never saw him?"

I shook my head.

"So what was he doing inside?" she asked.

"Not protecting Nicole," Merrill said.

"You gonna add him to your suspect list?" Anna said.

"Yeah," I said. "Near the top."

Rudy's was filled with a variety of people ranging from the president of the local co-op to a couple of pulpwood truck drivers. Several staff members from PCI were at a table together and a smattering of brown correctional officer uniforms could be seen throughout. I wasn't sure if Merrill felt it as forcefully as I did, but he was the only African-American in the entire establishment.

With Carla in school, our food was brought to us by Rudy himself—he was cook and waiter today. We had ordered off the menu rather than getting the buffet, in an attempt to be more healthy—a failed attempt, we realized, when the food was placed before us. We had ordered grilled chicken and baked potatoes. The chicken had been grilled in butter and the potato was filled with butter and sour cream.

"Here's to our arteries," Merrill said after I asked the blessing. "Just like Mom used to make."

Anna and I both laughed as we raked the small mountain of sour cream from our potatoes. The diner was set up with booths against the plate glass windows in front and a bar with built-in stools wrapping around the open galley. In the corner, a jukebox came alive with a country song that made me feel like drinking.

"I've looked at the files of the inmates in the hallway the night of the murder," Anna said. "Abdul Muhammin's a cold-blooded killer. What's he doing working in the chapel?"

"He's the one they sent when I said I wanted a well-behaved, knowledgeable Muslim clerk."

She shook her head. "I don't like him being up there so close to you," she said. "Watch him closely."

"I will," I said.

"And now I will, too," Merrill said.

"The best of them is Dexter Freeman. Then it's a toss up between Paul Register and Cedric Porter. But just because they're not violent inmates doesn't mean they couldn't've done this."

The bell above the entrance door rang as Dad and Jake walked in. Dad waved, Jake nodded and they took the only open booth, which was on the opposite side of the diner from us.

"Jake sure looked relieved when he saw a booth open in the white section," Merrill said. "I reckon he rather starve than eat in the colored section."

"Me, too," I said.

"Well, me, too," Merrill said.

Anna looked confused.

"We don't want there to be no colored section," Merrill explained.

From various tables around the room, I could hear sound bytes of southern living.

"They say that every year," one of the truckers said of the paper mill in Panama City closing.

"But it's just to make us grateful for our jobs and make sure we don't ask for a raise. It's not gonna shut down. It's just a rumor."

The other trucker shook his head. "You used to say the same thing about the one in Port St. Joe, and look what happened."

At another table someone in a suit was saying, "Affirmative action is just unconstitutional. There's no two ways about it. I'm for fairness. Give the job to the person who deserves it. It's unfair to do anything else."

The most amusing conversation came from the booth just over my shoulder where a man in blue jeans was trying to convince another man in a telephone company uniform to take out his ex-wife. "I know the two of you would hit it off. She's really great.... Really."

"I don't know," Telephone Company Man said.

"Just tell me you'll think about it," Blue Jeans said. "She really is great. And this alimony shit is killin' me."

As I scanned the room, I felt someone staring at me, and I turned to see Colonel Patterson glaring at me from a stool at the counter. Our eyes locked briefly, but then from shame and embarrassment over how I had behaved following Nicole's murder, I looked away. I hadn't told anybody what had happened—not even Merrill and Anna. It was just too humiliating.

Unable to bring myself to take another bite, I dropped my fork onto my plate.

"That's about all of that I can take," I said, pushing my plate toward the center of the table.

"You don't need to eat that shit anyway," Merrill said. "Your body's the temple of the Holy Spirit."

"So is your—"

"I'm not so sure about mine," he said.

I smiled.

"Any headway with the Caldwells yet?" Anna asked.

"Dad's working with NOPD on it," I said. "And I've asked to meet with them."

"That's it?"

"Except for rumors on the compound," I said. "And you know how reliable those are. But I have heard one over and over."

"Yeah?" Merrill said. "What's that?"

"That Bunny has a thing for black men," I said.

"Well, who doesn't?" Anna asked, winking at Merrill.

Vigorously nodding his agreement, Merrill said to her, "He'll get to them. He's got a secret weapon."

"Oh yeah, what's that?" she asked.

"Me," he said with a broad smile. "I a brother. And Bunny love herself a brother."

As I walked out of Rudy's, I spotted Tim Whitfield heading toward his new sports car parked in a pasture across the street.

Jogging to catch up with him, I noticed there were plenty of spaces in Rudy's lot.

"Nice," I said, nodding toward his new car.

"Thanks," he said. "It was a gift."

"A gift?" I asked.

"From God," he said.

Directly? I wondered, or through Bobby Earl?

"He wants his children to have the best."

The lonely old highway running in front of Rudy's was straight and flat and empty, stretching away for several miles in both directions. It was scarred and pocked and had deep ruts caused by loaded log trucks. I was surprised Tim would put his new car on it.

"How long have you had it?" I asked.

"Just got it," he said.

Payment for a job well done?

Pulling a handkerchief out of his pocket, he wiped a speck of dust off the front quarter panel. "I wasn't about to park it in front of Rudy's and get oyster shell dust all over it."

Glancing over at my old Chevy S-10, he said, "About time for you to get a new one, isn't it?"

I smiled. "I haven't gotten my other one broken in all the way yet," I said.

"Seriously," he said. "As a man of God, what you drive and where you live reflects on God. Brother Bobby has an eight-part teaching on prosperity that you need to hear. It's in the chapel library. You should listen to it."

"Speaking of Brother Bobby," I said, "you sure you didn't see his security guard that night? Maybe on the compound or—"

"I've told you," he said. "I didn't see him. You sure he was even there?"

"What about in the bathroom?" I asked. "Someone said he was in the bathroom the same time you were."

"You were in there," he said. "Did you see him?"

"They said he was in the stall."

"Well, I didn't look in any stalls," he said. "Who's they anyway? You talkin' 'bout some inmate?"

I didn't answer.

"I gotta go," he said. "Colonel Patterson'll chew my a—behind if I'm late getting back from lunch."

He jumped in, cranked and revved the loud engine, and turned around. I smiled when I saw the little Jesus fish on his bumper, but stopped as I caught a glimpse of the Louisiana license plate beneath it. Was all his religiosity, like Malcolm's extreme racism, just a cover?

I motioned for him, and he rolled down the window.

"You went all the way to Louisiana to get your car?" I asked.

He nodded. "It's where I could get the best deal."

As he peeled off and sped away, I said, "I bet."

CHAPTER 30

I loved the intensity with which children played, though watching them had always been a disturbing mixture of pleasure and pain. As I stood near the fence and watched the raucous play of the wild angels of Pottersville Elementary School, I had to blink back tears.

For several years I had been unable to see a child without thinking of Martin Fisher, but today, as I watched the children on the playground, it was Nicole I thought I saw among the others playing with such wild and reckless abandon.

After watching for as long as I could, I turned and walked down the sidewalk toward the inmates from the public works squad. They were repairing a section of the fence under the watchful eye of city employees.

I was used to seeing inmates working around Pottersville. Each year public works squads saved the city tens of thousands of dollars in labor, and only offenders without violent crimes could participate in them. Now I looked on the scene of inmates working so close to children with fear and suspicion, each child becoming as trusting and vulnerable as Nicole. Technically, the work crew wasn't at the school, and they were probably far enough away from the children to satisfy the regulation, but it was a lot closer than I would have liked.

"Did somebody die, Chaplain?" one of the inmates asked when I walked up.

I shook my head.

"Then what're you doin' here?" he asked.

I walked past them and over to Phillip Linton, the city employee in charge of maintenance.

"How's it goin', JJ?" he asked.

"Okay," I said. "You?"

"I'm great," he said. "Never better. If it got any better I wouldn't know what to do."

That was always Linton's response, and it always sounded the same way to me—like he was trying to convince himself as much as me that what he was saying was true.

"What brings you out here?" he asked.

"I need to speak to one of your inmates for a few minutes," I said.

"Sure," he said. "Which one?"

"Porter," I said.

"Cedric," he yelled. "Chaplain needs a moment of your time."

"Yes, sir," he said.

I walked down the sidewalk next to the chainlink fence to meet him.

"You got out of the infirmary awfully quick," I said. "I was surprised when they told me you were already back at work."

He shrugged. "I just a convict. I can work with a headache."

"Let's move down this way a little," I said, leading him away from the earshot of the others and further away from the children.

"You found Nicole's killer yet?"

"No," I said. "But we will. And again, I'm so sorry but I need to ask you a few more questions about the night she was killed."

"I hope y'all catch him soon," he said, "'fore he finally kill me."

"Who?"

He shook his head at me in disbelief. "Bobby Earl."

"You think he's the one who tried to have you killed?" I asked.

He nodded. "More than once," he said, pulling up his shirt to show me a jagged scar running down the side of his abdomen.

"Why haven't you checked in?" I asked.

If an inmate felt his life was in danger—for any reason: gambling debts, refusing to perform sexual favors, retaliation from an officer—he could check himself into protective management, where he would be locked in a cell and watched closely while the inspector investigated the matter.

"'Cause," he said. "If I in a cell, I can't run or hide or fight back. Least out here I can see 'em comin'. Anyway, don't worry about me. You just find out who killed my little girl. Then he better be the one lookin' over his shoulder."

I didn't say anything.

"You said you wanted to ask me about the night she was killed," he said. "What about it?"

"How long were you in the bathroom?"

"What?"

"We're trying to establish everyone's movements during the time when Nicole was killed," I said.

"You know where I was," he said.

"How long were you in there?" I asked.

He shrugged. "Don't know, but it was a while. My stomach was real upset. The later it got, the sicker I got. I missed work the next day. You can ask Mr. Linton."

"Who all'd you see while you were in the bathroom?"

"No one," he said.

"No one?"

"It was empty when I went in," he said. "Once I was in the stall, I couldn't see anyone. I heard a few people, but I didn't see anyone."

"Well, who'd you hear?"

"You," he said with a smile. "Abdul. Freeman. Somebody came in and washed they hands near the end, but they didn't say nothin', so I don't know who it was."

"When was this?" I asked.

"Near the end," he repeated. "Because it wasn't long after that I went back in the service. Bobby Earl and Bunny were giving they altar call."

"How long was the hand washer in there?" I asked.

"A while," he said. "A long time now that I think about it." His eyes growing wide in alarm, he added, "If I was that close to her killer and didn't…"

He looked away and thought about it, tears forming in his eyes. "I hate to think I was that close to him and didn't kill him."

"Why were you even at the service that night?" I asked.

"Whatta you mean?"

"You don't normally come to church, do you?" I said. "Was it just to see Nicole?"

He nodded.

"Not Bunny?" I asked.

He hesitated.

"You still love her, don't you?"

He looked away, glancing back at the other inmates. Without looking back at me, he nodded.

"Did you see her?"

"Bunny?" he asked.

"Nicole."

"Of course," he said.

"I mean did you get to talk to her?"

He shook his head. "How would I do that?"

"You tell me," I said. "How'd you use to meet Bunny?"

He shook his head. "I didn't see her. Not except on stage when she's singin'. Bunny and I used to meet in the back of the chapel—the kitchen or the cleaning closet—when she worked at Lake Butler. Not since."

Over at the school, a bell rang and the children began to scatter, most of them racing back to class. A few stragglers had to be goaded by the teacher on duty, but soon the playground was empty, its abandoned equipment looking sad and useless like a body without life.

"I'm sorry to have to ask this," I said, "and I'm sure it'll seem like a stupid question since you had a child together, but did you and Bunny use condoms?"

He nodded. "She always made me. And she still got pregnant," he added, shaking his head. "I think she did it 'cause she went with so many different mens."

Looking down the sidewalk toward the other inmates, I hesitated to ask my next question, wishing I didn't have to. True to form, the inmates on the work crew were quiet, respectful, and hard working, their interaction lacking the cruelty, horseplay, and profanity that was typical of many of the inmates on the inside.

"I'm doing my best to find out who killed Nicole," I said. "And sometimes that means I have to do and say things I'd rather not, but I have to—and I have a good reason to ask what I'm about to or I wouldn't ask it."

"What is it? Damn."

"Did you and Bunny ever have anal intercourse?"

If he found the question intrusive or disturbing, he didn't give any indication. Shaking his head, he said, "It never came up."

I nodded.

"We weren't together long," he added, as if it were something that had to be worked up to. "But I don't think they was anything Bunny wasn't up for."

"She has a reputation for really liking black men," I said.

He nodded. "She does. Her dad was a real redneck racist. Used to catch her with black boys and beat her, but she keep on goin' with 'em."

"You see anybody in the hallway?" I asked.

He shook his head.

"What about in my office or near the door?"

"I saw the teacher sorta hangin' out," he said.

"Mr. Malcolm?"

He nodded.

All around us, spring was turning into summer. The tops of the oak trees above us were filled with thick green growth. The flowers spilling out of the planter in front of the school, already past their zenith, were in the heat of the increasingly warmer days beginning to wilt.

"What about Bobby Earl's bodyguard?"

He shook his head again.

"Is there anything else you can tell me that might help us?" I asked.

He shook his head.

We both fell quiet a moment. Tears filled his eyes, and he wiped at them absently.

Slipping his hand into the pocket of his inmate uniform, he withdrew a soiled and crumpled piece of paper, unfolded it, and handed it to me. It was a picture similar to the one Nicole had colored for me.

"She colored this for me," he said. "I carry it everywhere I go."

I nodded.

"My little girl was being used," he said, his voice weak and small. "Anyone who'd do that... well... sometimes I think I'd be better off dead," he said. "I don't care what happens to me. I really don't."

I nodded.

"Would you do something for me?" he asked.

I didn't respond.

"When you find out who did it, will you tell me first?" he continued.

I just might, I thought.

"And if it's Bobby Earl," he said, no attempt to conceal his contempt, "would you invite him back for just one more revival service?"

CHAPTER 31

Later that afternoon, I took Highway 20 into Tallahassee and picked up I-10 heading west toward Greensboro. Greensboro was a small town in Gadsden County, which borders on the Georgia state line. It was originally settled by wealthy slave owners, and is still famous for its large plantations, substantial black population (joined now by Mexican migrant workers), and tobacco crops.

In Greensboro, I bought a pack of Certs at a convenience store and then drove over to the AME Church near the high school where Pottersville regularly got beaten in every athletic competition. The church was actually a small white clapboard house with a chimney that had been converted into a steeple. However, I suspected, that like most of the conversions that took place inside the church, the process was incomplete and didn't seem to be working out too well.

Perhaps because everyone else was running on CPT, I was one of the first to enter the small sanctuary. I walked down to the front where the casket was centered between the two altars and looked at the lifeless shell that used to be Dexter Freeman's mother. Even in death, she was beautiful, and I could easily see Dexter's handsome face in her features. She wore a delicate white dress with lace around the neck, and in her hands was a Polaroid picture of herself and Dexter that had been taken in the visiting park of Potter Correctional Institution. You could tell by her expression that the blue inmate uniform her son wore didn't diminish in any way the fact that her boy was the apple of her eye.

A small door to my right opened, and I turned to see Dexter enter the sanctuary, his wife and daughter at his side, his son in his arms. He wore a navy blue double-breasted suit and a burgundy silk tie over a crisp white shirt as if he had come from a GQ photo shoot rather than a Florida state prison. His son's suit matched his, and his wife and daughter wore matching navy dresses with white lace collars. They were the picture-perfect young American family.

When he saw me, his face lit up, and he rushed over and wrapped me up in a hug that included his son.

"I can't believe you're here," he said. "Honey, this is Chaplain Jordan, the one I was telling you about." He looked at me. "This is—"

"Honey," I said, and took her outstretched hand.

"I'm Trish," she said with a smile. "And this is Moriah." She touched her daughter on the head. I held my hand out and she took it.

At the mention of Moriah, I couldn't help but think of Abraham and Isaac; Bobby Earl and Nicole.

"And this is Dexter, Jr.," she added with a big smile.

"What's up, DJ?" I said, and held my hand up for a high five, which he gave me with no hesitation.

When I looked back at Dexter, he was shaking his head, and staring at me. "Thanks so much for coming, Chaplain. You'll never know what it means."

"You're welcome," I said. "You have a beautiful family." I winked at Moriah.

"Thank you," she said, as she shrugged her shoulders and looked down, an embarrassed grin spreading across her adorable face.

Standing there with Dexter's family, attempting to offer support and perhaps comfort in their time of crisis, I thought about how strange it was. Only a sometime-investigator and all-the-time prison chaplain would be caught in the seeming contradiction of trying to minister to one of a handful of suspects in a murder he was investigating.

"Am I early?" I asked.

Dexter shook his head. "Everyone else is running on CPT," he said.

"That's Colored People Time," Trish explained.

"Oh," I said, and winked at Dexter.

He shook his head. "Honey, he works in a prison that runs on CPT. He knows words and phrases Chris Rock doesn't."

I smiled. "I'm going to slip back there," I said, nodding toward the back, "and give you all some time together."

"Thank you," he said, "but I'd like for you to sit with us. We don't have any other family."

"I'd be honored to," I said.

After the funeral and interment, I stood with Dexter and his family beneath the canopy of a towering oak tree in front of the small church as they underwent the tearing of their souls at having to say good-bye again so soon. The air wasn't as cool as it had been, but the gentle breeze made the shade beneath the shelter of the oak tolerable.

I was facing the church and Dexter when I saw the expression on his face change. I turned to see what was behind me.

A Greensboro City police car crept by, as if in slow motion, the two young, white police officers inside glaring at Dexter in a manner that indicated they had no intention to protect or serve.

I looked back at Dexter. The muscles in his jaws were flexing and his eyes had narrowed to slits. Trish continued to hug him, only now it was about restraint as much as affection. "Don't," she said. "We're not going to let them keep us apart one more day than we have to."

He seemed to relax a little, and when I turned back, the police car was gone.

"The one in the passenger's side is Larry Lassiter, my brother," Trish explained. "He's the one who set Dexter up."

I nodded.

"We better get you back," she said to Dexter.

"Okay," he said.

"Would you mind if I followed you?" I asked.

"Mind?" Trish said. "I was going to ask if you would." We walked over to our vehicles. "Now that Mama Freeman is gone," Trish said, "we'll be moving, too. We're going to get away from them. If we can just make it until then."

"An actual innocent inmate," Anna said. "I've become so jaded I didn't really believe they existed."

I had called Anna from a convenience store in Greensboro and asked her to check with FDLE about Larry Lassiter. What she had discovered, that Lassiter was under investigation and Dexter was believed to have been set up, so surprised her that she had rushed up to tell me the moment I arrived at the institution. I had just been buzzed through the sally port when she rushed up and gave me the news.

"They gonna get Dexter a new trial?" I asked.

"It has low priority," she said. "They're not going to do anything until they arrest Lassiter. Don't want to warn him."

"So Dexter could EOS before anything happens," I said.

She nodded and frowned. "At least it'd be taken off his record."

I shook my head. "That's not enough," I said.

"Not much we can do."

"I'll talk to Dad, see what he can do."

She shook her head to herself in disbelief again and said, "An actual innocent inmate."

CHAPTER 32

In seminary, I had read *On Death and Dying* by Elisabeth Kubler-Ross. In it, she shared her experiences with the dying and what she had learned from them. Kubler-Ross witnessed each of her patients experiencing the same five stages when faced with a terminal condition. I read the book as a part of a class on hospital ministry and experienced its truth first-hand while I served as a student chaplain at Emory Hospital. Memories of those days drifted over me like the sounds of a sad love song that brings both pleasure and pain as I drove over to Mom's.

I had watched helplessly as the initial denial began with the first shake of their heads as the doctor delivered the grim prognosis, listened as they shared with conviction the opinion that this was a mistake, just a mix-up of records or an invalid test result. After a while, the light of their denial burned out, and then, like a lightning flash in a dark sky, their anger bolted out of nowhere and struck with rage at whatever happened to be in its path. I was usually called in on the next stage, for when it came to bargaining, everyone wanted to talk to the 'Man upstairs.' I heard confessions and received numerous vows that would be kept if only God would allow them to live. When this failed, which of course meant I had failed them as much as God had, they sank slowly into the quicksand of depression, emerging much later, as if from baptism, new and clean in their acceptance.

My mom, who would die soon from the disease of alcoholism if she didn't receive a liver transplant, was in the midst of a lengthy stage of bargaining, and had grasped the religion of the dying with all the fervor and desperation of a falling rock climber clinging to the last safety line.

When I arrived at Mom's, an extremely overweight lady in ill-fitting polyester pants and an untucked religious T-shirt that read "Turn or Burn" over fiery flames met me at the door. She wore thick glasses, and her labored breathing whistled out of the numerous gaps between her too few teeth.

"You the son who's a preacher?" she asked with a smile that scrunched up her face, lifted her glasses, and narrowed her eyes.

"Yes, ma'am," I said. "I'm John."

"I'm Sister Bertha," she said. "Come on in. I came over here to pray for her. You wanna join us?"

"You go ahead," I said. "I'll—"

"You're a preacher, aren't you?" she asked. "Prayin's what you're paid to do."

"Actually, I have to do most of my praying on my own time," I said. "You go ahead. I'll see her when you're finished."

She turned back from closing the door and eyed me skeptically. "You don't want to pray with us?" Her question was filled with accusation and disdain.

"Well, I—"

"Listen," she interrupted. "Your mother's under the attack of Satan. She needs prayer warriors now more than ever. She has become a precious saint and this whole thing is just Satan trying to snatch her life."

I nodded as she spoke, but I didn't say anything.

"What?" she asked angrily. "You don't agree? I can't get an amen from a supposed-to-be preacher?"

"Actually," I said. "Her condition is the direct result of her actions. Not the work of the devil. As unpleasant as it is, in truth, she's reaping what she's sown, and I believe that it is to her benefit to deal with the reality of what she's done and what she's experiencing because of it. She needs our compassion, but love doesn't involve lying to her or supporting her in denying her responsibility."

She shook her head, her face scrunching again, this time as if she smelled a bad odor. "My God," she said. "No wonder we're in the shape we're in, when preachers are so deceived. Do you know anything about spiritual warfare?"

"Lady, I'm a recovering alcoholic," I said. "I know all about spiritual warfare."

She snorted and rolled her eyes. "Do you know how to bind and loose the enemy? Do you have the Gifts of the Spirit?"

"I—"

"I bet you don't even speak in tongues," she said and turned and waddled down the hallway to my mother's sickroom.

I went to the kitchen to wait. While I was there, I noticed how dirty it was. Dishes were piled in the sink, plates of discarded food lined the counter, and the kitchen table was covered with letters and bills.

I began to clean.

Sister Bertha prayed long enough for me to clean nearly the entire kitchen. Her prayers were loud and demanding, formal and austere. She addressed God, the Devil, demons, and even cancer, though my mom's condition was cirrhosis of the liver. She also prayed against her "blind and deceived family" and rebuked us for being a hindrance to her healing. When she was finished, she paraded out of the house without saying a word to me.

I continued to clean the kitchen long after Bertha had left. She disturbed me, and her irresponsible, judgmental religion left me angry and embarrassed. I was certain that her pseudo-spiritual, superstitious cocktail was eating away at Mother's soul. When my anger had subsided, I walked down the long hall that awaits every son, to the room where my mother faced her mortality like the single raised finger of a Ferris wheel operator signaling that only one rotation remained on the ride of her life.

I quietly entered the room where I found her sleeping, and sank into the chair beside her bed. I studied her face as if seeing it for the first time. The gravitational pull of desperation in her eyes was held in by her heavy lids, and I could examine what was normally too painful. It was the guilt and pain she felt when she looked at me that hurt me most.

Her stress-creased face radiated a calm glow, and the corners of her mouth were turned up in a small pleasant smile. She looked peaceful. She looked only vaguely familiar. Perhaps I had been wrong about Sister Bertha. Perhaps I had been guilty of judging her for judging me. She must have been doing some good—she must have wanted the same thing I did.

My head fell into my hands and I began to pray… for Mom, and for her son, who needed forgiveness once again. After a while, I sensed she was looking at me, and I looked up to see the wide-eyed, adoring face of a mother—one I didn't recognize as my own—gazing at me lovingly. I looked away for a moment. I was used to the glazed, out-of-focus gaze, the bobbing-head, confused leer, but not the compassion only a mother was capable of.

When I looked back, she asked, "Were you praying for me?"

"Yes, ma'am," I said. "And for me."

"For you?" she asked. "Why?"

"Because I'm quick to judge and slow to learn."

"No, you're not," she said, and I got the impression she thought I was talking about her. "Why didn't you pray out loud?"

"I didn't want to wake you," I said. "But I probably will before I go, if you will allow me to."

"Allow you to?" she said, shaking her head. "Allow you to? I'm your mother, John. Don't be so bashful. You don't have to ask me if you can pray for me. You act as if I'm a stranger."

I could tell by the quick flash of pain in her eyes that she had read my thoughts. "In a lot of ways we are strangers, Mom, and you know it. We really don't know the people we've become."

"Well, you've become a man of God," she said.

I shook my head.

"Don't," she said and reached for my head. "I mean it. You've got to get more bold about your faith, that's all… like Bertha. I want you to lay your hands on me and cast out this foul demon of sickness."

"Mom," I said slowly, my mouth suddenly dry, my tongue thick. "I don't think it is a demon."

"You don't?" she asked, her face narrowing into a concerned question. "Not the attack of the enemy?"

I shook my head.

Her face clouded over, but I could tell she was still focusing, contemplating.

"It's like sobriety," I said. "We're all responsible for our own. No one else can be. Or my divorce. Do you know how much I would like to say that Susan had a demon." I laughed. "Or how I would like to blame her or someone or something else. No. I've got to take responsibility for me, for my part, for my actions."

She began to cry.

"I'm sorry," I said.

"Are you trying to hurt me?" she asked in a soft, wounded voice. "To pay me back?"

"No, ma'am."

"I need you to go right now," she said. Her voice was firm, but not mean.

"Can I pray for you?"

She shook her head.

I nodded, and slowly walked out of the room. I was three steps down the hall when I realized what I needed to do. But it was ten steps before I was able to do it. I stopped, turned, and went back to her bedroom.

"Would you like for me to call Sister Bertha for you, Mom?"

CHAPTER 33

"Bobby Earl's in serious financial trouble," Dad said. "At least he was until Nicole was killed."

I had stopped by Dad's on my way home from work, and as usual, found him in the corral behind his house feeding his cows. In addition to being a sheriff, Dad had, as of late, become a cowboy, transforming his five-acre lot into a small farm and having more fun than he had had in years.

"He had a life insurance policy of a million dollars on her," he added.

I shook my head, anger spiking anew inside me.

"So far there doesn't seem to be any mob connection, but he's got money problems of the magnitude that make a person impetuous."

"His TV show doesn't bring in—"

"That's just it," he said, "it brings in shiploads. So it's going somewhere. Either it's being grossly mismanaged or he's got an addiction or he is laundering it for the mob."

Where's all the money going? I wondered.

"And get this," he said. "He's hired a high-powered attorney to file a wrongful death suit against the State of Florida for a few more million."

I shook my head in disbelief as I thought about it.

We were quiet a moment, then he started shaking his head. "Religion," he said. "War. Hate. Judgmentalism. Money. Power. Pride. Theft."

I nodded, but didn't say anything.

"How can you be associated with them?" he asked.

"Who?" I asked. "The Caldwells?"

I knew I was about as far from the Caldwells as a person of faith could be, but it bothered me it wasn't obvious to him. I had broken away from my family years ago. Our relationship now was that of adults, not parents and child. We had little in common, and though I loved them, we weren't close, yet I still cared what they thought about me—especially Dad—and I didn't like it. It made me feel immature and insecure.

"All the crazy fanatics and fleecers."

"I don't see myself as associated with them in any way," I said. "I feel about organized religion the way you do. I find it tragically ironic that they do what they do in the name of Jesus, the poor peasant who refused power at every turn."

"Hell, they hide behind him," he said.

"I just wonder what exactly they have to hide," I said, attempting to change the subject. "We need to interview them."

"That'll take an act of God," he said.

"Well, don't count that out," I said.

He ambled over to where I was leaning on the metal corral panel and draped his arms over the top so that we were nearly a mirror image of each other.

"You get anywhere with FDLE on the Dexter Freeman case?" I asked.

He looked at me incredulously. "You just called me about it this afternoon," he said. "I haven't even called them yet. What's the rush?"

I shrugged. "His family needs him. Prison's a dangerous place. He's innocent."

"We'll get it taken care of," he said. "It'll just take a while. I'm sheriff, not king."

"I wasn't aware there was a difference," I said.

He smiled. "There's not in Potter County," he said. "But that's as far as my reign extends."

We fell silent and his smile faded.

"You think they brought that little girl all the way down here and into that institution just to kill her?" he asked.

"God, I hope not," I said and prayed. "But," I added, "can you think of a better place to do it?"

"I'm havin' a hard time thinkin' about it at all," he said, looking down at his feet. He was kicking at the dirt with the point of his boot, then covering over the divot with the heel of the other one.

On the other side of the small corral, three cows ate grain out of a trough that hung from one of the panels, two of them with calves sucking milk from them as they did. One of the calves seemed to be getting more than her fill, but the other continually nuzzled the sack with his nose attempting to get the milk to let down.

"Probably going to have to bottle feed him," Dad said when he looked over at where I had been staring in wonder. "Her milk's not flowing right."

A small breeze blew over us, carrying with it the fresh scents of livestock, the sweet smell of hay, and the dusty smell of grain. The stillness and peace of the moment was interrupted as three violent sneezes erupted from me in quick succession.

"Excuse me," I said.

"Bless you," Dad said.

"Thanks," I said.

"We haven't gotten any results back on the condoms yet," he said, "but the pathologist said that the one found in the visitor's restroom was definitely covered in feces like we thought. The fluid on the two found in the kitchen was saliva. So I guess we're talkin' oral, anal, or something else altogether—like muling, but we don't know who—or why there're two with saliva, and DNA's gonna take a while."

"One of the inmates says DeAndré Stone was there that night," I said, "but so far no one else has corroborated it."

"You believe him?"

"I'm inclined to," I said.

"Well now, that changes things, doesn't it?"

"Have you seen the crime scene photos?" I asked.

He nodded slowly and looked down.

"I was only in there a few minutes, but I thought I saw something," I said.

He wiped at his eyes, then looked up at me and said, "What's that?"

"Staging," I said.

"The body or crime scene?" he asked.

I nodded. "I noticed her skirt and top had been pulled up and her panties down," I said, "but if she wasn't sexually assaulted, then it was staging—made to look like a sex crime when it wasn't."

"As I recall," he said, "staging is most often done by people who're close to the victim. They do it to throw us off."

"Like the ransom note in the JonBenet Ramsey case," I said. "And the photos show that her skirt and shirt were up and her panties had been pulled down?"

He nodded very slowly and deliberately.

"So if she wasn't sexually assaulted, which we don't really know," I said, "then it probably was staging."

"It'd have to be," he said.

Beyond the corral, a handful of cows grazed the short green grass. Bunched together, they lazily moved through the field, bending down, pulling the grass with upward and sideward jerks of their heads, raising to chew, then back down again.

After a few moments of silence, he said, "You're wasting your talents as a chaplain. How'd you know about staging?"

"Worked with a profiler from the FBI on the Stone Cold Killer case when I was in Atlanta," I said.

I worked for the Stone Mountain Police Department while in college during the late eighties and early nineties, part of which coincided with the reign of a serial killer who became known as the

Stone Cold Killer because of his murder weapon—Stone Mountain itself.

"And on Martin Fisher's," I added. "He taught me a lot. Since then, I've read his books and others."

He nodded.

"But," I added, "if I weren't a chaplain, I wouldn't be working this case."

He shrugged. "I guess you're right," he said. "We've got to find out for sure if she was assaulted."

"Yeah," I said. "The thing is even with her panties down and shirt up, she was facing down, which meant her most private parts were covered up."

"Yeah?" he asked, his face expressing his confusion.

"That's just what someone close to her would do," I said. "Stage it to look like a sexual murder, but then preserve her dignity as much as they possibly could."

"What the hell is the motive?" he asked. "Is there one, I wonder?"

The smell of the livestock was pungent, and I realized I was breathing through my mouth.

"I don't know," I said. "But the means is probably a clue. She was beaten and strangled to death."

We were both silent for a moment, and I shook my head as I thought about what I had said. "Unless…"

"Unless what?" he asked.

"Unless it was a sex crime," I said. "Then the anger wouldn't've been personal. Nicole would've merely been an object for it."

He stopped kicking the dirt and looked up at me, our eyes locking for the first time. "When I think of what the sick bastard did to her, I want to kill him, John."

"Yeah," I said, "the thought's occurred to me, too."

Just then, his cell phone rang and he answered it.

While he talked, I walked a few feet away to think about what we knew—or believed—and what it meant.

"You said not to count out an act of God," Dad said when he got off the phone.

"Come again," I said.

"You get to talk to Bobby Earl Caldwell tonight," he said. "How?"

He smiled and shook his head to himself again. "On national television."

CHAPTER 34

I picked up Susan at the newly remodeled Driftwood Motel, which had been forced into renovation because of hurricane damage. From Mexico Beach, we drove east along the coast on Highway 98 through Port St. Joe and into Apalachicola, where we ate at Caroline's.

On the drive down, we had mostly made small talk about the events in our lives since we had last seen each other, and our conversation had all the charm of a first date without the mystery and possibility. But as we neared Apalachicola, we both seemed to relax, the iceberg on the armrest between us beginning to thaw, and as we really began to talk, the stranger beside me only occasionally sounded like the person I used to know.

"Are you seeing anyone?" she asked.

I shook my head. "You?"

"I'm a married woman," she said as if she were appalled.

For a while, we sat speechless and I considered the beautiful woman across from me as if for the first time. She no longer seemed awkward or uncomfortable with herself, and she obviously had overcome her dislike of silence.

"Well, aren't we a faithful pair?" she asked with a smile.

"That or pathetic," I said.

Caroline's faced the marina, her windows overlooking the choppy waters of the boat-filled bay. The full moon bathed everything in a romantic glow, casting long shadows that seemed alive, its pale particles of light gently slow-dancing on the small waves of the water.

Earlier in the day, a harvest had been gathered from this place where all life began, that included fresh amberjack, which we ordered grilled with baked potatoes and the sweetest iced tea around.

After we had ordered, she said, "Dad told me about the case you worked together last summer. He was very impressed with you."

"Yeah," I said sarcastically. "He's been a fan since way back."

Only two other tables were occupied in the small restaurant. At one, an elderly couple sat in silence waiting for their food. They seemed perfectly content not to speak to one another, as if through their long life together they had said all there was to say. In stark contrast, a young couple sitting across from them attempted to talk with each other in between feeding their baby and entertaining their little girl.

"No, really," Susan said. "He would never say anything to you, but—"

"He tried to have me fired," I said. "And tried me for rape in the media."

She shrugged. "So he has a funny way of showing it," she said. "When it was all over, he said he respected you as an investigator."

"Sure," I said. "It's just as a human being that I disappoint him."

She laughed. "Actually, it's only as the man who broke his little girl's heart."

"I guess I did, didn't I?" I said. "You were so angry… I thought I repulsed you more than hurt you."

The elderly couple's food arrived, and as their disfigured hands met in the middle of the table when they bowed their white heads in prayer, I wondered if I would ever find someone to grow old with, and if there was any possibility it could be Susan.

From deep within, a voice whispered that it could never be anyone but Anna, and that it could never be Anna.

"Are you ready for this?" she asked, taking a deep breath and sighing. "The anger was designed to hide my true emotions, my love and hurt. It's taken nine months of therapy and support groups to be able to say that."

I smiled.

"And it wasn't your addiction, but your recovery," she said. "I could handle an alcoholic. I was comfortable around one of those, but the person you became... well, frankly, he scared the hell out of me."

I nodded, encouraging her to continue.

The laughter of the little girl drew my attention away, and Susan and I both turned to see the toddler hurling French fries at her dad, who ate them with monster sound effects that brought a smile to my face.

Nicole Caldwell's face flashed in my mind like heat lightning over the Gulf on a hot and sleepless night.

"Good dad," I said.

She nodded. "Anyway, you were so different," she said. "So... you didn't need me anymore.... So when you were accused of having an affair, I knew it had to be true because you didn't want me anymore."

"But," I said, and she held her hand up.

"That's how I felt," she said. "I realize now that it wasn't that you didn't want me. It was that you didn't need me, but I had always seen them as the same thing."

My mouth must have been hanging open, because she said, "What is it? What's wrong?"

"You're so different," I said.

"Now you know how I felt," she said. "It was freaky. I was living with a stranger. Plus you had the whole new God-thing going on, too, and that was extra-freaky. You became like this saint. The last thing I wanted around was a saint."

"It's the last thing I am," I said.

Our food came, and as we ate the fresh grilled fish in the glow of the full moon, I found myself being pulled to the enigmatic woman sitting across from me. The combination of her familiarity and mystery was even more hypnotic than the moonlight shimmering atop the gentle ripples of the bay.

But my feelings were out of sync with my thoughts, as if a war were waging between my head and my heart. I felt physical, sexual attraction to someone I wasn't sure I could ever like as a person again. She seemed so different, but anyone could for an evening.

After dinner, we continued east along the coast into Tallahassee.

"Sorry this has to be part of our evening together," I said. "I just found out late this afternoon."

"Are you kidding?" she said. "It'll be fun. I still can't believe you're going to be on *Larry King*."

"Yeah," I said sarcastically, "if you want my autograph, you better get it now. The price'll probably double after the show."

"Maybe," she said, "but double of nothing I can afford."

CHAPTER 35

The familiar music swelled then faded in the small teardrop earpiece I was wearing, while on the twenty-inch Sony monitor beside the camera in front of me, a shot of the *Larry King Live* logo dissolved into a live shot of Larry King.

I was seated in the Channel 7 news room where, via satellite, I was joining four other guests around the country for *Larry King Live*.

"Tonight," he said, "I'm joined by Evangelist Bobby Earl Caldwell. He'll be here for the full hour to talk about the death of his daughter inside a Florida state prison facility where he was conducting a crusade. Plus, theologians from the new PBS special on Abraham along with John Jordan, chaplain of the prison where Nicole Caldwell was murdered."

The monitor in front of me filled with an earnest-looking Bobby Earl Caldwell wearing a thousand dollar suit, makeup, and slicked back hair.

"Welcome, Reverend Caldwell," King said. "Before we begin, let me say again how sorry I am about your daughter."

"Thank you, Larry."

"Now let's meet our panel," King said. "First, Rabbi Daniel Rosenberg, author of *Abraham: Father of Faith*, Father David

O'Donnell, author of *Abraham: Figure of Faithfulness,* and Imam Syed Jumal, author of *Our Father Abraham.*"

As Larry King introduced each of them, their faces appeared on the monitor before me. Both the priest and the rabbi were handsome young men in their early thirties, dressed smartly in black suits, the priest wearing a Roman collar, the rabbi wearing a black yarmulka. The Imam was a thin black man in his fifties with graying hair, large glasses, and a white koofi.

"All three men can be seen on the PBS special *Abraham: Father of Nations* airing later this month.

"And from Florida, prison chaplain, John Jordan."

Suddenly, the camera was on me, and it was my face filling the screen in front of me, as I assumed it was on screens around the world. It was an awkward moment. My first reaction was to smile, but then I thought it inappropriate, so I just nodded instead. The camera lingered long past the time it took me to nod.

"Okay," King said, "first question is an obvious one: What was your little daughter doing inside a state prison facility?"

"Singing with her mother, my wife, Bunny, as a part of our evangelistic outreach."

"But prison?" King said, turning his hand palm up. His eyes grew wide, his brow furrowing as his large glasses rose on his nose.

"Our Lord and Savior, Jesus Christ, has called us to reach out with love to the least of these his brethern—the ones the rest of the world has forgotten about. We've done it all of Nicole's life and never had an incident."

"You've come under a lot of criticism lately for taking her inside," King continued, "but there seems to be just as many supporters coming to your defense."

"I think they understand Bunny and I are just doing what God's called us to do," Bobby Earl said. "And that we took every precaution."

"What precautions did you take?" King asked.

Bobby Earl told him.

"So, Chaplain Jordan, Nicole was in your office when she was murdered?"

Suddenly, my face was filling the screen again.

"Yes," I said.

When I didn't elaborate, King smiled at my awkwardness and announced it was time for a break.

During the break, Susan walked over from where she had been standing against the back wall of the studio.

"Let the others talk, too," she said.

I smiled. "I'll try not to prattle on during the next segment."

"Chaplain Jordan," King said when we came back from the break, "do you know if there're any suspects in the case?"

"Yes," I said.

"There are?"

"Yes."

"But no arrest?" he asked.

"No, sir," I said. "Not yet."

"Chaplain, are the Caldwells suspects?"

"No one has been ruled out," I said.

"How does that feel?" King asked Bobby Earl.

"Just awful," he said. "Anyone who knows us knows how much we loved Nicole, knows we could never do such a thing. But the good book tells us to expect to suffer for righteousness."

"And Nicole was adopted, right?"

"Yes," Bobby Earl said.

"But it doesn't hurt any less losing an adopted child."

"No."

"Now, let's bring in the rest of our panel," King said. "They're all members of the group discussing Abraham on PBS in an upcoming special. Reverend Caldwell, last week on your broadcast you compared yourself to Abraham, didn't you?"

"Well, I think I was misunderstood," he said.

"Let's take a look at the clip," King said.

The screen filled with Bobby Earl preaching in his New Orleans studio. And if there had been any question before, there was no doubt now—Bobby Earl had indeed compared himself to Abraham and Nicole to Isaac.

For the next few minutes, Bobby Earl tried to explain why he had made the comparisons between himself and Abraham and Nicole and Isaac. The longer he talked, the more defensive he became, until eventually he told Larry King that until God had tested him in a similar manner, he could never understand. No one could.

"Fair enough," King said, and took another break.

"Rabbi Rosenberg," King said after the break, "what is it about the story of Abraham and Isaac that makes it so enduring?"

"Well, first," Daniel Rosenberg said, as his faced filled the monitor in front of me, "we must remember what having an heir meant to Abraham, his culture and religion—it was everything. And God had promised this childless man that he would become the father of nations. But for twenty-five years, his wife remained barren."

"Think about how cruel that was," Father David said, jumping in before the director could cut to him. "Twenty-five eternal years waiting for a child, all the while being called the father of nations."

"And now," Rosenberg said, "after all the waiting, all the testing, all the suffering, all the years of feeling like the biggest fool on the planet, Abraham is given a son—"

"Only to have God ask for him back," Larry King said. "Right, Chaplain Jordan?"

"No," I said, my face filling the screen. "God doesn't just ask for Isaac back. He asks Abraham to kill him."

As the camera cut back to King, my mind exploded with a terrifying thought: *Maybe Bobby Earl had compared himself to Abraham because he had done what Abraham had been willing to do—kill his own child. Was Bobby Earl subconsciously confessing?*

"'Take your son, your only son whom you love,'" King was saying, "'and go forth up to the land of Moriah and offer him up on a high mountain that I will show you.' I mean this was the ultimate test, wasn't it?"

"Yes," Father David said, "and he failed it."

"What?" Larry King asked in surprise.

"I think he failed," Father David said. "I know everyone says what a great act of faith this was on Abraham's part—how he was willing to sacrifice his only son—but the real test was how he would respond to God, or to the voice inside his head he thought was God. He should have said no."

"Wow," King said, "I never thought of it that way. But it's kind of like a father sending his son off to war, isn't it? No one wants to do it, but sometimes…"

"Wait a minute now," Imam Jumal said, breaking his silence at long last. "We've got to view this from an eternal position. Obedience to God is all that matters. Whatever we give up or even sacrifice in this life will be given back to us a hundred-fold by God in the next."

"Amen," Bobby Earl said.

"Of course, the Qur'an teaches that it was Ishmael, not Isaac, that God asked for and Abraham offered."

Bobby Earl seemed unable to respond to that, and we went to break.

"So you believe you'll be back with Nicole one day?" Larry King asked Bobby Earl after the break.

"Absolutely," he said, tears filling his eyes. "It's why I can rejoice. My loss is heaven's gain. God will reward me and Nicole for our faithful service."

"But you know people can't understand that," King said. "If Abraham were alive today, and he told us God told him to kill his son, we'd lock him up in a mental institution."

"It's interesting," Rabbi Rosenberg said, "that the Hebrew word for prophet has a connotation of madness in it."

Maybe Abraham was mad, I thought. Just a crazy old man who'd been out in the desert heat too long… Or maybe, just maybe, he trusted God beyond what I can even begin to understand.

"Really?" King said. "That is interesting, but I guess that's true, most of the things the old prophets did, we would think of as crazy today, wouldn't we, Chaplain Jordan?"

"Yeah," I said. "There's a very fine line between faith and foolishness. Most acts of faith are illogical—they don't make any sense from a practical standpoint."

During the next break, Susan waved and blew me a kiss, and when I asked how I was doing, she gave me two thumbs up.

"Does it offend you men that Reverend Caldwell compared himself to Abraham?" King asked after the break.

"Deeply," Imam Jamal said. "I am very sorry for the loss of his daughter, but her death does not make him Abraham, the father of our faith."

"Larry," Bobby Earl said, "I never said I was Abraham. I only meant that I know what it's like to offer everything up to God."

"How could God ask such a thing of Abraham, Rabbi Rosenberg?"

"Maybe God views death very differently than we do," he said. "Maybe God expects everything from us."

"But we can't forget," I heard myself saying before I knew what I was doing, "that in the story this test came at the end of Abraham's life, after he spent twenty-five years learning he could trust God. This was like his final exam. And, God didn't accept Abraham's sacrifice of his son. He tested him, yes, but didn't allow him to follow through with it. He instead provided a lamb. The God who tests is also the God who provides."

"Which is a beautiful picture of Christ," Father David said. "Think about Isaac carrying the wood for the fire up the mountain the way Christ carried his cross to Calvary."

"And it's certainly a picture of resurrection," Rabbi Rosenberg added. "Ultimately, nothing is lost, for God redeems and returns to us everything in the end."

"Chaplain Jordan, since this story has been getting so much attention, you've received a lot of criticism for not adequately protecting Nicole while she was in your chapel."

My face filled the monitor, the growing pink glow of my embarrassment obvious.

It wasn't a question and I wasn't sure what to say.

"Yes?" I asked.

"Well," King said, "do you have anything to say to that?"

"What can I say?" I asked. "I deserve the criticism. I should've never left her side."

"Okay," he said, hesitated a moment, then asked, "Who's responsibility was it to keep her safe?"

"Mine," I said.

"Bobby Earl," King said, "why take the chance?"

"Ah," Bobby Earl said, seeming at a loss.

"Why take her in such a dangerous place?" King added. "Why ask people like Chaplain Jordan and others to do such a difficult job?"

"Larry," Bobby Earl said, "this is what God has called me to do. You'd have to ask him."

"God?" King asked with a laugh.

"Yes," Bobby Earl said sincerely.

"Chaplain Jordan," King said, "do you think Nicole's killer will be found?"

"I'm certain of it," I said.

"Bobby Earl," King said, "do you think most people sitting at home watching us tonight think you killed your daughter?"

"Heavens, no," Bobby Earl said. "I think they realize—"

"But as I understand it," King said, "you and your wife were the only two people to go in or out of that locked office where Nicole was killed. Are you saying your wife did it?"

"Absolutely not," he said. "Bunny could never do such a thing. She's a—"

"Looks like we're out of time for tonight," King said. "I want to thank my guests—"

"One more thing before we go," Bobby Earl said. "Earlier you asked if we were suspects and Chaplain Jordan said no one had been ruled out, which might have sounded like we were, but I have been assured by the governor this week that we have been cleared and that they're not going to waste time investigating innocent people."

"Oh," King said. "So, Chaplain Jordan, the Caldwells are not suspects in the investigation?"

"As I said before, Larry, no one has been ruled out."

"But the governor said—" Bobby Earl began.

"The governor," I said, "is not conducting the investigation."

CHAPTER 36

"He killed his daughter, didn't he?" Susan said.

We were back in the car riding toward Mexico Beach on the brightly moon-lit barren highway next to the coast.

"I don't know," I said. "But if he did, he sees himself as Abraham."

"I bet everyone wondered why you said you were certain her killer would be found," she said, "but I knew."

"Yeah?"

"Yeah," she said. "You're certain because you won't stop until you find him."

I nodded.

"But what then?" she asked. "What will you do with a monster like that?"

"I may make a little sacrifice of my own," I said.

We were quiet for a long time before she said, "Probably not a good idea to make the governor mad at you."

"Why should he be any different?"

She smiled. "Can you believe we're still married?"

"No," I said. "I can't. Why didn't you sign the papers?"

"I meant to," she said. "But I didn't want to, so I procrastinated. And then when I began recovery, I don't know, I guess I just began to see things so differently." She turned toward me suddenly, eyes moving rapidly, voice pleading. "You didn't cheat on me, did you?"

"No," I said. "I never did." Then I laughed out loud. "Still haven't."

"You haven't?" she said. "You mean this whole time you thought we were divorced, and you haven't..."

"Sad, isn't it?"

"No," she said. "Of course not. It's sweet. It's wonderful. It's just what I'd expect."

She reached over and took my hand, lacing her fingers in mine, and laid her head on my shoulder, the scent of her hair drifting pleasantly over me. Her hand felt right in mine, her body like it was made to be beside mine, but an uneasiness, blinking like a warning light at the edge of my mind, whispered that my body was betraying me.

"What're we gonna do?" she asked.

"About what?"

"In the eyes of the law," she said, "we're still married."

"I know," I said. "But that's not how we've been living. The law doesn't change the fact that we reached a place where we both felt like we had to separate. It can't heal us or make us right with each other again. It's powerless to create love."

"So there's no hope for us?" she asked, releasing her hold on my hand and rising off my shoulder. "No chance of—"

Just then, a black van pulled out of a small side road and rammed into us. My truck fishtailed, but I managed to keep it on the road, and when I had it back under control, I slowed, but continued moving forward.

"Aren't you gonna stop?" Susan asked.

"On a dark road in the middle of nowhere without a gun?" I asked.

"Why don't you carry a gun?" she asked.

"I tend to shoot less people," I said.

"But with all the criminals you work around, all the crimes you still investigate..."

"Now's probably not the best time for this conversation."

I checked the rearview mirror again. The van was still sitting in the middle of the highway, its lights on.

"We've got to go back and help them," Susan said.

"I've got to find a safe place to drop you off first," I said.

"I'm going with you," she said.

"On a dark road in the middle of nowhere without a gun?" I asked. "Are you kidding?"

She smiled at me, reached into her purse, and pulled out a small snub-nosed .38. She pointed it at me and said, "Go back."

"What?" I asked in shock.

"Just kidding," she said with a smile. "It's not loaded."

She then reached back into her purse, pulled out a small box of cartridges, and loaded the gun.

At first I was surprised she had a gun, but then on second thought: *Of course she would. She's a single woman living in Atlanta and her dad's been in law enforcement all her life.*

"How many of your dates come this prepared?" she asked with a wry smile.

"Not many," I said. "Usually they have a very different idea of protection."

When I checked the mirror again, the lights in the van had gone off, and just as I was about to turn around, I caught a glimpse of it racing toward us.

"What's he doing?" Susan asked.

"Probably not trying to give me his insurance information," I said, and floored it.

My truck did zero to sixty in less than sixty minutes, so the van had caught up to us in no time, and as soon as it did, it rammed us again. And then again. And again.

I knew I could never outrun or out-maneuver him, so I tried to think of an alternate plan.

"Could I borrow that?" I asked Susan, nodding toward her gun.

She handed it to me.

"Thanks," I said. "Now, cover your ears."

I rolled down the window, and, with my left hand on the wheel, reached out with my right and squeezed off two rounds.

Both missed.

"How many rounds you got?" I asked.

"Not many," she said.

"Uh oh."

"Don't miss and it won't be an issue."

"Oh, okay," I said with as much sarcasm as I could muster at the moment.

I fired two more rounds. Both of them missed again.

"This is embarrassing," she said with a laugh.

"Yeah," I said, "laugh it up. It's all fun and games until they kill us."

This was a different Susan—witty, charming, cool under pressure. Not to mention, she carried a gun—how cool was that?

"I've got an idea," she said, unbuckling her seatbelt and turning around in the seat. She reached back and slid open the center panel of glass. "I'll steer and you shoot through there."

"Couldn't get less results," I said.

When I turned toward the van, I thought I noticed something about the plates, but it was too dark to be sure. So before I fired again, I reached under the passenger seat and pulled out a Q-beam spot light, plugged it into the cigarette lighter, and shined it on the van.

The van started slowing immediately, but I fired the last two rounds anyway. One ricocheted off the bumper, the other missed completely.

"It's another couple of miles to East Point," Susan said, "Why'd they stop?"

"They didn't want me to see their bumper," I said.

"What?" she asked in surprise. "Why?"

"Because," I said, "it held a Louisiana license plate."

When we reached the Driftwood, she asked me up to her room, and I politely declined.

"I just don't want this night to end," she said. "Not yet.... Take your wife for a walk on the beach. Please, John."

"It's not that I don't want to," I said. "It's that I want to too much."

"Remember what you were saying earlier," she said. "About the law being unable to create desire?"

I nodded.

"Well, if you have the desire," she said, "the law is on your side. I'm still Mrs. John Jordan."

CHAPTER 37

I knew sleeping with my ex-wife was a mistake before our clothes hit the floor.

We had just come up to her room to change clothes before taking a moonlit stroll along the beach, but she looked and smelled and felt so familiar, and over a year without physical intimacy had been an eternity too long.

Her eyebrows arched into a question that meant only one thing. It was how she had initiated sex during our marriage—never verbally, not once, just an expression that I couldn't resist.

I would never again underestimate the power of shared history, like the connection that binds you to school friends for life, though you have nothing but school in common. Susan and I had shared a life together, and that shared experience wrapped itself around us like elastic bands that allowed for only so much separation before they snapped us back together again. I hadn't thought about her in nearly a year. Now as beauty, softness, and a sweet scent filled my senses, my mind could think of little else, and my body couldn't quit wanting her.

We lunged at each other, kissing so hard and long that I was sure we had drawn blood, as we unceremoniously ripped each other's clothes off. My mouth found her breasts as my fingers danced around her wet and waiting body. I knew what she liked.

"Oh, God, John," she said breathlessly.

She was still beautiful, her brown hair lighter and shorter, her eyes still the color of brandy—windows of the deep decanter of her soul. If her body had changed at all, it was firmer and fitter, the muscles in her arms and abs hard and tight. But she was still soft in all the right places. Her bottom and breasts were still full and not too firm and her secret place was still as soft and as wet as a kiss in the rain.

She grabbed me hard with her hand, grabbed the throbbing anger, guilt, discipline, denial, and frustration and it took all I could do to hold back the flood threatening the dam of my determination.

On many occasions, Susan and I had made love. We had become lost in each other's souls even as we entered each other's bodies. We had been enraptured. This was not one of those times.

On other occasions, Susan and I had just had sex. We had searched each other's bodies for what was missing in our souls. This was one of those times—a time after the end of the innocence. This was not about love. This was about sex. About desire. It was also about anger and regret.

I was reminded of my sex life with Susan—how she had run hot and cold. How she had found the safety and security of monogamy in a loving and committed relationship monotonous and restricting, longing instead for forbidden fruit; passion without permission.

For Susan, I thought, *stolen bread is sweeter*, and I wondered if she had lied to me in the truck about not having been with anyone else while we had been apart. *Actually, she had avoided the question.*

I should stop.

But I couldn't.

As my body went limp, collapsing onto hers, a wave of guilt and regret swept over me, tugging me down, the force of its undertow too much for me to resist.

What have I done? I wondered.

"I'm sorry," I whispered.

"For what?" she asked in shock. "That was great. So intense."

We were lying side by side on the floor between the two double beds, never having made it to either of them.

I felt empty, the void in my heart matching the absence in the room.

What was it? I wondered. What was missing?

And then it blew me back like the vacuous whirlwind of Job. Love was missing. God was missing.

"Wasn't it? God, it was good."

I nodded.

"But it always felt good," she said. "And we had it good there for a while, too, didn't we? I mean in every way. We were good together."

Susan was always chatty after sex, which was all right with me, because I was always mellow and reflective. I used to love to listen to her, to the stuff that came pouring out of her with the wash of hormones orgasm produced.

She was quiet for a moment, then said, "God, that was good."

Suddenly, I was overcome by an oppressive and overwhelming sense of loss for what might have been. We had been in love, we had dreams, we had—

"Hey," she said, leaning up on her elbow, "did I ever tell you I was sorry?"

I nodded.

"Well, let me tell you again. I really am," she said, her eyes filling with tears. "I'm so sorry for… for what happened… for all that I've done."

My hard heart melted and I had to blink back stinging tears of my own.

"I'm sorry, too, Susan," I said.

She smiled at me, tears at the corners of her eyes. "I still love you," she said. "I've tried to stop, tried to convince myself that I don't anymore, but I do."

She waited, but I couldn't say the same thing back to her exactly. Not yet. An awkward silence crept into the room like a fog, and I could feel the distance between us increasing.

"I want to make love to you," I said.

"Whatta you call what we just did?"

"Sex," I said. "But I'd like to love you body and soul."

"Take me down to the beach," she said.

I did.

We walked down the beach, holding hands as we followed the twisting and turning path of the tide as if mirroring the path of our lives.

After a while she stopped and turned toward me. When she looked up at me, I took her face in my hands and kissed her gently.

With tears in her eyes, she whispered, "Make love to me."

I did.

And this time love, as well as the God who is love, was present.

No anger, no hate, no blame, and no shame. Just love and appreciation for the love we once had, for the people we once had been.

Our love-making on the beach beneath the warm glow of the full moon was tender and sweet, our bodies quickly finding familiar rhythms, seeming to nurture each other with a desire to warm and heal. She felt like home in my hands, and I experienced a rush of emotions similar to our first times together before the cops, before the booze, before the Stone Cold Killer.

Her climax, though quiet and sweet, was as intense as it had ever been, and she cried softly afterwards.

Tears of grace.

Chapter 38

The morning after.

Looking at myself in the bathroom mirror of my small, dilapidated trailer, dark circles beneath bloodshot eyes—the only color on an otherwise pale face, I strained for recognition. Who was this stranger staring back at me?

I looked bad. I felt worse.

I'd had a lot of mornings after in my life, and this one was like all the rest, filled with guilt and regret. I had made love to a woman I wasn't sure I could ever love again, and the fact that she was still my wife couldn't justify that. The pain inflicted, though not yet felt, hung over me like a dark cloud.

Like the stranger in the mirror, my surroundings seemed foreign to me. Dangling hollow door, paper-thin paneling, curling linoleum-covered creaky floor, rust-spotted lime-green sink beneath a leaky faucet, and cabinet doors that no longer fastened shut—it was bad. I deserved worse.

I needed to talk to someone, to share the dark thoughts slamming into the walls of my mind, to release the conflicting feelings swirling inside my chest cavity, but who? Who could hear my confession, who could offer compassion, comfort, and wise counsel?

A moment later my phone rang.

"Hey," Susan said, her voice sultry and sleepy.

"Hey," I said. "I was just thinking about you.... about us."

"I figure you've got a lot of that to do," she said.

I didn't say anything.

"I'm going back to Atlanta today," she said.

"Why?" I asked.

"To let you think," she said. "I'm a different person, John. If you think there's any possibility we can be together again, we'll have to start over—get to know the people we've become. I'm in no hurry. I won't rush you."

"Thanks," I said.

"I don't regret last night," she said. "No matter what happens. So please don't feel guilty about it. I'm a big girl and not nearly as fragile as I used to be. Don't worry about me.... But think about me."

"I will," I said, and I felt an enormous weight begin to lift, as if the newness of the morning might bring hope rather than regret. "Thank you."

"I know you," she said. "You're predictable in such a good way. I loved who you were.... I love more who you've become."

"I love who you've become, too," I said.

"Becoming," she said. "Becoming."

"Of course."

"Good-bye," she said.

"Good-bye."

"No regrets."

"None."

"The investigation's over," Fortner said.

He had been standing in the parking lot waiting for me, and had quickly walked over to my truck as soon as I pulled in.

"What?" I asked in shock as I got out of my truck and closed the door.

"At least for us," he said, and we began walking toward the admin building. "Tom Daniels showed up this morning and took over. Didn't you take his daughter out last night?"

"Yeah," I said.

"Isn't he your ex-father-in-law or something?"

"Or something, as it turns out," I said. "We're still married."

He shook his head in disbelief and smiled. "I'm not even assisting him this time," he said, his face growing angry. "He's got a team from FDLE. Evidently, Bobby Earl called the governor."

I shook my head wearily.

Across the street, near the employees' softball field and next to the training building, several news trucks were setting up, as reporters, mics in hand, were checking makeup and hair as camera men were making final adjustments to tripods and video cameras.

Following my gaze, Pete said, "Oh, I saw you on *Larry King*. Did you talk to Bobby Earl?"

"We were in different states," I said.

"Oh," he said. "Hey," he added, stopping suddenly, "what the hell happened to your truck?"

I told him.

"Van was from Louisiana?" he asked. "You sure?"

I nodded.

"But it couldn't've been Bobby Earl," he said. "He was with Larry King at the time."

"Which was very smart," I said.

Further down the road, past the training building and obstacle course, members of the pistol team were practicing on the firing range, preparing for a tournament this coming weekend. From this distance, the .38 rounds sounded like the small pops of firecrackers.

"Did you see who it was?"

"Who was what?"

"In the van?"

"Just a glimpse," I said, "but it looked like DeAndré Stone."

"Oh shit," he said. "He came into the institution last night."

"For what?"

"Evidently his uncle has given him a volunteer badge and made it clear to the control room sergeant that he can come and go as he likes as a representative of Bobby Earl Caldwell Ministries."

"But what did he do?" I asked.

"I'm not sure," he said. "I just saw his name on the control room log. But guess who's back in the infirmary?"

"Cedric Porter?"

He nodded.

"Is he okay?"

"No, but he's gonna live."

"We need to—"

"Assign security to him? Already done."

"Great," I said. "Good work."

"Thanks."

Correctional officers, most of them in mud-covered trucks with tall CB antennas bobbing up and down in the wind, and employees began to trickle down the long road that leads to the prison, each of them straining to look at the news vans and reporters. Soon the empty parking lot was filling up, doors slamming, alarms twerping, the last bites of breakfast being eaten, and Pete and I, suddenly in a crowd, had to lower our voices.

"This has got to stop," I said. "Dad's still working with NOPD on the Caldwells, but I'm gonna try to work it out so I can interview them in the next day or so."

"Speaking of which," he said, "your dad's off the case, too."

I nodded.

"Stone wants to see us in his office," he said. "Says if we continue to investigate, he's going to send us home and file criminal charges."

I didn't say anything.

"Are you going to stop?"

"Of course," I said. "I always do what I'm told."

Tom Daniels was waiting for me in Stone's outer office with his best glare. I tried not to quake. The door to Stone's office was ajar, and I could hear that he was on the phone.

I walked over to Daniels, and in a low voice that Stone's secretary couldn't hear, said, "Dad."

"Son..." he whispered back, "... of a bitch."

Tom Daniels' puffy face was lined with tiny broken blood vessels and looked far older than its fifty-seven years. His gin-soaked eyes were bloodshot and gray like his hair, which was in disarray.

"You've always had a way with words," I said. "And always been way too sentimental when it comes to family."

"We're not family," he said.

"Oh, but we are," I said. "My wife, your daughter, never filed our divorce papers. We discussed the whole thing over dinner last night. We're thinking of getting back together and moving in with you and Mom."

He was speechless, his anger seething beneath the fiery surface of his skin.

"I'm overcome, too," I said. "Let me see if I can find us a tissue."

CHAPTER 39

When we were all seated inside Stone's office, he said, "I'll make this brief. Inspector, Chaplain, you are no longer to investigate the murder of Nicole Caldwell."

"We can't just stop," Fortner said. "We're too far in. Getting too close to finding the killer."

"That's my job," Daniels said. "I appreciate what you've done, Pete, and I'll use it, but you can't work on this one anymore."

Fortner started to continue his protest, but Stone stopped him by raising his hand. "I didn't call you in here to discuss it," he said. "Merely to inform you. Do you understand?"

I nodded, but Fortner shook his head. "Do y'all want the killer to get away for some reason? Is he a family member, something like that?"

The sudden rage from Stone was palpable, but he spoke very calmly. "If it matters," he said, "this was not my decision. I'm confident in your abilities. Both of you."

"But—" Fortner began again.

"The media attention changes everything. This is coming from the top," Daniels said. "And not just of the department. Your warden's dangerously close to losing his job. If you want to join him, then persist in your insubordination. If not, back off and stay the hell out of my way. Both of you."

Fortner nodded and Daniels looked over at me. "Understand?" he asked.

I nodded.

"I'm not playing here," he said. "Don't nod your head in here and then go out there and fuck up my investigation. I've been empowered to fire and or file criminal charges against anybody who gets in my way on this thing. So don't fuck with me."

"The thought never crossed my mind," I said with a smile, and Fortner laughed out loud.

"I mean it," Daniels said angrily.

"Me, too," I said.

When no one else said anything, I looked over at Stone. "Are you doing this to protect DeAndré?"

He looked genuinely perplexed. "If it turns out that Bobby Earl is guilty—and I seriously doubt it will—DeAndré can find another job."

You're either a very good liar or your love makes you clueless, I thought, *wondering which was more likely.*

When we had left Stone's office, Pete stopped me out in front of the gate.

"Did you see Nicole with a coloring book and crayons when she was here?" he asked.

"Yeah," I said. "She colored a picture for me."

"Coel said she had them that night," he said. "Carried them in your office to color while she was waiting for Bobby Earl to preach his sermon."

"Yeah?"

"They weren't in the stuff we inventoried from the crime scene," he said.

"What?" I asked in shock.

"They're not still in your office, are they?" he asked.

"Well, I'm the last person who wants to be investigating when I've been ordered not to, but let's go have a look."

We walked through the sally port, down the sidewalk, and into the chapel.

Several inmates were seated in the chapel library listening to tapes, reading books, pestering my clerks, and by the anxious look on a few of their faces, waiting to talk to me.

After greeting the rest of the inmates and the officer who was babysitting them for me, Pete and I walked into my office. It was the first time since the night of Nicole's murder I had been inside.

Before I turned on the light, the still, stale air of the room was as dark and dank as a tomb. The wet copper smell of blood was in the air and breathing it in left a bad taste in my mouth.

I felt a presence in the room. As it swept past, its touch felt like the shredded gown of a gothic ghost floating above us, and the hair on the back of my neck stood on end. I wondered if Pete sensed it. No longer was this room my sanctuary from the insanity and brutality of prison, but a haunted and defiled death chamber, and turning on the light did nothing to vanquish the spiritual and psychological pain echoing through it.

"My God," Pete said. "It's worse now than when it happened."

We spent the next few moments in silence looking around the room, trying to breath shallowly and only through our mouths.

It didn't feel like my office anymore. It looked pretty much the same—especially if you avoided the blood-stained carpet, but it wasn't, and I wondered if it ever could be again.

"We found her body there," he said, indicating the bloody outline on the floor. "The envelope and cash next to it there," he continued, "the card there, and the candy there."

"That's just where they were when I came in," I said.

"Still no coloring book and crayons," he said.

The statement was so obvious I couldn't think of a response that wasn't sarcastic, so I didn't say anything.

"You think the killer took 'em?" he asked.

"If he did," I said, "it tells us a lot about him."

"Whatta you mean?"

"Many sexual murderers and serial killers take something belonging to the victim in order to relive the experience over and over again."

He shuddered. "That would point away from Bobby Earl to Register or one of the other inmates."

"Or it could point to someone close to her," I added. "Were Bobby Earl and Bunny searched before they left the institution that night?"

"No," he said. "They had just lost their daughter. They were victims at that point, not suspects." He shook his head. "The stuff could've been inside Bobby Earl's Bible cover."

I moved past him, edging around my desk to take a better look under it, but froze when I reached its corner.

"What is it?" Pete asked.

"Look," I said, pointing to the piece of paper on the floor. It was another page Nicole had colored and removed from her book.

"What the hell?" he said in shock. "That wasn't here before, was it?"

I shook my head, still pondering what it meant.

"And there's no way we'd've missed it," he said.

I didn't say anything, just continued to stare at the picture.

"It's not the one she did for you, is it?" he asked.

I shook my head.

"You think it was in here somewhere—bookshelf, desk, chair, and fell down after we left?"

"No."

"Me neither," he said. "I'll be damned."

We were quiet a moment. I stepped around the picture and searched the desk and bookshelf thoroughly. No crayons. No coloring book. Nothing.

"This means someone's been in here since we have," he said.

I nodded.

"Her killer?"

"Possibly."

"Well," he said, "it was pretty damn dumb. Now we know it had to be a staff member with access to keys."

"Not necessarily," I said. "See how close it is to the door? It looks like someone could've slid it right beneath the door."

"But there again, that points away from the Caldwells," he said. "Bobby Earl hasn't been here."

"No," I said, "but DeAndré has."

CHAPTER 40

I found Theo Malcolm sitting at his desk grading papers, his inmate orderly, Luther Albright, standing behind him with his arms folded like a bodyguard. From a boom-box in the corner, the aggressive sounds of gangsta rap polluted the air in the room. When he had said, "Enter," and I walked in, he briefly looked up, shook his head, and looked back down at his papers.

"You don't seem happy to see me," I said with a big smile.

"I'm very busy," he said. "What can I do for you?"

The rapper was rapping about killing white policemen in the war of the streets—about takin' his nine and smokin' the pig's cracker ass until they were all just traces on the pavement.

I shook my head.

"If you don't like our music," Albright started, but Malcolm held up his hand.

Our music? Was Albright an orderly or a buddy? Getting overly familiar with an inmate was a dangerous decision to make. I had seen more than a few careers destroyed because of it, and I wondered if Malcolm realized how foolish he was being.

"You probably think that African Americans believed OJ was innocent," he said.

"Actually," I said, "I don't."

"Well, we didn't," he said, as if contradicting me. "We's not's dumb as y'alls thinks we is," he said in his best slave dialect, before gliding smoothly back into his regular condescending tone. "We knew he was guilty. We didn't care. We were glad he got away with it. Killing a white woman and a white man—even a cop—can't come close to the multitudes of young black men y'all've killed."

Albright smiled.

I shook my head. "Are you for real?"

"An eye for an eye, brother," he said.

"Leaves everybody blind," I said.

"It's very good that you know the quote, though the quote itself is naive," he said, "but do you know who said it?"

"Dr. King. Will that be on the final?"

"Well, if you all really believed it, I guess you wouldn't have shot him down like a dog, would you?"

"Actually," I said, "I had nothing to do with it."

Malcolm stood, walked over, and stopped the music. When he turned to face me again, Albright put his hand on his shoulder. "I don't have time for this," he said. "I'm really busy. If you need something, you better ask now."

"Have you been back to the chapel or my office since the night Nicole died?"

"No, why?"

"I found something in my office that wasn't there before," I said.

"Well, I haven't been back," he said. "Is someone saying I have?"

Ignoring his question, I said, "On the night Nicole was killed, why'd you stop by the chapel? I mean beside to check the program for racism."

"I was there to see Bunny," he said.

"What?"

"We worked together at Lake Butler," he said. "We're just friends."

"Did you see her?" I asked.

He shook his head. "She was on the stage singing, so I left."

"Did you see Officer Coel standing at the sanctuary door?"

He shook his head.

"Did you see anyone in my office?" I asked.

"Just Nicole," he said. "And she was fine when I left. If you suspect me of her murder, you're wasting valuable time you could be using to find the real killer."

"You sound like OJ," I said.

"Look—" he began angrily, but I cut him off.

"What're you trying to hide?" I asked.

"I have nothing to hide."

"Why was I attacked right after I talked to you last time?" I asked. "And why were you the only suspect they told me to stay away from?"

Before he realized what he was doing, he glanced at Albright.

"I thought I recognized your voice," I said to Albright.

He didn't say anything, just glared.

"I'll be in the chapel if you want to give it another go," I said.

"We know where to find you," Albright said.

"And vice versa," I said.

When I got back to my office, I called Chaplain Rouse at Lake Butler again.

"Chaplain Rouse," he said after the second ring.

"Where's your secretary?" I asked.

"I'm in between secretaries at the moment," he said.

"You have two?" I asked.

"Huh?"

I wasn't sure if he didn't get it or didn't approve of the humor, so rather than taking the risk of being sued for sexual harassment, I let it go.

"They've been promising me one for about a year now," I said. "A staff chaplain, too."

"Can't imagine where the state gets the reputation of being mired down in bureaucracy," he said. "What can I do for you?"

"Tell me what you can about Theo Malcolm," I said.

"Don't know him."

"Says he knows Bunny from working with her there," I said. "He's a teacher."

"Well, he hasn't taught here," he said.

"Angry young black man," I said. "You're sure?"

"Positive," he said.

"Maybe he had a different job," I said.

"What's he look like?"

I told him.

"Nope," he said. "Never worked here."

"Okay," I said. "Thanks."

"Wonder why he'd make that up?" he asked.

"Why indeed?" I said, then sat there and thought about it for a long time after he had hung up.

I could come up with only one reason—to hide his real purpose for being there that night, and if he wasn't there to see an old coworker, what was he doing?

CHAPTER 41

"Couldn't Malcolm know Bunny from somewhere else and just say it was Lake Butler?" Anna asked.

It was late afternoon, the inmates had returned to the compound and the chapel was empty. Anna and I were alone in my office.

"It's possible, I guess," I said, "but why?"

She shrugged.

"Abdul Muhammin also said he knew Bobby Earl from Lake Butler," I said.

"But he did," she said.

"Uh huh," I said.

"Uh huh what?" she asked, puzzlement on her face.

"Muhammin would know that Bunny worked there," I said, "and could have told Malcolm."

"For a cover story," she said. "Which shows a connection between them and that they have something to cover up."

"Unless Malcolm heard it somewhere else," I said, frowning and letting out a long sigh. "It's thin. Maybe they're not connected."

I shook my head.

"Are you okay?" she asked.

I didn't say anything.

Eyes narrowed in concern, she stared at me for a long moment.

"I'm worried about you," she said. "I got some information about the Stone Cold Killer case off the Internet. You should've told me there were children involved."

"Probably," I said. "But I never thought it was him. Still don't. The crimes were too different. And how many serial killers do you know kill adults *and* children?"

"But you worked a case in which children were killed?"

I nodded.

"And this case has dredged it all up again?" she asked.

"It's never very far away," I said.

"And you've been dealing with it all alone?"

I shrugged.

"You are so alone down here, aren't you?" she asked.

I didn't say anything. I couldn't, but I thought, not just here. I had yet to find a place where I really fit.

"And having someone in your life…" she started and then stopped, letting it float between us like a wish tied to a balloon, "wouldn't change that, would it?"

Having you would change everything, I thought, but said, "No, probably not."

We fell into a silence pregnant with all that was left unsaid between us.

Eventually, I told her about still being married to Susan.

She shook her head in disbelief. "Why didn't she sign them?" she asked.

I told her.

"She trying to manipulate you in some way?"

"I don't think so," I said. "She really seems different. She came down to Mexico Beach and we went out last night."

"What?" she asked in shock.

"She's in an ACOA support group, and—"

"A what?"

"Adult Children Of Alcoholics," I said.

"I don't know what to say," she said. "I couldn't be more shocked."

Oh, I bet you could, I thought, but decided not to tell her about sleeping with Susan.

"I have no right to feel the way I do," she said. "I have no claim on you, but…"

"I could say the same thing," I said, *but we know differently.*

We were quiet again, and I began to think about the women in my life, and like a Polaroid image finally coming into focus, I realized how much Susan resembled Anna—physically anyway.

She was the woman in my life. The woman by which all other women were judged, to which none could compare.

My phone rang, breaking the silence, and as I answered it, Anna whispered, "I'm going to the restroom."

I nodded to her and then said into the receiver, "Good afternoon. Chaplain Jordan."

"Chaplain Jordan, it's your wife," Susan said.

Heart pounding, heat spreading across my face, I felt as if I had been caught cheating, and was glad when Anna stood up and left the room.

"Are you sure?" I asked. "Because I don't have one."

"It's a long story, but you do."

"Well, supposing I do," I said. "How is she?"

"Actually, she's wonderful," she said. "She's still after-glowing."

"Wow," I said. "Her husband must really be amazing."

"He has his moments," she said.

I heard a noise from the hallway like someone bumping into the wall and then a scream.

"Can I call you back?" I asked.

"Sure," she said, but I was already dropping the phone and running out of the office.

CHAPTER 42

In the hallway, I looked around. No one was there. Nothing was out of place. To the right, through the glass of the double doors, I could see that the sanctuary was dark and still. To my left, the chapel library was dark and empty as well. In front of me, a narrow hallway led to the restrooms, kitchen, and fellowship hall.

I ran down the hall and without stopping, burst into the women's bathroom. I hit the door hard and it slammed into the wall behind it. I held my gaze wide, trying to take in the whole room, so that any movement, no matter how small would be perceptible. Nothing. I looked around. I still saw nothing.

"Anna," I called.

No response.

I pushed open the doors to the two stalls and looked inside. They were both empty, but one of them had toilet tissue hanging down from the holder to the floor. I ran out of the bathroom and back into the hallway. I looked around the front door, saw no one, locked it, and decided to search the building room by room, starting with the library.

In the library, blue plastic chairs sat neatly beneath folding tables, books evenly lined the front of wooden shelves, and religious magazines and pamphlets were stacked on wire literature racks. There were only a couple of places to hide—behind the counters or in the storage closet. I started with the counters. I ran over to the counter where Muhammin normally checked out books and tapes and looked behind it. I then rushed over to the other one.

My mind filled with images of Anna bound and gagged, her body trembling with terror. I closed my eyes and shook my head, a feeble attempt at exorcizing the unwelcomed images from my head. I opened my eyes and frantically began searching again as a dark sense of dread descended upon me.

Rushing over to the storage closet, I turned the handle and snatched it open, slamming the door into the wall behind it, the handle puncturing the sheetrock. At first glance, I saw nothing. But in the back behind a large stack of boxes in the center of the floor, I thought I saw movement. I moved toward it, running to the left of the stack without slowing, coming up quickly behind the boxes.

The tower tilted and fell. The top box, full of left-over Christmas and Hanukkah cards, hit me squarely on the back of the neck, scattering a thick mist of dust as it did. I went down, but the moment I hit the floor, I was moving. I bucked the box off my back and crawled around to the other side of the stack. No one was there. I looked back towards the door. No movement. No one.

I sneezed several times before rushing back out of the library, pausing only long enough to shut and lock the door, and then ran across the hall to the extra office I had been using and checked it. It was locked. I unlocked it and looked inside, locked it again and then ran down and rechecked mine. After locking my office door, I searched both bathrooms. I hurriedly locked them behind me and ran into the kitchen, the odor of damp and soiled dishcloths filling my nose.

In the kitchen an island composed of cabinets and a counter top was the only thing that blocked my view. I ran around behind it. When I did, an inmate scurried around the other side on his hands and knees. He was out of the kitchen and moving to the left before I could stop and turn around.

I ran out of the kitchen and followed him into the fellowship hall. When I ran through the door, he swung a metal chair like a baseball bat, two of its legs striking the top of my back and the base of my neck. For the second time within five minutes, I hit the floor. As I attempted to roll over, he hit me again, and sharp streaks of pain bolted along the nerve endings in my back and head, and splotches of bright yellow distorted my vision.

He swung again, and the chair connected with the back of my skull, causing my face to slam into the hard tile floor.

Without thinking, I began rolling toward the inmate. I had no idea where I was, but I rolled. And I rolled into him. Then I rolled through him, knocking his feet out from under him. He went down. I turned. I was face to face with Luther Albright, the inmate orderly who worked for Theo Malcolm.

He reached down into his pocket and brought out a shank, which had once been a toothbrush. The handle had been filed to a sharp point, the brush covered with putty, and two razor blades protruded from it.

He slashed at me. I flung myself back, but not far enough. He sliced both my shirt sleeve and the flesh beneath it with the razors. Then, with the flick of his wrist, he turned it and stabbed at my arm with the sharp spear of the handle. I screamed out as he plunged it into my shoulder.

Reflexively, I began kicking at him. I hit his boots at first, but as I continued, I landed a couple of solid blows to his shins. He then made the mistake of pulling his legs back so I couldn't reach his shins, and I kicked him in the groin. His eyes widened, his face contorted, and, after a moment, he began to heave.

I stumbled to my feet as he began throwing up. I heard Anna scream from the sanctuary, and I turned to run, but then turned back and kicked Albright in the head. The blow was hard and knocked him out cold.

I ran back down the hallway and into the dark chapel, pausing to let my vision adjust. As soon as I could see, I scanned the entire sanctuary. I didn't see anyone. And then, the split second of a heavy blow to the base of my skull and I was out, a black hole opening up before me and sucking me into it.

Later, when I opened my eyes, I saw the base of one of the brass candle holders—presumably the blunt instrument that had kissed me goodnight. I rolled over and looked down toward the front. Anna was gone. When I stumbled slowly to my feet, my head grew light and I fell back down again.

Then with the help of the pew, I slowly pulled myself up and held on. When I had my balance, I saw Anna stumbling up the outside aisle.

"You all right?" I asked.

"Nothing that a bottle of Extra-strength Excedrin and a week of sleep won't fix," she said. "How about you?"

"The same."

"Who was it?"

"You don't know?" I asked.

"No," she said. "There were two. I think one of them was Abdul Muhammin, but I couldn't swear to it."

"Come on," I said, and we walked into the fellowship hall.

"This the one you saw?"

Luther Albright didn't look bright at all as he lay unconscious on the floor.

She shook her head. "Who is it?"

"Albright," I said. "Theo Malcolm's orderly, and trained investigator that I am, I'm beginning to observe a pattern: Interview Malcolm, get attacked."

We walked back up to the main hallway to find my keys in the door. I looked at my watch. It was a few minutes after five. I retrieved my keys, unlocked my office, and called security and medical.

"My God," Anna said, her eyes growing wide as she looked at the shank sticking out of my shoulder.

I looked down at it. "Albright," I said. "In my excitement to see you alive and well, I forgot about it."

"It's not killing you?"

"No," I said. "I don't feel anything." I reached down, took hold of the shank, and yanked on it.

Anna screamed, "NO, JOHN, DON'T," as the shank pulled free. The dam now gone, the river of blood came gushing out. I stood dumbfounded and watched as a flash flood of my blood rained down on my desk top.

CHAPTER 43

While I was being treated in a small outpatient room at the Pottersville Medical Center, Pete Fortner walked in and stood beside me. Seeming oblivious to the doctor's put out sighs and incredulous looks at his intrusion, he made no attempt to talk softly or stay out of the way.

"Albright's in confinement," he said. "You want me to lock up Muhammin too?"

I thought about it.

"I can lock him up for thirty days while we investigate," he said. "Don't have to have a charge or any evidence now."

"Let's leave him out," I said. "I've got an idea for a little trap and we'll need him for it."

"When we gonna set this little trap?"

"How about tonight?" I said.

"They should've never messed with Anna," he said.

"When I think what could have happened to her while I'm laid out on the floor, I…"

"But it's obvious it was just to scare you," he said. "All they did was threaten her."

"Well, it worked," I said.

"If this is you scared, I don't want to see what you call anger," he said.

I smiled. I knew what he meant—that anger far more than fear was motivating me—but he was only partially right. After what had happened to Nicole, what had almost happened to Anna scared me plenty.

"You ready?" I asked.

"Sure," he said, "but in this little trap, is Muhammin the spider or the fly?"

"I'm not sure they have a term for what he is," I said. "In prison vernacular he's the fly's bitch."

Later that night, as a special program was taking place in the sanctuary, Merrill, Pete, and I were hiding in one of the stalls of the visitors restroom in the back. The lights were off and it was extremely dark, only a hint of hallway light peeking beneath the bottom of the door.

Like all toilets in the prison, the one in the stall had no lid, and we were all standing far closer to one another than we would have liked—especially Merrill and Pete.

"Pete, you get any closer and it'll be sexual harassment," Merrill said.

I laughed.

"How much longer we got?" Merrill asked.

Pete pushed a small button on the side of his watch and it lit up, bathing his round face in an eerie green glow. Looking at his watch, he said, "The GED class should already be out," he said. "Shouldn't be much longer."

"Tell me again how this works," Merrill said.

"Malcolm knows that when his class is completed, one of the officers from the chapel service is called to escort his students back to the compound," I said, "so he slips in over here virtually unseen."

"For a little butt lovin'," Pete said.

I shook my head. "I can't believe we're arresting somebody for sex."

Merrill laughed. "I'm sure some shit we've done is illegal in some states."

"Sex with an inmate is a crime," Pete said.

"Still," I said.

"It's not the sex," Merrill said. "It's the assault. They could've killed Anna, and a little higher and that shank in your shoulder could've been in your eye."

"I know," I said. "It's like Watergate, but I still feel like one of those people who scare me the most—rigid, repressed, xenophobic, homophobic—"

"Watergate?" Pete asked.

"Not the crime as much as the coverup," Merrill said.

"Merrill, you're pretty smart, aren't you?" Pete asked.

"But he hides it well," I said.

"I is on occasion able to muster up a thought or two."

I noticed we were all breathing through our mouths, avoiding as best we could our sense of smell. The unpleasant odor permeating the air was a pungent combination of human waste, mildew, stale smoke, and too many chemicals/too little cleaning.

We froze when we heard approaching footsteps followed by the metallic clicks of a key being inserted into the lock.

"How far along do we have to let them get?" Merrill whispered.

"We'll have their DNA from the condom when the lab finishes processing it," I said. "So not very far."

"Thank you, God," he said.

"Amen," Pete said.

Like most straight men, they found homosexuality about as appealing as a lengthy prostate exam by a large-handed doctor who enjoyed his work, and I knew they were anxious to make the arrest before they saw or heard anything that might scar them for life.

That's why the moment Malcolm and Muhammin were inside with the door shut behind them, they were slinging the stall door open and yelling for the two men to get on the ground.

Coming out of the stall behind them, I laughed.

"What's so funny?" Merrill said.

"Not taking any chances, are you?"

"These are very dangerous men," he said with a smile.

Within just a moment, Pete had them cuffed and on their feet, but it had given Malcolm enough time to collect himself.

"What the hell is the meaning of this?" he asked me.

"For assault."

"First of all," he said, "nothing went on here tonight. Second of all, if it had it would have been consentual."

Merrill smiled. "Like little slave girls on the plantation, inmates can't consent," he said. "They not free to choose."

"Not sexual assault," I said. "Physical. The attack you had him and his friends make on me in the education building and on me and Ms. Rodden in the chapel."

"This is absurd," Malcolm said. "This'll never stick. You can't even prove we've ever—"

"Actually," I said, "we have a used condom, so one of you better be the first to flip and let us know everything—including who helped in the education building attack."

They looked at each other suspiciously, and I knew it was only a matter of time before both would spill in hopes of a deal.

Looking back at me, Malcolm asked, "How'd you know?"

"When I found out you hadn't worked with Bunny I knew you had come over here for a different reason," I said. "Your over-familiarity with your orderlies, your attempt to cover it up by having me attacked—their willingness to do it for you, the used condom, the fact that it was in the visitors bathroom."

"Did Nicole see them?" Pete asked. "Is that why they killed her?"

"Whoa, wait just a minute," Malcolm said. "I didn't have anything to do with the death of that little girl. I swear."

"Sort of makes you wish we cared and you could afford Johnny Cochran, doesn't it?" I said.

CHAPTER 44

When I walked into my trailer, the phone was ringing, and some-thing about hearing the unanswered rings echoing through the emptiness made me sad.

"Is everything okay?" Susan asked. "The sergeant in the control room said there was an incident in the chapel."

"Sorry I didn't call you back," I said. "Everything's fine."

"You sure? You sound sad."

"Well, I'm not anymore."

"Good," she said, pausing before adding, "How do you feel about phone sex?"

"I'm in favor of it," I said.

She laughed. It was a good laugh. Warm, genuine, slightly seductive.

"I'd like to see if I could make you come from three hundred miles away," she said.

"You just did," I said with a laugh.

She laughed again, then said, "I'm serious. Wanna try our hand at it—so to speak. You up for it—or could you be?"

I laughed again.

"Well?" she asked.

I thought about it, another idea occurring to me. We'd miss a little sleep, but I didn't sleep much anyway.

"We could," I said, "or..."

"Or what?"

"Don't get me wrong," I said. "It's not that I don't like your idea."

"But ... ?"

"But," I said, "we could both jump in our cars and in two-and-a-half hours meet at a motel in the middle."

"Oh," she sighed. "I like that idea. I like that idea a lot." She started to say something, but broke off.

When she hesitated, I said, "But...?"

"No buts," she said. "I was just thinking, with cell phones we could try both our ideas—mine on the way, yours when we got there."

"I like the way you think, woman," I said. "And I know what I want you to get me for Christmas."

"What?"

"A cell phone," I said. "The only one I have belongs to the prison."

She laughed. "Honey, after tonight," she said, "you won't be able to wait for Christmas. You'll rush out as soon as you can and buy one for yourself."

"And what do I tell them when they ask me why I want the one with the headset?"

"That you're a very lucky man," she said. "Where do you want to meet? Are we really gonna do this—drive all that way just for one sexual experience?"

"You're right, that's ridiculous," I said. "We better make it six or seven."

"I see you haven't lost your appetite," she said.

"No," I said, "Webster's still has my picture by the word 'insatiable.'"

"Can you wait two-and-a-half hours?" she asked. "I want you hungry."

"Don't worry," I said. "I'll be starving."

Without hesitating, I rushed out of my empty trailer and jumped into my truck, driving as if I hadn't just gotten a ticket.

Only a sliver of moon peeked out from behind a smoky cloud, leaving the night dark and shadowless, and I could see just the short distance that my headlights illuminated.

What all am I not seeing? I wondered.

Before I could even begin to consider all that question implied, I turned on the radio.

Tonight's not the night for contemplation and introspection, I thought, *but pleasure and passion.*

And though the second thought set off a little alarm inside my head, I ignored it, concentrating instead on singing with Christopher Cross on the radio and riding like the wind.

When I arrived in Phoenix City, I found the motel "up on a hill, with a little blue general or admiral or some little soldier thingy on the sign" just like she had described.

Even better was the fact that I also found her waiting for me.

When I pulled in beside her, she stepped out of her car, and as quickly as I could jump out of my truck, we were devouring each other. In the small space between my old Chevy and her new Lexus, we kissed and hugged and groped like a couple of teens with no place of our own to go.

Eventually, she touched my shoulder and I winced.

"What happened to your arm?" she asked.

"Got in a little fight," I said. "It's nothing."

As we continued to kiss, she slid along her car. I followed. Before I knew it, we were in her backseat tearing at each other's clothes.

"Why waste time checking in?" she asked.

Beneath her black leather skirt with the off-center slit, I found thong panty style sheer hose—all that stood between me and Eden. Pulling her black sweater off not only tossed her hair in the most seductive of ways, but revealed a sleek black satin Miracle Bra with a gold embroidered heart-shaped cut-out.

For a long breathless moment, I sat back and drank in her beauty like wine. Forget the bra, she was the miracle, and in no time I was intoxicated.

She leaned forward, reached back, unhooked her bra, tossing it in the front seat where it landed on the steering wheel.

"Bon appétit," she said, then, cupping her hand behind my head, brought me to her breast.

When we had finished the appetizer, she said, "I brought you something."

"That wasn't it?" I asked. "Because I was thinking you could just give me that again."

"I will," she said. "Again and again and again. As often as you like. I'm the gift that keeps on giving."

I smiled. "You are a—" I started, but stopped as my cell phone rang.

"Hello," I said, my voice still hoarse with passion.

"Chaplain Jordan," the unmistakably smooth voice of Bobby Earl Caldwell said.

For a long moment after I hung up, I sat there in stunned silence.

"What is it?" Susan asked. "What's wrong?"

"Bobby Earl Caldwell wants to see me," I said.

"What for?"

"Apparently to offer me a job."

"Threatening you hasn't worked," she said, "so now he's gonna try bribery?"

CHAPTER 45

Bobby Earl's 19th Century plantation home was smaller than a Hollywood sound stage—if you didn't count the garage—and as gaudy and distasteful as a televangelist's studio set.

"I believe God's children should have the best," he said, leading me through large, lavishly decorated rooms with ornately hand-painted ceilings and faux marble fireplaces toward his back porch.

"Obviously," I said, "but did you ask God how she felt about it?"

Ignoring me, he said, "I think our prosperity is directly related to our spirituality."

The dingy little trailer I called home flashed in my mind, and I thought, *you might be right,* but then I pictured Mother Teresa, and thought, *then again maybe not.*

"What do you think?" he asked.

"That God wants what's best for us," I said. "Not necessarily for us to have the best."

He nodded and looked as if he were intently considering what I had just said. "I like that," he said. "But couldn't that be the same thing?"

"Not often," I said.

Taking the day off without explaining why, I had left early, driven fast, and arrived by midmorning.

Beyond his oversized pool, the sun-dappled back yard, which was canopied by enormous oaks, led down to a bayou whose moss-shrouded cypress trees reminded me of home.

"You're really a man of God," he said. "I can tell. And you have a great reputation. Very well respected in Potter County."

"Depends on who you talk to," I said.

He smiled. "Ah," he said, "but beware if all men speak well of you."

I didn't say anything. And he didn't either for a minute. Then, "I wish chaplains made more money. Y'all deserve it. Do such important work."

When I didn't respond, he said, "You do. Don't be ashamed of what you do."

"I'm not," I said. "If I were, I wouldn't do it."

"Right," he said. "Integrity. That's the reason I wanted to talk to you. I'd like for someone with your integrity, deep spirituality, and obvious knowledge of prison chaplaincy to oversee the outreach prison ministry of BECM."

"BECM?" I asked.

"Bobby Earl Caldwell Ministries," he said, as if I should've known. "We send in tapes and books to most of the major institutions. We conduct crusades and healing services, but I want us to do more. And I want you to help."

I shook my head.

"You wouldn't have to move here," he said. "Could if you wanted to. Think about how much more good you could do. You'd be reaching so many more souls. You'd have enormous resources at your disposal. You'd be making six times what you make now. And you'd get to work with me."

I smiled.

"Thanks," I said. "But, no thanks."

He was genuinely shocked. "I don't understand," he said. "Think about the opportunity I'm offering you. Think of what it could mean for your ministry."

"I'm not a prison chaplain at PCI because I don't have other options," I said.

"I can't tell you how much I respect that," he said, nodding to himself, then looking off in the distance.

A white egret at the bank of the bayou stood perfectly still as a sun-baked man with long hair beneath a soiled baseball cap and a Ragin' Cajun T-shirt glided by in a flat-bottomed boat.

"You're right," Bobby Earl said. "You don't need to be anywhere other than right where you are. And they're blessed to have you."

I didn't say anything.

"I know," he said in a sudden burst of enlightenment. "How about letting me retain you as a consultant? You could sit on our board. Help us make decisions about our prison ministry. That way you could continue doing what God has called you to do, help us, and supplement your income as well."

"I just can't," I said. "But thank you."

"Think about it for a while," he said. "The offer stands open. Just pray about it. You can get back with me any time. You could be instrumental in helping so many inmates."

"Was there a chaplain who was instrumental in your life?"

"Actually there was. That's why I believe in what we're doing in prisons. My chaplain was truly a man of God."

I nodded, and then we were quiet for a moment.

I had waited to bring up Nicole until now to see if he would. He hadn't, so I did. "How are you and your wife doing?" I asked.

"Huh?" he asked, as if somewhere else, his forehead furrowing in incomprehension.

"Since Nicole died," I said. "How are you?"

"Oh," he said, shaking his head sadly. "I accept it as the will of God. I know she's better off—a lot better off than us, right? But Bunny's still all broken up about it. She believes in heaven and all, but she still misses her a lot. I do, too. She was such a special child."

"Yes, she was," I said. "We'd like to hold a memorial service at the chapel for her. She meant so much to all the men, all of us."

"That's a very lovely thought," he said. "I appreciate that."

"We'd like for you and Mrs. Caldwell to be there."

"Oh, we couldn't," he said. "I'm sorry, but we're way too busy and it'd just be too painful."

"Perhaps you'll feel differently when the time comes. I hope so," I said. "I'm still trying to figure out what happened that night. I was wondering if I could ask you and Mrs. Caldwell some questions?"

"I'd be happy to answer them," he said. "But Bunny's not home right now. And I wouldn't subject her to that even if she were."

"I understand," I said. "When you finished preaching and Bunny came back out to sing, was that planned?"

"Whatta you mean?"

"Does she normally come back out and sing at the end?" I asked.

"Yes," he said, nodding his head.

"Does Nicole usually sing with her?"

He nodded. "Yeah," he said. "I was surprised she didn't that night. That's why I went into your office while Bunny was singing. You know, to check on her."

"But while Bunny was still singing, you went back out to begin your altar call," I said, "so for at least ten minutes she was alone in there."

"That must be when it happened," he said, shaking his head.

"How was she when you went in to check on her?"

"I don't know. She was in the small bathroom in your office. I didn't even see her. I just assumed that's why she wasn't with her mother. When I asked Bunny later, she said that Nicole's stomach had been bothering her."

"So you never saw her after she left the stage the first time?" I asked.

"No," he said softly, looking down, "I didn't. I wish I had. Wish I could've taken her in my arms just one more time before she woke up in the arms of Jesus."

"Did you talk to her?" I asked. "Through the door."

He shook his head. "The fan in there was so loud," he said. "I knew I wouldn't be able to hear her, so I just waited for her to come out, but eventually I had to go back out."

"It would really help if I could talk to your wife."

"Absolutely not," he said. "She's a very fragile woman. It's too soon."

"Do you know who Nicole's parents are?" I asked.

He studied me for a very long time, then said, "Before Bunny and I were saved, we were sinners living in the world, committing sins of the flesh. Bunny is Nicole's mother.... But you already knew that, didn't you?"

I nodded. "And her father?"

"To be honest," he said, "we don't know. And I almost feel it's better that way. I became her father. And loved her as much as any father ever loved his child."

It was only through years of discipline and training that I kept from laughing at that.

"How long have you known?" I asked.

"About Bunny?" he asked. "She was pregnant when I married her. It was a test from God. I passed. I accepted her, the way Hosea did Gomer, the way God did Israel, his beloved, even when she played the harlot."

"Is there a possibility that Nicole's biological father could've been at the service that night?" I asked.

He tried to act surprised, but didn't pull it off well. "Like I said, we don't know who he is."

"But he might've been?"

"It's possible," he conceded. Then glanced at his watch. "I'm sorry, but I've got to go. I've got a meeting and then a prayer luncheon to speak at."

"Just a few more questions, please," I said. "What exactly does DeAndré Stone do for you?"

"Provides security for and assists Bunny," he said. "He's part of our Freeing the Captives program. Sometimes a judge will actually send a troubled young man to us rather than putting him in prison. I have several men on parole and probation working for me—I want prison outreach to be the center of my ministry. God's given me a heart for them—I am *them*."

"Did you know there are a lot of rumors of criminal activity in your organization?"

"No, but it doesn't surprise me," he said. "You know how people envy and talk about successful people—especially ministers. Besides, as I said, I employ a lot of ex-offenders and parolees. Not all of them are saved. We're working with them, but they're still fallen human beings. I'm sure some of them are still in the life. But it really surprises me that you listen to rumors."

"Did you know that DeAndré was at the prison this past Monday night?"

"What?" he asked in what appeared to be genuine shock. "Are you sure?"

"Positive," I said. "He attacked Nicole's father and later, after the *Larry King* show, me and my wife."

"Did he say why?"

He had flinched when I said 'Nicole's father,' but quickly recovered and apparently wasn't going to pursue it.

"I figured he was doing it for you," I said.

"*Me?*" he asked in even greater shock and I was convinced it was authentic. "Why would I—I invited you here to offer you a position on my staff. I really respect you... but even if I didn't, I wouldn't have anybody attack anybody—I can't believe you could think such a thing about me."

Standing, Bobby Earl led me back through the opulent mansion that made me think of a thriving Victorian whorehouse more than anything else.

"He works for you," I said. "It's not as if I made an enormous leap."

"He works for my wife," he said, "but not any longer—if you're certain he did these things."

"I'm certain," I said. "Did you know that NOPD has an ongoing investigation into you and your organization?"

"I knew the IRS did," he said. "They hound every major ministry in the country. Are the police helping *them*?"

Either he was truly out of touch with what was going on in his organization or Bobby Earl Caldwell was a tremendous loss to stage and screen.

I shook my head. "They're looking into allegations of abuse, extortion, and homicide."

"*Homicide?*"

"Yeah."

"No wonder you don't want to join my staff," he said. "But I can assure you there's some kind of mistake and I'll get to the bottom of it."

"I've noticed that a lot of inmates donate significant amounts of money to your ministry," I said. "Why—"

"Chaplain," he said in a voice that sounded scolding. "You know good and well most inmates don't have much money. It is true that some of them make small contributions, but I can assure you that they don't even cover our expenses when we conduct a crusade."

"The really large amounts go to a post office box here in—"

"I don't have a post office box," he said. "All our mail is delivered directly to the headquarters."

"Well, I'm telling you an awful lot of money payable to you is leaving our prison addressed to you at a post office box over here."

He hesitated a moment, his eyes moving around as he thought about it. "I have a very large organization," he said. "I guess some of our departments may have post office boxes to keep things separate. I'll check into it. I will, but right now I've got to go."

"Okay," I said.

"Please consider coming to Nicole's service," I said. "I'm sure the media would like to get a statement from you about it."

"The media's gonna be there?" he asked.

"Yeah," I said, as if I knew, "I think Larry King may even do a follow up show afterwards."

"I'll do my best," he said. "And you please consider my offer. I can assure you the rumors you've heard are not true. You'll get three times what you're making now just to attend a few meetings a year and answer the occasional question about prison ministry from time to time. Plus, I'll give you a signing bonus of say, a hundred K."

"No," I said, as he ushered me out the door, "I'm not worth that kind of money."

"Maybe not, but what you know is," he said, just before closing the door, and I left wondering if what he thought I knew had anything at all to do with prison ministry.

CHAPTER 46

That evening, with the sun beginning its descent behind St. Louis Cathedral, I bought a bag of beignets and a large coffee at the Café du Monde, crossed Decatur to Jackson Square, and found an empty bench on which to enjoy them.

Slowly, the sounds of jazz bands were dying out, the street artists, mimes, and magicians being replaced by fortunetellers, tarot readers, and guides for vampire, ghost, and graveyard tours.

The breeze blowing off the Mississippi filled the air with a briny pungency and humidity that mixed with the cooking food and confections of the Quarter, riding on its currents the soft, sad sounds of a lone saxophone coming from Pirates Alley.

With the crowds and noises of the day gone, I had hoped to think about the case, integrating what I knew with what I had learned since arriving in New Orleans, but it was not to be.

Both the bag and the beignets were filled with powdered sugar that stuck to my fingers and face, a light dusting of which was accumulating on my clothes. I was trying to wipe it off when Bunny Caldwell walked up.

"I heard you and Bobby Earl talking at the house," she said.

She was wearing dark shades and a hat that hid much of her face, her nervous moves and paranoid glances highlighting the fact that they were intended as a disguise.

"How?" I asked.

She looked confused.

"That was a crack about its size," I said. "Have a seat."

Glancing around furtively, she sat down next to me without trying to avoid the powdered sugar covering the bench.

"Bobby Earl grew up poor," she said.

"Well, he's making up for it now."

She smiled. "Trying."

"Except you can't," I said.

"You can't make up for anything you didn't get in childhood, can you?"

"Sounds like maybe you've been trying, too," I said.

She nodded. "Yeah," she said, more to herself than to me, and I knew some of what I had heard about her was true.

Across the way, a homeless man rose from where he had been sleeping on the grass, walked over to the fountain, and began washing his face and hands.

Figuring there was a reason she had sought me out, I didn't prod, but instead waited for her to tell me in her own time what she had to say.

"There's a few things I want you to know about Bobby Earl," she said.

"Okay."

"He's not like me," she said. "When he gave his life to the Lord, he did it all the way. He really is a new creature in Christ. I've never seen someone change so completely. I mean, yeah, he spends too much money and he's still a kid in many ways, but he really is one of the good guys now."

The woman sitting next to me was different from the one I had met in the institution just two weeks ago, as if in addition to aging her, grief had stripped her of all illusions. She was now disillusioned in the most positive, if painful, sense of the word.

"He judges people—especially inmates—by what happened to him," she continued. "If they say they've changed, he believes they have."

"And the ones who work for him…"

"Haven't," she said. "For the most part anyway. Not like him. Some, not at all. His transformation and love blinds him. He can't see what's going on around him—and that includes the things I do."

She didn't elaborate and I didn't press her.

The three towers of the cathedral and the cross on the center one were now silhouettes backlit by the soft orange gleam behind them, as all around us candles on the tables of palm readers blinked on like the first stars of twilight.

When I caught her looking over her shoulder again, I asked, "Who are you afraid of?"

"No one," she said. "Why?"

"Who gave you the bruises on your arms?"

"He said if I say anything, he'll kill Bobby Earl," she said.

"Who?"

"DeAndré."

"Did he come back into the institution with you the night Nicole was killed?"

She nodded.

"Have you ever worked at Lake Butler?"

"In the chapel," she said. "It's where I met Bobby Earl."

"And Nicole's father?"

She whipped her head around and stared at me in shock. After a few moments, she nodded. "Yeah."

"What about Theo Malcolm?"

She squinted, her brow furrowing, then began to shake her head.

"He's a school teacher."

"I don't know him," she said. "Why?"

In between the intermittent breezy sound of traffic on Decatur behind us, the whinnying and clip-clop of horses could be heard.

"Chaplain Jordan, I didn't kill my little girl," she said.

I was inclined to believe her.

"But I'm responsible," she said. "We should've never taken her in there."

"Why were y'all there?" I asked. "What's a guy like Bobby Earl gain from preaching in a prison?"

"He has a heart for inmates," she said. "Though we weren't scheduled to go back to PCI for quite a while, DeAndré begged him. Bobby Earl saw it as doing a favor for DeAndré and his uncle, but I think DeAndré just wanted an excuse to go in there and deal with Cedric."

"Nicole's father?"

She nodded. "I thought he was going to pay him off or something, but maybe he meant to kill him," she said. "I don't know. I do know Bobby Earl likes preaching in prison because of what happened to him when he was inside. But we should have never taken Nicole. We just didn't—"

Breaking off abruptly, she stood up and said, "I've done a stupid thing. I should've never gotten involved with—he's always been insanely jealous—even of Nicole. Just seeing us talking together like this—be very careful."

As she began to walk away, I looked to see who had spooked her. Across the square, seething beneath a street lamp, was DeAndré Stone, a look of unadorned rage on his face. When I turned to stop her, Bunny was gone, having disappeared in the darkness. Deciding to settle a little business with Stone, I spun around, but found that he had vanished, too.

CHAPTER 47

"Where the *hell* you been?" Tom Daniels asked as he stormed into my office.

I was back in my office because he had removed the crime scene tape and had it cleaned, and he had asked me to meet him there.

"Miss me?" I asked.

There was no evidence that an unspeakable act of violence had taken place here, no blood crying out from the ground about the murder of innocence, but I felt uncomfortable, as if a residue of horror hung in the room like a lost spirit hovering aimlessly.

"You better not have been screwing around in my investigation," he said.

"Wasn't within a hundred miles of it," I said with a smile.

"Don't get cute with me, dammit," he said. "I'm not your buddy."

"We may not be buddies," I said. "But we are family."

He shook his head.

"Susan and I—"

"That's just a technicality," he said.

"Actually, Dad, we're trying to patch things up," I said.

He started to say something, but instead shook his head, his contempt seeming to indicate the comment wasn't worthy of a response.

"I'm not your enemy," I said. Then amended, "Well, you're not mine. Why'd you even notice I was gone?"

"I've got some questions for you," he said, pulling a pen out of his wrinkled suit coat and opening a file folder. His movements, like his words, were often exaggerated, a compensation for his alcohol-induced unsteadiness. "You're a witness. This thing happened right here in your office. Hell, you're a suspect."

"A suspect?"

"You had access to this office. Hell, it's yours. You were here. What can you tell me?"

"I didn't do it," I said.

He laughed. "Well, who did?" he asked.

Outside my window, the last of the first shift officers ambled past the last of the second shift arrivals rushing to their post. Both groups carried lunch boxes or small coolers to help them get through their eight-hour shifts in posts they could not leave.

"Was she sexually assaulted?"

"Let me explain how this works," he said, holding up his pen. "I ask the questions, you answer them." When he noticed that his pen was shaking, he pulled his hand down and rested it on the folder. "Now, let's try that. I ask. You answer. Got it?"

"Is that one of your questions?" I asked.

His eyes narrowed into bloodshot slits, his face turning red and strained as if his blood had become mercury and was rising.

"Look," I said. "I've just got a couple of questions. If you answer them, I'll answer all of yours."

He closed his eyes and took a deep breath, then let it out very slowly. He then sat there in silence for a long time before he opened his eyes again. When he did, they seemed calmer, if not clearer.

"I'll cooperate either way," I said. "But I'd really like to know just two small things."

"You got anything really good you could trade me for them?" he asked as if we were on a school yard.

I nodded.

"Let's have it," he said.

"Was Nicole sexually assaulted?" I asked.

"No," he said.

"Was there any indication that she ever had been?"

"Inconclusive," he said. "But we don't think so."

"Was—" I began.

"That's two questions," he said.

"Actually," I said. "That was two parts of the same question."

"You really are a sneaky SOB," he said wearily. "What's your other question?"

"Was there blood in my office bathroom?" I asked. "Nicole's blood?"

"Yes," he said.

"There was a greeting card and a wad of cash under the desk," he said. He pointed at the small stack of greeting cards on the corner of my desk. "Tell me about those."

"Each month I give the inmates cards to send to their families and significant others," I said. "Did it match one of the ones on my desk?"

He nodded. "I think it fell off while they were struggling," he said. "But what about the money?"

"I don't give it out," I said.

A metallic clanging drew my attention toward the window. Outside two inmate-powered push mowers were beginning to cut the grass between the chapel and visiting park. The dew on the blades of grass and rose petals glistened in the morning sun, and the wet clippings stuck to the metal mowers.

"So where'd it come from?" he said.

"Sounds like a payoff to me," I said.

"Yeah, I came to that same conclusion," he said. "Any idea who?"

I shrugged.

"Maybe Bobby Earl's paying off someone to do his business behind bars or to turn their heads while someone else does it."

"Maybe," I said.

He didn't respond, and we sat in silence for a few minutes.

"I didn't look for very long," I said. "But it looked like her face had been beaten very badly."

"Yeah?" he said.

"So her killer probably knew her pretty well," I said.

"Possibly," he said, pulling a small plastic bag from his coat pocket. "We found this on the floor near the door." Handing me the bag, he added, "I think he hit her so hard it flew out of her mouth and across the room. It's a piece of candy."

I held up the plastic bag and examined its contents. It held a round pink piece of hard candy that was circled by red and white streaks.

I swallowed hard, my heart and stomach in my throat, my forehead breaking out into a cold sweat.

"Not finding very much about the Caldwells," he said. "We need to get them back down here, but that's not gonna happen."

"I don't know," I said.

"Yeah?"

"I'm doing a memorial service for Nicole," I said.

His eyebrows shot up along with the corners of his lips and he nodded in appreciation. "That just might work, but I thought you were against her coming in—why memorialize her in front of all the inmates?"

"To see what happens," I said. "And not *all*—just those who were here the night it happened."

"I like it," he said. "Still, we don't have any real evidence yet."

"We will," I said.

"We?" he said.

"You," I corrected. "You will."

"When is the service?"

"*This afternoon,*" I said.

"This afternoon," he yelled, jumping to his feet and heading toward the door. "Thanks for the heads-up."

"Where're you going?" I asked.

"To try to get enough evidence to build a case by then."

CHAPTER 48

As I began to study for my homily, I noticed again the stack of greeting cards on my desk. I picked them up and rifled through them. To my surprise, all the cards had envelopes. More to the point, all the envelopes had cards. Finding an actual clue, I almost didn't know what to do. And before I could do anything, Pete Fortner knocked on my door and walked in.

Sitting down, he looked around my office uneasily. As he stared at the spot where Nicole's body had lain, I remembered that he had been the second one at the scene, and I knew he still saw her broken little body there just as I did.

"How can you—" he started, but stopped when his eyes rested on the picture Nicole had colored for me. I had framed it and hung it on the center of the wall behind me. The most prominent place in my office.

"How can you work in here?" he asked.

"I don't," I said. "I mean, I haven't. I've pretty much just been working her case. And she helps me with that. It's like she's still present. I don't know… I feel her guiding me. I like being in here. I think soon the violence will fade and just her precious spirit will remain."

He nodded without saying anything. There was nothing in his body language or facial expression to suggest it, but I got the sense that I had made him uncomfortable.

His mustache had thickened and he rubbed at it absently. When he turned to the side the sunlight outlined his profile, illuminating several nose hairs which had grown so long they blended with his mustache.

"That was good work with Malcolm and Muhammin the other night," he said. "But are you sure they didn't kill Nicole?"

"As sure as you can be about such things," I said.

"You're probably right. Guess what we found inside a small hole in Paul Register's mattress?"

"Nicole's crayons?" I asked.

His mouth dropped open. "Just how the hell did you know that?"

"I didn't until just now," I said. "You told me to guess."

He shook his head and smiled appreciatively.

"Who found them?" I asked.

"Officer Coel," he said.

I nodded. "When?"

"Yesterday," he said. "The hole was tiny. I don't see how he ever found them."

"Did you ask him what made him look there in the first place?"

"Yeah," he said. "At first he said it was just part of a routine search of the cell. They toss them every two weeks or so, but then when I pressed him on it, he said he got an anonymous tip."

"He say from who?"

"Never would," he said, shaking his head. "Said he'd lose his informants if he gave them up, but that the person was credible."

I thought about it.

"You wanna talk to him?"

"Who?"

"Either one."

"Yeah."

"Who?"

"Both of them," I said. "Please just help make sure all our suspects are here for the memorial service."

"Word on the compound is Nicole's killer'll be arrested today," he said.

I shook my head. "That's not good."

"Is it true?" he asked.

"You'd have to ask Daniels."

"You think he knows who did it?"

I shrugged.

"If he had any sense, he'd ask for your help," he said. "I—" he started, then paused for a moment before awkwardly beginning again. "I—I've got a lot of respect for you—as a man of God, of course, but as a... I don't know... cop, too. You're the best I've worked with. I can't believe you're not up in Atlanta working high profile cases."

"Pete, in Atlanta I was a small town cop," I said. "I wasn't APD. I was a cop for the little tourist town of Stone Mountain. I did it while I was in seminary. I had worked for Dad down here and it was an easy job to get. It just happened to be at a time when a high profile case was going on."

"You're the one who stopped him—the Stone Cold Killer. You'll always be the one who stopped him."

We were silent a moment and he shifted in his chair and re-crossed his legs. His movements were hesitant and awkward, his eyes seeming to search for criticism or ridicule. I felt sorry for him and regretted not having done more to encourage and edify him.

"And always the one who let the Atlanta Child Murderer get away," I said.

His eyes widened in surprise, his eyebrows popping up into question marks. "You worked the Williams' case," he said, adding quickly, "and let him get away?"

"No," I said. "He'd been in prison a good while when I went up there. But there was another one—some say a second one. I say he was working at the time of Williams and hid his victims like

trees in Williams' forest. The point is, I not only let him get away,
I let him kill a little boy I should've been protecting. There are no
experts in murder investigations. Not really. And if there are, I am
certainly not one of them."

"Well, I think you are," he said.

"Thanks."

"I got that information you asked me to," he said, pulling out
a folded sheet of paper from his shirt pocket. "Three inmates have
sent Bobby Earl Freeing the Captives Ministries very large contributions since you've been back from New Orleans."

"Any of our suspects?" I asked.

He shook his head. "Most of them don't send or receive much
mail. Porter hasn't gotten a single letter the entire time he's been
inside. Register is the only one who sends and receives a lot, but
none of it to or from Bobby Earl."

"The three who sent contributions mailed them to the post
office box, right?"

He nodded. "How'd you know they would?" he asked. "And
before Bobby Earl came, not afterward."

"Because," I said, "the checks aren't to support a ministry, but
a habit."

"Huh?" he asked, a look of confusion on his face.

"The inmates are buying drugs," I said. "They prepay for drugs
that are brought in from the outside."

Eyes wide, he sat there for a moment, then said, "What do you
need me to do?"

"Arrest Tim Whitfield," I said, "and see if you can get him to
give up his supplier."

CHAPTER 49

"'Take your son, your only son, Isaac, whom you love, and go to the region of Moriah and sacrifice him there as a burnt offering to the Lord,'" I read from Genesis to begin my homily for Nicole Caldwell's memorial service.

She had already been eulogized. Her life had already been celebrated. Now it was my job to deliver a message that spoke to the heart of the matter. To give reassurance and hope to her loved ones. And I would try. But I had no easy answers. No quick fixes for the ancient problem of evil and the unwelcome guest of grief.

I looked up from the Bible on the pulpit to the congregation before me. The Caldwells, dressed in black, were on the front pew, DeAndré beside Bunny. Behind them, in a sea of blue, were many of the inmates who had attended the service the night Nicole was murdered. Across the aisle from the Caldwells, Theo Malcolm sat stiffly beside Edward Stone, who sat even more stiffly. Next to him, Pete Fortner and Tom Daniels looked uncomfortable and out of place.

"These words are among the most shocking in all of sacred literature," I continued. "They resound throughout history as an echo of madness by a God who could only attract the deranged, the disturbed, and the fanatical. A God who, after making Abraham wait for twenty-five years to receive his promised son, the boy whose very name means laughter, because of how hard his decrepit old parents had laughed when they received the promise, demands that Abraham give him back. Not just surrender him, but sacrifice him with his own hands."

Several inmates in the congregation winced at my words, and gave me looks like they wondered where I could possibly be going with this.

My response to them, that which Frederick Buechner had convinced me should be the foundation for every sermon—most of all this one—came from Shakespeare: "'The weight of this sad time we must obey,'" I said. "'Speak what we feel, not what we ought to say.'"

If I was right about who had killed Nicole, there could be no better source for a quotation than *King Lear*, but if my audience perceived the message within the message, they didn't give any indication.

"I am here to tell the truth," I added. "No matter how tragic it might be."

The only response I got was a sea of blank stares.

"From the very beginning, Nicole has been compared to Isaac; Bobby Earl, her father, to Abraham."

Bobby Earl nodded earnestly as Bunny looked up at him admiringly.

"And though the connection was never obvious to me, it has caused me to meditate a lot lately on Abraham, his God, and his son.

"How could God ask for the sacrifice of this innocent lamb whose very life was the heartbeat of his father?

"How could Abraham do it? Was he mad? Or was he, as the three world religions that sprang from him claim, the most faith-filled and faithful man ever to live?

"These questions are as old as mankind, and they've been asked by so many of us at one time or another in one way or another. And in the deepest part of our hearts, I think we've all come to the same terrifying conclusion: We don't know."

Anna's intense eyes rested heavily upon me, her head nodding agreement and support. I looked at her often.

"Just as we don't know why God allows bad things to happen to good people. We don't know why God lets children suffer and die. We don't know.

"I'm not saying there aren't answers to these questions. In fact, there are some pretty convincing ones, but none of the answers, no matter how logical or convincing, can ever remove that wordless darkness from the corners of our hearts and minds that says we don't know. Not really.

"Let me ask you the real question in my heart and on my mind. Why did God allow little Nicole be murdered?

"I don't know. I wish to God I did. She knows I've asked that question a thousand times.

"But I've been thinking more and more that perhaps that's not the right question anyway. God didn't kill Nicole. God didn't ask for the blood of this little lamb to be shed. So, really, shouldn't the question be: why did *you* kill Nicole?"

Time seemed to stand still. No one moved. No one made a sound. No one looked directly at me.

Unfortunately, no one answered my question either.

"Whoever killed Nicole," I continued. "That's who we need to ask. Why'd you do it? How could you? We can ask God, 'Why'd you let them do it?' but only the murderer can answer 'Why'd you do it?'"

As I spoke, I thought about Susan and how often she had sat in a church and listened to me preach. She had been a good wife in so many ways, and now that there was a possibility that we might have a future together, I found myself missing her.

"So why was Nicole taken from us?

"I don't know.

"I *do* know that God was the first one to grieve. Tears fell from the eyes of God long before they fell from anyone else's.

"Abraham, the madman of faith, lifted his knife to plunge it into the heart of his son, Isaac, and God said: 'NO! Don't touch him. It was just a test. I just wanted to see how much you loved me. How much you trusted me.' Then Abraham looked, and there in a thicket was a ram. God had provided a lamb.

"One of the names of the place where Abraham did this unspeakable thing means: 'the Lord shall see.' God saw Abraham's heart. And that was the whole point. Not the sacrifice of innocence. Not murder. God provided a lamb. Not Abraham. God.

"The blood of the lamb shed in this building was not for God. Not because God wanted it, but because of the evil in her murderer's heart. And just like on Mount Moriah, God sees. Sees that heart of hate and darkness. Sees the heart that has rejected the lamb God has provided.

"I don't understand. I don't have the answers. But I trust in love. Trust in God. Trust that if my heart breaks for Nicole then God's breaks all the more.

"What can I offer you today?

"What Christianity, my religion, offers. 'Christianity,' in the words of Frederick Buechner, 'points to the cross and says that, practically speaking, there is no evil so dark and so obscene—not even this—but that God cannot turn it to good.'

"What do we do then? Let me tell you what I'm going to do. I'm still going to question, still going to doubt, still going to struggle, but I'm also going to hang on, to hold on, to have faith, to trust. Because...

"I believe. In spite of myself—in spite of all I've seen, I still believe. I trust. I choose love. Choose to believe that God is love.

"God asked for Abraham's trust. Not his son. Today she asks us for the same thing. To trust. To trust that her heart is broken even more than ours. To trust that Nicole is with her, in the warm embrace of her love.

"Trust God.

"Jesus did," I said.

And look what happened to him, a voice responded inside my head.

"Nicole did," I said.

"And I'm trying to."

CHAPTER 50

"I've been trying to get up here and see you," Dexter said, walking up to me as soon as the service had ended. "They said you were gone."

"I have been," I said. "Just got back today."

Most of the other inmates, staff, and visitors seemed to be getting out of the chapel as quickly as they could, including the Caldwells, though I had asked to speak with them when the service had concluded.

"I'm glad you're back," he said. "I've been needin' to talk to you."

"How have you been?" I asked, motioning for him to walk with me toward the back.

"I'm all right," he said. "I really appreciate you coming to Mom's funeral. It meant more than you'll ever know."

"I was glad I could," I said. "Would you mind waiting in here for me? I need to see the Caldwells before they—"

"Your dad's arresting Bunny Caldwell," Pete said, running up to us.

"What?"

"They're in your office."

Without waiting for Dexter's response, I ran across the sanctuary and into my office, Pete following right behind me.

Inside, Dad and Jake were cuffing Bunny Caldwell as Daniels read her rights. Bobby Earl stood behind them, demanding to know why they were doing it. Beyond Bobby Earl, next to the door, DeAndré Stone looked on without obvious emotion.

"What're you doin'?" I asked Dad.

"What's it look like?" Jake said.

"We're arresting her for the murder of her natural daughter, Nicole Ann Caldwell," Daniels said. "She—"

"Didn't do it," I said. "Don't—"

"I told you to stay the hell out of my way, boy," Daniels said, but Dad stopped what he was doing and looked over at me, eyebrows raised.

"I'm telling you," I said. "She didn't do it."

He nodded, his expression signifying his trust in me.

"Well, one of them did," Daniels said. "And—"

"No," I said. "They didn't."

"No one else could have," he said. "Hell, I'll arrest them both and let the courts decide—"

"And I guarantee my testimony would create enough reasonable doubt so they'd be acquitted."

As Daniels began to protest, Dad started taking the cuffs off Bunny.

"What the hell are you doin'?" Daniels yelled at him.

"Thank you," Bunny said to me.

"Yeah, thanks," Bobby Earl said.

"He's the one you need to arrest," I said, nodding toward DeAndré Stone. "He's the one behind virtually every crime the Caldwells have been accused of."

As if untouchable, DeAndré let out a little laugh, but his eyes remained hard and flat as a shark's.

"Aside from all his criminal activity in New Orleans and the abuse Bunny has suffered from him, he's been supplying the inmate population with drugs."

Bobby Earl put his arm around Bunny protectively.

A smile spread across DeAndré's face, but didn't reach his eyes. "I'd like to see you try to prove that," he said.

I turned to Daniels, Pete, and Dad. "Inmates send money to a post office box in New Orleans—supposedly to one of Bobby Earl's ministries, but it really goes to DeAndré for the drugs he brings in. That's why it's sent prior to Bobby Earl's coming in and not afterwards like all the others."

Though obviously still feeling invincible, DeAndré's smile begin to fade a little, the first cracks in the seemingly secure foundation of his crime fortress beginning to show.

"The two condoms we found with saliva and vomitus on them were not from someone having oral sex, but from DeAndré muling the drugs in to Officer Whitfield. He puts the drugs in the condoms and swallows them, then vomits them up once he's in the chapel. That's what he was doing with Whitfield in the bathroom the night of the murder."

Bobby Earl looked at DeAndré with contempt and disbelief, saying his name the way people have said that of Judas for the past two millennia.

The cold, hard, blank expression on DeAndré's face didn't change, his emotionless affect revealing the years of repression and hardening that had resulted in his current soullessness.

"The money found in here that night was Whitfield's cut," I continued. "For helping with distribution, he gets a shiny new sports car and stacks of tax-free contributions. Between the prints on the money and the DNA of the saliva on the condoms, there should be enough to bring charges, but in case they aren't, I had Pete arrest Whitfield ahead of time so he couldn't be here to receive the delivery. DeAndré's probably got a couple of condoms full of crack or heroin inside him right now."

Turning toward DeAndré, Jake started reaching for his cuffs, but before he could get them out, DeAndré pulled a 9mm from beneath his coat and pressed the barrel to Jake's forehead.

Dropping the cuffs, Jake raised his hands. "It's cool, man," he said, though his voice told a different story. "Just relax."

Having checked their weapons at the control station, Dad and Jake weren't armed. In fact, except for the shotguns in the towers and the weapons locked in the arsenal, DeAndré Stone had the only firearm inside the prison.

"DeAndré," Bobby Earl said, "don't—"

"Shut your stupid mouth, Bobby Earl," he said.

"But—" Bobby Earl began, then suddenly stopped as DeAndré pointed the pistol at him.

"I'm 'bout to walk outta this motherfucker," DeAndré said. "Any y'all follow me gonna get capped."

He eased out of the door into the hallway, turned to head out of the chapel, and saw Merrill coming in, .38 drawn. Before Merrill could say or do anything, DeAndré fired a round, missing Merrill and shattering the glass of the outer chapel doors, then ran into the sanctuary.

"Figured we might need this," Merrill said, holding up the revolver as we met in the hall.

Still shaken, Jake had yet to move, but Dad and Daniels weren't far behind behind us as Merrill and I rushed toward the sanctuary.

CHAPTER 51

"Black men not dying fast enough for you?" Merrill yelled to Stone.

DeAndré fired a round toward the back of the sanctuary for his response.

"I guess it's unthinkable for the control room to pat down the warden's nephew when he come in," Merrill said, as we ran toward the sanctuary doors.

A few inmates who had been hanging around after the service began pouring out of the doors in a panic and suddenly Merrill and I were running upstream.

We each pulled open one of the double doors, ducked in the sanctuary, and crouched behind the back pew.

"Don't fuck with me," DeAndré shouted from the front of the sanctuary.

I dropped all the way down to the floor and looked beneath the pews. I could see the black pant legs of his suit and the expensive black shoes beneath them, but I also saw another pair of legs on which were blue pants above inmate boots.

I edged to the end of the pew and glanced down the center aisle. DeAndré was holding Dexter Freeman in front of him, his gun jammed against Dexter's right temple.

"Come out where I can see you right now," DeAndré said, "or I'll splatter this nigga's brains all over the frontta your church house."

All I could think about was Dexter's family, of how Trish, Moriah, and Dexter Jr. were just about to get him back. I recalled his son's little navy-blue suit, his daughter's white lace collar and imagined seeing them wearing them again for their father's funeral.

When we didn't get up, DeAndré yelled, "NOW, GOD DAMMIT."

I glanced back at Merrill, and when I did, I saw Daniels edging toward the sanctuary door. As he stepped inside the sanctuary, a round fired from DeAndré's gun shattered the glass of the door beside him and he jumped back into the hall.

"I got nothing to lose," DeAndré said. "I'm probably gonna die anyway, so whoever gets close to me is going with me. Get my uncle in here."

Standing up very slowly, I walked over to the center aisle and faced DeAndré.

"What the fuck you doin'?" Merrill asked.

Dexter's eyes were wide with fright and moist with tears. The tendons in his neck were stretched taut under his shiny, sweat-covered skin, and when he swallowed hard, his Adam's apple rose and fell slowly.

As Merrill stood up, DeAndré loosened his grip on Dexter and turned his gun toward him. When he did, I took several running steps and dove, tackling both men to the ground.

As we went down, DeAndré fired his gun and I took a bullet in the right shoulder. My skin and muscle felt as though they had been branded, a searing pain arcing out in every direction like the phosphorescent tails of Fourth of July fireworks.

As we hit the floor, DeAndré fired again. The side of Dexter's head exploded and the pain in my shoulder was sucked into the vacuum in my soul. Suddenly, all the fight was out of me and I lay there on the floor, unable to move. Dexter was dead. I had failed again.

Merrill kicked the gun out of DeAndré's hand and it bounced across the floor. He then rushed forward and grabbed it.

Merrill said, "How's the arm?"

I shook my head. "I can't feel anything."

He glanced over at Dexter's body and shook his head. "He was dead before we got here."

We would never know—I would never know if I had done something differently, just one little thing, if the outcome would have been different and Dexter would have been spared.

After helping me to my feet, Merrill handed me the two guns. A violent wave of nausea swept over me as I realized I was holding the instrument of Dexter's death in my hand and I dropped both guns on the pew.

Merrill then grabbed DeAndré and jerked him up.

"We got unfinished business," he said. "Show me whatcha got, dog."

DeAndré lunged for him before he even finished saying it.

Grabbing Merrill by the throat with both hands, DeAndré did exactly what Merrill wanted him to do—leave himself open to body shots.

With the hand speed of a fast light heavyweight, Merrill threw a barrage of punches into DeAndré's abdomen. Unaware that Merrill was attempting to burst one of the condoms, DeAndré saw it as a challenge to keep choking him. As he did, Merrill continued to drive uppercuts into his gut, drilling them with such frequency and force that by the time he finally let go, DeAndré was coughing up blood.

Dad and Daniels ran up, Edward Stone on their heels.

"You all right?" Dad asked.

I shook my head and nodded toward Dexter.

"What the hell's going on here?" Stone asked when he saw Merrill using his nephew as a heavy bag.

"If he's still alive when Merrill gets finished, I'm arresting him," Dad said.

"What's the charge?" he asked.

"Narcotics possession with intent," he said. "Bringing a firearm into a state prison facility, and murder."

"*Murder?*" he asked, just as he caught sight of Dexter's body on the floor.

"And I'm sure NOPD'll have a lot of other charges to add before it's over," I said.

"He sure as hell didn't do that," Stone said. He looked at Daniels who nodded, then looked at me. "Is this your doing? Have you been *shot?* What're these weapons doing in here?"

"Your nephew brought one of them in and killed Dexter Freeman with it," I said.

"He did no such thing," he said. "And he's obviously not in possession of drugs, let alone trying to distribute them."

As if on cue, Merrill drove one final punch into DeAndré's gut and he doubled over, falling to his knees and beginning to vomit.

Among the contents emptying from his stomach were three condoms filled with what looked to be small crack rocks.

Stone's eyes grew nearly to the size of his glasses as he saw them.

"Looks like one of those has a hole in it," Merrill said. "Get enough straight in your blood stream and you'll save the taxpayers some money." He smiled broadly. "Not to mention how poetic it'd be."

"Inspector," Stone said to Daniels. "Secure this crime scene. The rest of you get the hell out of here."

"But—" I began.

"NOW," he shouted. "Get the hell out of my institution right now."

"Come on, Son," Dad said. "We need to get you to a hospital anyway."

CHAPTER 52

Three days later, I stopped by Anna's office to get some information.

"How are you?" she asked.

"The pain in my shoulder is manageable."

She frowned and gave me an understanding look, but didn't say anything, which I appreciated.

Vividly expressing her duality, Anna's office was both hard and soft, tough and tender. Like the other institutional offices, pale painted cinder block and tile floor conducted cold and enhanced echoes. However, Anna's warmth radiated from her large collection of porcelain, painted and cloth angels, and it was the soothing sounds of soft rock that echoed through the small room when her laughter did not.

"Can you tell me what kind of time Cedric Porter has left?" I asked.

"Sure," she said, immediately typing his name into her computer. "Why?"

"Because he killed his daughter," I said. "And I want to make sure he'll be around for a very long time."

She stopped typing. "He killed Nicole?"

I nodded.

"Can you prove it?"

I shook my head. "That's why I want to make sure he'll be around for a while."

"I'll check," she said. "But wait, he works outside the—"

"Not anymore," I said. "I had his gate pass pulled a week ago."

As she typed in information and clicked through the screens, she said, "What makes you think he did it?"

"Her face was very badly beaten, which usually indicates the killer knew the victim," I said. "Parents are the most likely suspects, which is why so many people thought it was the Caldwells. It was a parent—just not either of them."

She shook her head as she thought about it, lines of pain drawn across her face.

"Plus the body had been staged."

"Been what?"

I told her.

"But after staging it to look like a sexual murder," I said, "he undermined his own production by turning her over to cover her. I knew it had to be someone who knew her well, and of course Bobby Earl and Bunny knew her very well, but it really looked to be an impulsive act. Bobby Earl or Bunny could have done it impulsively, but they were more likely to have planned it, and if they had, they'd've had a much better alibi and not been anywhere near her at the time."

"How'd he get into your office?"

"I think Bunny let him in," I said. "I think they prearranged a visit between Nicole and her real father because he demanded it—probably blackmailed her. Bunny goes to the inner door that leads to the chapel and calls Coel over so he won't see Porter slip in the outer one from the hallway."

"That's right," she said. "Coel had a blind spot of about ten seconds each way—walking to the door and then walking back to his post. But when did he kill her? Was Bunny in there?"

I shook my head. "I don't think so," I said. "I think he did it shortly after Bunny went back on stage."

"But Bobby Earl went in there."

"Yeah," I said. "And he thought Nicole was in the bathroom, but really Porter and Nicole were. Daniels said they found blood in the bathroom."

"The sick son of a bitch," she said.

"No one else had a motive," I said. "And it wasn't a sexual crime. It was pure rage. She said something or did something, or Bunny did, to set him off."

"You really think he's capable of doing that to his own daughter?"

I nodded. "He really loved Bunny," I said. "When she had him transferred out of the chapel at Lake Butler and began her relationship with Bobby Earl, he was devastated. He's been on a downward spiral ever since."

"What about evidence?" she asked. "What do you have?"

"Everyone in the hallway and bathroom that night remembered seeing Porter. He stayed out of the service longer than anyone— almost the entire service. He was out there when I came in the first time and still out there after I returned from the control room."

She nodded slowly, and I continued.

"Then there was the evidence inside the office itself," I said. "A greeting card, a wad of cash, and a piece of hard candy. At first I thought the greeting card just fell off my desk during the struggle, but all the cards on my desk had envelopes. Since there wasn't an extra envelope, I knew it had to have been brought in. Only an inmate would bring in one of the cards I give out—he wouldn't have access to any others. But he didn't sign it. That was smart. That way he could give it to Nicole, but Bobby Earl wouldn't know it was from him. Or if she lost it, he wouldn't be implicated."

"He's bringing it as a gift for his daughter," she said.

"Exactly," I said. "And that's not all. He brought candy, too—a fire ball from the canteen. He was trying to endear himself in the only ways he knew. He was trying to be her father, buy her love. He didn't know what else to do, and didn't have anything else to give."

"What about the money?"

"DeAndré brought that in to pay off Whitfield," I said. "It couldn't've been for an inmate—and Porter didn't take it—because it wouldn't do him any good in the cashless canteen system on the compound. If a staff member or either one of the Caldwells had done it, I think they would have picked it up."

"Porter also stole Nicole's crayons and coloring book," I said. "He's in the same dorm as Register, so he planted the crayons on him, but he held onto the pictures. He showed me one he kept in his pocket, but according to the mail room he's never received anything from her—or from anyone—not a single letter. The picture was obviously from the same book mine was. He could've only gotten it from her the night she was here, but he said he didn't see her. Then later, he returned to the crime scene and slid another picture she had colored under the door between the sanctuary and my office. As a memorial I guess. He's the only one who could have."

She shook her head. "Not a single letter—from anyone. No wonder he's so angry."

"Yeah," I said. "The woman he loves and their child won't have anything to do with him. They're living indulged lives and he has no life at all."

She nodded. "Well, I'm convinced."

"But would a jury be?" I asked.

She frowned, pursing her lips tightly together. "Hard to say, but I doubt it."

"Exactly," I said.

"So what're you gonna do?"

I shrugged. "Depends how much time he has left," I said.

She looked down at her monitor again. "Mandatory twenty on a third offense drug charge," she said. "He'll be with us quite a while."

CHAPTER 53

It was June now, nearly three weeks since Nicole had died, and the full heat of the day bore down on Cedric Porter as he picked up trash along the fence near the front gate. The road leading away from the institution, toward freedom and opportunity, shimmered like a mirage, waves of heat rising from the sizzling asphalt.

Walking toward Porter, I noticed how often he paused from picking up the trash to gaze down the road, as if continually making sure it was still there.

"I heard you had my gate pass pulled," he said, when I reached him.

I shuddered inside as I recalled how close he had worked to the children at the elementary school, and though, like most parents, he probably wouldn't hurt any child but his own, we couldn't take the chance.

I nodded.

"Why?" he asked.

"You know why," I said.

As he stooped to pick up another piece of trash, I noticed his futile attempt to endue his menial task with dignity.

"I want to know why you did it," I said.

"What?" he asked, standing and facing me haughtily.

"Don't," I said.

He started to say something, but I continued.

"I could let it be known on the compound that you're a child killer and you wouldn't last much more than a day," I said, "so don't play games with me."

Joining the thick sheen of sweat, a tear rolled out of his eye and down the shiny black skin of his cheek.

"I didn't mean to," he said, his body slumping and more tears coming as the dam of denial broke within him. "I… " he began, but broke off. "That son of a bitch was using her," he began again in a trembling voice. "My daughter. To get some bunch of convicts to think he not the most racist motherfucker on the planet. My daughter. Her mother's a whore. They not better than me."

He paused and I waited in silence, standing firm as a witness against his evil act, allowing him to face his accuser.

"They usin' her," he said again, his voice cracking. He swallowed hard before adding, "And she think they all she got. She say I not her daddy. Say Bobby Earl her daddy. Look at me like I's not worthy to be in the same room with her. Like I a nigga. Like the thought of my blood runnin' through her veins make her wanna slit her little wrists."

When he paused again, this time to wipe tears from his eyes and sweat from his face, I noticed how much smaller he seemed, as if he were imploding from the emptiness the absence of his denial was causing.

"'Cause she think she white," he said. "They straighten her hair and keep her away from little black children and got her convinced she white. That she his daughter. I loved her. I not gonna let her be used by that bastard. He not gonna take what mine. I told her to say she was mine," he said, his voice gaining strength. "To say it with pride. 'Cause Cedric Porter somebody to be proud of." The defiance was back in his eyes, joined by hardness and madness. "She wouldn't say it. She say she gonna tell her daddy. I say, 'I'm your daddy,' and I said to say it. But she won't."

All around us the world had faded for me and unaware of anything else, I entered his world and relived with him the last moments of Nicole's life.

"She say she not gonna say it no matter what I do," he said. "So I spank her. 'Cause my daughter gonna do what I say, but she don't. So I spank her again. Hard this time. And I spank her again. But she still won't say it." Now tears were flowing as fast as his words. "She never would say she mine. Never would say, 'Cedric Porter my daddy.'"

When he finished, I still didn't say anything, just remained a silent witness to things I could only see in my mind.

"I didn't mean to kill her," he said. "I loved her. I just wanted her to say she mine. That I her daddy and she love me, too, but she wouldn't."

Inept and aberrant as it was, what Cedric Porter was trying to do was be a daddy to his daughter, to love her in his twisted way and get from her the love he so needed.

For a long time after he finished his story, neither of us said a word.

I though about Nicole, about what he had done to her. The compassion I had for him felt like a betrayal of her, but there was nothing I could do for her now. I had failed her. I had failed Dexter. I would try not to do the same with Cedric.

Finally he asked, "What's gonna happen to me?"

"I'm not sure," I said.

"You gonna tell the compound?"

I shook my head.

"I am going to turn everything I have over to the inspector and DA," I said. "But I doubt what I have is enough for them to bring you to trial."

He nodded slowly, seeming to think about it.

"You could tell them," I said. "Confess to them like you have to me."

He didn't respond, but seemed to be considering my suggestion.

"It'd be the right thing for you to do—the best thing you can do now," I said.

He nodded.

"You've lost your daughter," I said. "Don't lose your soul, too."

As repulsive as I found his act, I couldn't help but feel compassion for this wounded man, and I knew where it came from—knew I had to tell him, though it would most likely come out as awkward and contrived as an altar call at a funeral service.

"But regardless of what you decide to do," I said, "there's something I've got to tell you."

He turned and really looked at me full on for the first time.

"What you've done is horrible," I said. "It's evil in so many ways, but… it doesn't change the fact that God loves you. Your actions, ungodly though they are, don't—can't separate you from the love of God unless you allow them to."

His tears started streaming again, his body beginning to convulse as they did.

"The best way you can receive and respond to God's forgiveness and grace is to take responsibility for what you've done and accept the consequences it brings, but no matter what you do, it won't—it can't change the fact that God loves you. Nothing can."

That night I went to bed early.

The only light came from the bathroom down the hall, and the dim room was a chalky gray like moonlight defused through thick clouds. I lay on my bed staring up at the gray, thinking about all that had happened. Concluding a murder investigation—no matter how seemingly successful—is always incomplete and bittersweet, and, as usual, I was depressed. I had found the murderer, solved the mystery, but that did nothing for Nicole. It couldn't bring her back, couldn't undo what had been done to her, couldn't wake her from the nightmare she had lived through, had died in. It couldn't absolve me from failing her in the first place, from failing Dexter.

Only God could do that, and, as I lay there looking up at nothing, I prayed for forgiveness.

Later, when I answered the phone, my mouth was dry, my voice sleepy, though I was still wide awake.

"Hey."

It was Susan.

"Hey," I said.

"How'd it go?" she asked.

I told her. And as I did, the three hundred miles between us shrank to nothing, our connection seeming to bypass circuits and lines and everything mechanical to become direct and intense and intimate.

"My God," she said.

"That'll teach you to ask."

"No," she said. "I'm glad you told me. I want you to tell me everything." She was silent a beat before asking, "Do you think he'll confess?"

"Already has," I said. "Went with me right then and did it."

"How do you feel about the inmate—what was his name?"

"Dexter," I said. "Guilty."

"I figured you did," she said.

"If I hadn't staged the whole memorial service in the first place," I said, "or confronted him in such an uncontrolled environment or dove for the gun…"

"Have you talked to anyone?"

"You mean besides you?"

"Yeah."

"No," I said. "Not about how I feel."

"Oh," she said, a little startled. "Thank you."

I didn't say anything.

"Sounds like you need to get away for a while," she said. "That's the reason I was calling—to invite you up for the weekend. I'd really love to see you and—"

"I'm sorry," I said. "I just can't. I—"

"I told myself I wasn't going to do this. I let you know how I felt, and I was going to just wait on your response, not push it. I'm sorry."

"No," I said. "That's not it at all. I'd love for us to get together. Really. I'm just not ready to come back to Atlanta yet. It's too soon, wounds too fresh. Could we go somewhere else?"

"Yeah, sure," she said.

"What about that bed and breakfast we stayed at near Charleston?" I asked.

"Oh, John," she exclaimed. "That sounds wonderful."

After we made the plans, she said, "I feel so hopeful about us," she said. "But I want you to know that even if we don't wind up together, I'm glad we're doing this... getting to know the real us."

"Me too."

We were quiet for a while and I could hear her breathing. It reminded me of making love in sweet silence, caught up in passion beyond words, and it made me want her even more.

"I don't need you, John," she said.

"What?"

"I don't need you," she said. "For over a year now, it's been just me. And I'm comfortable with that. I'm learning who I really am and I like me very much. I don't have to have someone in my life—that's why I haven't been looking. I'm not looking for someone to rescue or complete me."

"Good," I said. "That's really good."

"I'm not finished," she said. "I don't need you... but I do want you. I want you very badly. I want you in my life, in my body, in my soul."

Images of being in all three filled my mind, and I lost myself in the sound of her breathing.

"I don't want to hang up," she said after a long, comfortable silence.

Lying in the dark, listening to her words, her silences, reminded me of when we were first dating, the hours we spent tethered together by phone cords, unseen radios playing the same songs in the background, the darkness keeping the rest of the world at bay. Like everything about her, this felt familiar, comfortable, like a home I had only briefly known.

"So, don't," I said.

"I don't really have anything else to say," she said.

"Just breathe," I said.

"What?"

"I like listening to you breathe," I said.

"But I'm about to fall asleep," she said.

"That's okay," I said. "I like listening to you sleep."